"How did you get in here?"

"Oh, hi there." The woman got to her feet.

"Hi there? Are you out of your mind?"

"Um . . . Good evening?" she offered instead.

Scowling, Kahari advanced, and the woman withered backward, stopping when she hit the wall.

"You answer me, and you answer me right now. How did you get in my r—"

Kahari stopped abruptly as he suddenly recognized the woman. Her hair was pulled back, unlike the way she had worn it on Sunday, which is why it had taken him so long.

"Oh God. I know who you are," he said with a sinking sense of dread. "And you can stay right there, because I'm calling the—"

The woman leapt at him like a corner from an opposing team coming at him for the tackle. But where he was normally grace under fire on the football field, here, in unfamiliar territory, he was too stunned even to move.

He was even more stunned when she threw her arms around his neck and kissed him.

By Kayla Perrin

How to Kill a Guy in 10 Days
(with Brenda Mott)
The Sweet Spot
Gimme an O!
Tell Me You Love Me
Say You Need Me
If You Want Me

KAYLA PERRIN

THE SWEET SPOT

AVON
An Imprint of Harper Collins*Publishers*

This book was originally published in trade paperback by Avon Trade in June 2006.

This is a work of fiction. Names, characters, places, and incidents are products of the author's imagination or are used fictitiously and are not to be construed as real. Any resemblance to actual events, locales, organizations, or persons, living or dead, is entirely coincidental.

AVON BOOKS
An Imprint of HarperCollins*Publishers*
10 East 53rd Street
New York, New York 10022-5299

ISBN: 978-0-06-114392-2
ISBN-10: 0-06-114392-8
www.avonbooks.com

First Avon Books paperback printing: October 2007
First Avon Books trade paperback printing: June 2006

Printed in the U.S.A.

10 9 8 7 6 5 4 3 2 1

This one's for my fans.
Thanks for all your support!

One

This is fast turning into the worst day of my life.

My friends will tell you I say that a lot—that whatever crappy day I'm going through is the worst day of my life—but this time I mean it. *Reeeally* mean it. I may as well find a hole and bury myself alive, that's how completely hopeless I feel right now.

I'm stuck in traffic just south of NoHo (a.k.a. North Hollywood), and horns blare as car after car whizzes by me. Like people actually think I chose to break down in a live lane in the middle of busy traffic. And not one person offers to help me.

"Okay," I begin, hoping my calm tone will appease my car. "You can do it, Betsy." I rub the dashboard lovingly, trying to coax my car into submission. "Now come on, engine. Turn over." I turn the key, but Betsy's engine only whines in protest. "Come *on*!"

The engine sputters and burps, then magically comes to life. Energy shoots through my veins, renewing my hope.

"Oh, thank you, Betsy. Thank you, thank you, *thank you*!"

Betsy's clock long ago stopped working, so I glance at my watch as I start to drive. Ten thirty-five. I have to get to the NBC studios by eleven if I want to have a shot in hell of changing my life for the better.

I've been trying not to be too excited about this opportunity, but I just can't help it. NBC is launching a new sports show, and I actually have an audition/interview for one of the three host positions. One of the hosts is the legendary quarterback Lionel Griggs, and they're specifically hiring two new faces, probably a man and a woman.

This is the break I've been waiting for. No, the break I've been dying for. The reason I've worked for the past three years at a pathetically low-paying job, in the hopes of building up a decent video reel. Today's audition is the chance of a lifetime in this City of Angels where everyone has a dream but only a small percentage will ever make it.

Something my mother, back home in Cleveland where I was born and raised, reminds me of every chance she gets.

But I'm not thinking about that now. You have to have faith if you're ever going to make it.

My heart pounds as I get closer to Burbank. I want this job so bad, I can practically taste it. *Zoë Andrews reporting for Inside Sports! The Lakers will have some tough competition today . . .*

A loud screech-thud sound jerks me from my daydream just as Besty's sudden halting jerks me forward in the car. My stomach twists painfully. *Oh God. Not again.*

And this time, no matter how much I try to get Betsy going, she just won't cooperate. No sputtering, no screaming engine. *Nada.*

There is, however, a burning smell, and I know that can't be good. Betsy's radiator busted four weeks ago. Two weeks before that, it was the transmission that started acting up. God only knows what it is today.

I try again to turn the engine over, and absolutely nothing happens.

"No, no!" I cry out in frustration. "Not *now*, Betsy! Please not now . . . " Groaning, I drop my head against the steering wheel, knowing that my situation is grim. What am I going to do? I will never make it to NBC on time now. And I know firsthand that showing up late for an audition is the kiss of death.

I grab my things and jump out of the car, feeling only a mild sense of guilt that I'm going to abandon Betsy here in the middle of the road. She gave up on me first, I justify. And after all we've been through together.

Just like most of the men in my life.

Of course, people protest my leaving Betsy with a barrage of horn-blowing, and one guy even gives me the finger. I ignore him as I dig my cell phone out of my purse. I've got more important things to worry about right now.

I call my boyfriend, Marvin. He was actually sick today and didn't head in to work on the set of *Passion's Shore*, a soap opera for which he's a production assistant. But like the first time I called him when Betsy began giving me trouble, Marvin doesn't pick up our home line. And he doesn't answer his cell, either.

"Answer the phone, Marvin," I say as I listen to it ring again. "It's not like you were dying when I left you less than an hour ago!"

But Marvin doesn't answer, and I've just wasted a few more minutes I should have used to try and hail a cab, or to even call one. Not that calling a cab would be much help. I have exactly one dollar and twenty-two cents in my wallet.

I start walking somewhat aimlessly along this industrial stretch of road, not sure what to do. Should I hitchhike? I know I'm too far to make it to the studio on time, and I wonder if I should bother going if I know I'll be fifteen to thirty minutes late.

As I realize I'm fighting back tears, I also realize that I *can't* give up. I have to keep going. I have to hope for the best. I have to believe that when I walk into the studio, some exec will see me and instantly realize that I'm the perfect person for the job. "You're hired," he'll say in a corny Donald Trump-like imitation, which I'll laugh at, relieved that my pitiable life is finally going to take a turn for the better.

Damn it, why don't I have money in my purse?

Marvin always gets irritated with me because I hardly ever carry cash. "You need *something* in your wallet," he often tells me, "in case of an emergency."

I think this classifies as an emergency, but unfortunately I'm shit out of luck.

Quickly assessing my options, I whirl around. My stomach sinks. There are none.

I *could* hitchhike, but I don't want the job so badly that I'm willing to get in a car with a possible serial killer for it.

With a sigh of resignation, I do the only thing I can do given the situation. I slip off my heels, grip them in my hand, and start to run.

I sense cars slowing and people staring at me, but I don't stop my stride. At five feet ten inches, with my thick, curly hair bouncing in the wind, I know I'm going to get attention. I probably look like some kind of Amazon warrior.

But I don't stop.

Soon, however, I'm out of breath and not sure I can take much more of this. And then my toe hits something hard. Faltering, I cry out in pain.

"Dammit, dammit, dammit!"

I double over, catching my breath as pain shoots through my leg. I hobble around, fighting tears of frustration at just how bad my luck can be.

And then I see some flowers a couple feet away from me. I raise my gaze, and there's a fruit stand as well. My heart rate picks up speed as I realize that I've keeled over outside of a convenience store.

Oh, please . . .

Yes! I almost scream a *hallelujah!* when I see the large sign: ATM.

Remarkably, I am only half an hour late when I arrive at the studio. Screw the patches of sweat at my underarms, and screw my ruined makeup. Maybe the Amazon warrior look will work for me in a career field mostly filled by men.

There is a roomful of people in the waiting area, mostly men in fact, as I step up to the receptionist to check in. I blow out a long breath and force a smile.

"Hello, I'm Zoë Andrews. I'm sorry I'm running a bit late—"

"Your audition was at eleven."

"I know, but my car broke down in NoHo, and I couldn't catch a cab for a while . . . " My voice trails off when I see that the woman's expression is as hard as a granite slab.

"I'm sorry." She shrugs in such a casual way that I know she isn't sorry. "You're late, and we can't fit you in."

No, no, no. Not after the morning I've had. "Please. I'll wait until everyone else has gone through, even if it takes four more hours. Just give me a chance, see how I read with Lionel Griggs."

The woman's eyes roam over me slowly, and I realize she's checking out my disheveled appearance. "I have makeup in my bag. I can fix myself up."

"Wish I could help. But we have a strict policy."

"Don't do this, please," I whimper. "I've had such an awful morning. If you only knew how hard I worked to get here."

But the receptionist is already looking beyond my shoulder, and I turn to see that another woman is standing behind me. This one is probably five feet eight, at least ten pounds lighter than I am, and blond. And like the average bimbo in Hollywood, she's got a chest so huge there's no way it's God-given.

You're at the wrong studio for the porn audition, I think, and am almost tempted to say it. I mean, really. Brains must be part of the requirements for this gig, and this woman doesn't look like she's got much upstairs.

Okay, call me catty—and maybe I am. But if they're willing to give this woman a shot, shouldn't I have my opportunity to shine? Seriously, this bimbo can't be the type of person they want for the job . . . can it?

I quickly turn back to the receptionist and place both hands on the desk. "I will do *anything.*"

"Sorry," she says again. Then, to the other woman, "Name, please."

"Candi Caldwell."

Jeez, she's even got a porn name.

Once again, I look toward the receptionist, but this time she won't even meet my gaze. *Bitch.* It's so obvious she's the kind who enjoys her position of power, the kind who loves stepping on others when they're down.

Am I supposed to suffer because she's only qualified to be a lowly receptionist?

Cool it, Zoë. Who's being the bitch now?

I want to tell this woman that my father used to play football with Lionel Griggs, but I know that will be a futile attempt at gaining favor. It's over.

My chance at stardom blasted to hell.

Sometimes I just want to shoot myself.

Two

To say that I'm despondent is an understatement, and when I call the small cable station where I work and tell my boss that I'm sick, it's not a lie. I *am* sick. My feet are blistered and hurt from all the running I did, and I have the Migraine from Hell.

Phil doesn't question me, I guess since I lied to him and told him I had a doctor's appointment this morning. I couldn't exactly tell him I had an audition for a host position at a rival station.

Not that it isn't a bit of a laugh to call NBC a rival station to LASN. Sometimes I'm not even sure LASN is real TV. LASN stands for Los Angeles Sports Network, and sure, the name sounds big and important, but it's really not. LASN is a Mickey Mouse operation (no offense to Mickey Mouse!), a small-time cable company trying to make a dent in the sports market. We get second, third, or fourth dibs at the big sports stories and the big-name athletes. But we cover many semipro games, and alternative sports. Like curling. And bowling tournaments. You would think I'd be out of a job, but some people are really into this alternative stuff.

Then there are high school football games, which are always fun. All those crazy parents certain their kids are future stars.

I was supposed to cover some high school game today, and I can't say I'm disappointed to have missed it. I'm really getting sick of working at LASN. How can I not be? The job doesn't even pay the rent. And it doesn't challenge me, nor has it given me the opportunities I'd hoped.

I'm so ready to move on. I want a real job, with real opportunities for advancement. I can't be working for LASN in ten years. Hell, it's not even on my five-year goal plan.

I'm depressed enough to splurge on a taxi ride home, even though I only have sixty-three dollars in the bank. But I really don't want to be stuck on public transit today. And what the heck—I figure I'm saving money. If I had my car, I'd drive to a mall and shop till I dropped.

Not that I can afford that either, but isn't that why God created plastic?

A long, relieved breath whooshes out of me when I step into my apartment twenty minutes later. Marvin and I live in a pretty good-sized one-bedroom unit in a low-rise building in NoHo. North Hollywood is really artsy, which is a large part of why I love it. A lot of aspiring actors live here, musicians, painters, screenwriters. A real eclectic group of artsy farts, with every artistic neurosis in the book. Bipolar, fatally low self-esteem. You name it, I know someone who's got it.

My neighbor Charlotte, for example, is an actress who gets bit parts here and there but has yet to land anything substantial. She's stunningly beautiful, yet thinks she's horribly flawed because she can't land a decent gig. I know she's anorexic. Jill, another neighbor, had a starring role in a B movie, one in which she was naked most of the time, but hasn't landed another acting role since. She's taking antidepressants to get through the day.

Me—well, you know all about me. I'm working at a lowly cable sports station but have aspirations for bigger things.

I don't pop pills to survive the rejection, and I don't puke my guts out. I guess I'm not yet ready to let this business get to me.

Don't get me wrong. I'm not saying everyone who lives in NoHo is a nutcase. In fact, it's a great place to live, with lots going on, and a generally great group of people who are a lot of fun.

My shoulders drooped, I kick off my shoes at the apartment door. I'm sweaty and achy and want to take a bath, but I'm more tired than anything else so I head straight for the bedroom. I want to crawl under the sheets and die for a few hours.

A groan escapes my lips when I open the door and see that Marvin didn't make the bed. As usual. I think he believes that making the bed and doing some cooking on occasion is against the laws of nature for guys.

I take a few steps toward the bed, then stop abruptly. Wait a minute. Where is Marvin? He legitimately called in sick to work, so why isn't he curled up in bed, moaning and groaning like the baby he becomes every time he gets a cold? He sure as hell made sure to have me pamper him this morning, even as I was trying to get ready for my audition.

Despite my fatigue, I head back out of the bedroom to look for Marvin. He's not sprawled out on the sofa. He's not lying on the lounger on the balcony. And he's not bent over the toilet in the bathroom.

Where on earth is he?

I'm grateful to see the bottle of Advil on the bathroom counter, and I open it, pop two pills into my mouth, then stick my mouth under the faucet to slurp up lukewarm water.

Accepting that Marvin is nowhere to be found, I go back to the bedroom because I really need to sleep. I slip out of my clothes, climb into bed—and then notice the note on my night table.

> I hope you knocked 'em dead, honey. I was feeling better after all, so decided to go out and get some stuff done while I have the day off! See you later.
>
> xoxo Marvin

Well, that explains where he is. I should feel relieved, but I don't. Instead, I feel empty inside. Damn, I really wish Marvin was here so I could lie next to him and pour out my soul. I need to talk to someone about my disaster of an audition, and I'm not in the mood to call any of my friends right now. I don't want to even lift up the telephone's receiver. I simply want to cozy up to my man and have the kind of intimate chat lovers have, where you know that you're putting your most personal feelings in the hands of the person who also has your heart.

I curl the note in my hand and close my eyes. I probably need sleep more than a chat right now, anyway.

I have barely gotten comfortable when there's loud pounding at my door. At least I think it's the door. There's a possibility the pounding is in my head.

Thump, thump, thump.

Dammit, that *is* the door. Oh Lord. Not now.

Forget it. I'm not getting up. Whoever it is will have to go away. I'm not in the mood.

But the pounding persists, and now it's louder and more annoying. It's pretty obvious that whoever is at the door isn't going to go away anytime soon.

Cussing under my breath, I throw off the duvet cover and get out of bed. On my way to the bedroom door, I scoop up my bathrobe from the back of the armchair and slip it on. "Dammit, this had better be good."

I stare through the peephole. Gail, my friend and neighbor from one floor down, is standing there in tears. And since she's standing there in tears six weeks after the last time she did this, I know it's got to be boyfriend drama.

I open the door and she barges right in, sobbing like a colicky baby.

I follow her into my living room. "Gail, what's the matter?"

She faces me, her eyes puffy and red. "It's Bob. He's gone."

"Gone?" I knot the tie on my bathrobe. "What do you mean, gone?"

"I mean he left! Packed his stuff and took off not more than an hour ago!" She hiccups between sobs. "He said I've been smothering him. Do you *believe* that?"

I put my hands on Gail's shoulders to try and calm her down. She sounds like she's going to suffocate in all those tears and snot. In the six months I've lived here with Marvin, she's been through four boyfriends, all of whom she's been sure would marry her. She falls hard and fast whenever she gets involved with anyone.

But I say, feigning disbelief, "Smothering him?"

"Yes!"

"Wow. That's awful."

"I don't get it! Just because I asked him how many children he wanted. Suddenly he's not ready to 'commit' and he thinks it was a mistake moving in with me!"

Gail is five feet nothing, has flawless dark skin, and quite frankly is gorgeous. She's sweet and caring—but doesn't realize that she's doing everything wrong where men are concerned. Not that I'm anyone to talk, given that before Marvin, my longest relationship was only three months, but even I know better than to talk about marriage and kids before you've built a solid foundation.

"Gail, sit down." I lead her to the sofa and guide her to a sitting position. "You've got to calm down."

"How can I calm down when I've lost my soul mate?"

Her soul mate? She said the same thing about Andy, and Jerome, and Mitchell, and Brian.

"Gail," I begin gingerly as I take a seat beside her, "if Bob is really the guy for you, you know he'll come around. Maybe he just needs some time to cool down, don't you think?"

Snot and tears merge on Gail's upper lip, and I snatch a wad of tissue from a nearby Kleenex box. I pass the wad to her and she wipes it across her face, then loudly blows her nose.

"Why can't I hang on to a guy?" she asks. Her eyes are wide and pleading, as though she is desperately hoping I can answer this question for her.

And for a moment I contemplate telling her the truth—at least as I see it. That she moves far too fast and doesn't really know the guys she gets involved with.

But God, how can I say that? She's looking at me with such hopelessness, there's only one thing I can do.

I reach for her knee and squeeze it. "Gail, you know that's not true. Bob will be back."

And why shouldn't he be? Gail is entirely too generous, and at least three of her former boyfriends have been out-of-work actors who couldn't afford a cup of coffee, much less an apartment. Including Bob.

What I'd like to do is tell her that she needs to stand on her own for a while, but I know she's not ready to hear that. She's the kind of girl who can't bear to be without a man for even five minutes, which is why as soon as one relationship is over, she's on the hunt for someone new.

She's still crying, snorting and sniveling, and I simply can't take it anymore. I have to do something to get her to stop. "Let me get you a drink."

"Oh yes, a drink."

"Iced tea? Soda?"

"You don't have anything stronger than that?"

"Sure."

In the kitchen, I snatch up a bottle of tequila and a glass tumbler. But when I hand both to Gail, she opens the tequila bottle and puts the spout directly to her mouth. And gulps.

In disbelief, I watch her, not sure what I should say. When she drinks more tequila like it's Kool-Aid, I debate warning her to slow down. But I also consider leaving her to drown her sorrows while I go back to the bedroom to sleep. Right about now, I don't think she'd miss me.

I feel for Gail, I really do, but I have the Migraine from Hell and I've already had the worst day a person could have.

"Gail, will you be okay out here on your own?" I finally ask. "I'm not feeling well, and I was just trying to fall asleep when you came to my door."

"Oh." She shoots to her feet. "I'm sorry. I didn't even think—"

"It's okay."

"No it's not. Here I am, being so selfish and self-absorbed, and not even thinking about you. What's wrong with me?"

"Gail, you're more than welcome to stay here if you like."

She closes her eyes tightly as she shakes her head. "No, I'll just go. Let you get some sleep. Just one more sip, though."

Shamelessly, she downs more tequila before placing the bottle on my coffee table. My eyes widen in shock as I look at the bottle. She's polished off a good third of what was left.

Gail sighs. Sways. I reach for her to steady her.

"How do you do it?" she asks.

"Do what?"

"Hang on to a man? Keep a happy relationship?"

"Gail, honestly—I think you're making yourself sick with worry for nothing. Honestly. Bob is probably already on his way back to your apartment." I give her a bright smile. "You don't want him going home and not finding you there, do you?"

Her eyes light up at that. "Oh my God. Zoë, you're probably right. What if he comes back to talk and I'm not there . . . " Her voice trails off on a hopeful note, and she starts running toward the door. Her behavior is a bit odder than when she normally gets dumped, and it occurs to me that she was probably already drinking before she showed up at my apartment. Which would explain why she came to my door in the middle of a workday.

"Call me later," I tell her as she disappears down the hallway. I'm not sure if she hears me.

I close and lock the door, thankful I escaped answering her question as much as I am thankful that I can finally get some sleep. Because I don't really have an answer as to how to keep a relationship happy. Given my track record, the question is almost laughable.

Gail, of course, doesn't know that. She's only known me for the past six months since I moved in with Marvin.

But my track record with men is tragically dismal. I left Cleveland for L.A. when I found out that Quinn, my boyfriend of two months, was screwing my sister. She still thinks she didn't do anything wrong.

And sure, Marvin and I have been together for nine months, longer than I've been with any other guy (except Lance, whom I dated for a year, but that was tenth grade). But what Gail doesn't know is that while I can't put my finger on anything concrete, lately I've been feeling like Marvin's slipping away from me.

He still says he loves me, and we still make love two times a week. But something's different. I can't put my finger on it, but I know it.

Three

Go, go, go!" His hands around his mouth like a funnel, Kahari Brown yelled as he stood at the side of the basketball court. J'Ron, the kid with the ball, was holding his own as he dribbled down the court. "That's it, J'Ron. Take the shot, take the shot! You got it!"

J'Ron threw the ball. It sailed right into the basket, giving his team another two points.

"Yeah!" Kahari screamed, clapping till his hands were sore. "That's the way you play the game, J'Ron. Good job!"

All smiles, J'Ron was quickly swarmed by the rest of his teammates. They hoisted him into the air on their shoulders, whooping and cheering as they did. J'Ron had just won the game for his team.

Kahari couldn't help smiling. He was equally encouraging to all the kids, but he had a special place in his heart for J'Ron. The kid had endured more in thirteen years than anyone should ever have to, and he was finally building some self-confidence.

Kahari trotted onto the court, heading straight for J'Ron.

"Good job, Shorty," he said, rubbing his head in encouragement. "I knew you could do it."

The twelve- and thirteen-year-olds from the winning team were still caught up in the excitement of winning. Seeing them so happy did Kahari's heart good. When he and his best friend, Anthony Beals, had decided to build a community center in Compton, it was because they'd wanted to give back and make a difference in the lives of young people who didn't have the best influences around them. Kids like J'Ron, whose father had been in and out of jail since before he was even born. He had lived for years with a mother who had often turned tricks to put food on the table. Now that she, too, was in jail, J'Ron was being raised by his older sister.

Kids like J'Ron needed this place. A place where they could go and forget their problems, and learn that the world had more to offer them than horror.

The Rita Brown Community Center had been named after Kahari's grandmother, something that meant a lot to him and with which Anthony had graciously complied. Considering he'd been raised by his grandmother because both his parents hadn't been there for him, Kahari knew he owed his ultimate success to the strong foundation she had provided for him.

Stepping back, Kahari let the kids celebrate among themselves. But then he saw the look of displeasure on Shawn's face, one of the boys from the losing team.

So he said, "Y'all played a great game. I know only one team can win, but what do I always say?"

"It's how you play the game that makes you a winner," the kids said in unison.

"That's right. It takes two teams to make this game—any game—fun. And the most important thing is being a good sport." Kahari's eyes bounced over the crowd. Shawn was still scowling. "Now come on, y'all. You know how we end every game."

The boys slowly formed two lines facing each other. One team walking toward the other, the opposing teams shook hands.

But when Shawn, another of the troubled teens who came from a one-parent home, met J'Ron at center court, instead of shaking his hand, he gave J'Ron a shove that landed him flat on his back.

Among gasps from the boys, J'Ron shot to his feet, immediately charging for Shawn. Anger burned in his eyes as he shoved Shawn's chest with all his might. Shawn toppled backward, his sneakers squeaking as he tried to regain his footing. But he couldn't, and he landed on his butt before his head collided with the hard floor.

"Hey, hey, hey!" Kahari ran forward, quickly jumping between the two teens.

"You saw what he did!" J'Ron shouted.

"You deserved it!" Shawn countered, as angry as J'Ron.

Kahari placed a hand on a shoulder of each of the boys, holding them away from each other. "What did I just say about good sportsmanship?"

"I ain't the one—" J'Ron protested.

"I don't care," Kahari said firmly. "You both know better than that."

"Ain't you gonna talk to him?" J'Ron asked.

Kahari now leveled his gaze on Shawn. "There is *no* fighting here. Period. This is a game, that's all."

"Yeah, but—"

"But nothing, Shawn. If you can't deal with losing, then you should stop playing. But starting a fight because you're angry—that's not cool."

Shawn muttered something under his breath.

"All right, Shawn. Next game, you're sitting out." Letting

go of the boys, Kahari faced the rest of them. "It's all right to be competitive. It's not all right to get violent over the game."

"Then why're guys always fighting on the football field, or when they play hockey?" Mike asked. Mike had been in three different foster homes in the last two years.

"Those guys are stupid," Kahari told Mike, even if that wasn't exactly true. Part of his goal in opening this center was to have a spot where troubled teens could come and learn how to socialize with others. It was a tough battle with some of them, one that took time, but Kahari knew he was getting through to them for the most part.

"J'Ron, Shawn. Shake hands."

J'Ron's eyes flew to Kahari's in shock. Kahari gave him a stern look, then turned and leveled the same look on Shawn. "Go on. Shake hands."

Reluctantly, J'Ron extended his hand. Shawn extended his a moment later, and the two shook hands.

"All right." Kahari patted both kids' shoulders as he smiled. "That's what I like to see. Y'all up for another game?"

There were nods and "yeahs" among the crowd.

"Good." The boys started to take their places on the court. "No, Shawn—you come with me."

"Aw, Kahari," Shawn groaned.

"I meant what I said. We all have to face the consequences of our choices."

Kahari turned—and noticed Anthony standing several feet behind him.

"But I'm sorry," Shawn stressed. "I was just mad, cuz—cuz he was playin' real well, and I missed all my shots."

"All right," Kahari said, more because he wanted to talk to Anthony than anything else. "You want to play, you go and apologize to J'Ron."

"A'iight, I will."

Kahari watched as Shawn jogged onto the court. He went right up to J'Ron, who seemed to greet him warily. But after a moment the two teens shook hands—and this time looked like they meant it.

"And the award for Hero of the Year goes to . . ." Anthony ended his statement with a round of applause.

Kahari walked toward his friend. "Hey, T."

Anthony continued to clap. "Congrats on the nomination, man."

"Thanks." Kahari and Anthony knocked fists and slapped hands in their normal greeting. "It's no big deal."

"No big deal? Man, this is huge."

Kahari shook his head. "I wouldn't say that."

"What's up?" Anthony asked, chuckling softly. "Getting bashful all of a sudden?"

Kahari shrugged. "Naw. I'm just not making a big deal out of it."

"You know you're a shoe-in."

"We'll see."

Pass on the Dream, a national African-American organization geared at helping provide mentors for underprivileged youth, had an annual awards ceremony where they celebrated those who made a difference in the black community. Kahari had just been nominated in the "Unsung Heroes" category, a label he felt uncomfortable with. Both he and Anthony had also been given a nomination for founding this community center, but Kahari had gotten the additional hero nod because he'd saved one of the kids from a knife attack.

The fight had broken out in an instant, and it took Kahari only a moment to realize that one of the older teens—one who'd always had a bad attitude—was brandishing a knife and threatening to use it on a younger teen. Kahari had immediately run in front of the attacker, and ultimately wrestled him to the ground. As a result, he'd taken a sizable slash on the arm which had required eleven stitches. The media was impressed, as were all the parents of the kids who came to the center. They'd started calling him a hero, but as far as Kahari was concerned, he hadn't done anything that anyone else wouldn't have done under the very same circumstances.

"Who's the guy with the camera?" Anthony asked.

"Oh, him." Kahari had forgotten the guy was there. "Someone from the *L.A. Times.* He's here photographing me 'at work.' You know—because of the nomination."

"I am humbled in your presence."

"I could do without all this attention. You know how I feel about not getting too close to the media."

"You've got nothing to worry about. Everybody loves you."

"Until some fool from the press decides to twist some aspect of your life and run with it."

"This is all good, Smooth," Anthony said, calling Kahari by the nickname he often used. It was a nickname he'd earned on the football field as a wide receiver, considering he was so "smooth" catching most of the passes thrown to him.

"Is it?" Kahari asked. "I feel like they're intruding on my life."

"It's not like you've got anything to hide," Anthony commented.

"Maybe not, but I'm hardly perfect."

"Hmm." Anthony pursed his lips in thought. "That's a good point, Smooth. I can see why you're concerned. You think the *Times* is gonna find out that you cheated on a few college papers? Cuz if they do, it could be the end of your career."

Kahari's face twisted in a mock scowl. "It was one paper, dude. And I didn't exactly cheat. I just got some help."

Anthony grinned at his friend. "And who can blame you? That girl was sweet. What was her name again? Molly?"

"Melanie." Kahari paused. He knew Anthony was playing with him, but felt a moment of panic nonetheless. "Damn, you think that's something that might come out—that I got help writing one of my college papers?"

"Relax, Smooth." Anthony clamped a hand on his shoulder. "If that's the worst anyone can dig up on you, consider yourself a happy man. No one's taken a picture of you with some hooker. And if I can survive that fiasco, anything the media might throw your way will be a piece of cake."

Anthony was referring to his own issue with the media about a year and a half ago, when his ex-wife had set him up to be photographed with a prostitute in hopes of discrediting his character and forcing him to pay her a huge sum of money. Anthony had stood his ground, and fought tooth and nail to clear his name.

Kahari drew an uneasy breath. "And Estela Rivera?"

"There's a reason that only the *Daily Blab* ran her story. Every legitimate reporter knows that woman is crazy with a capital C."

Maybe so, but the woman's allegation that he had fathered her child still hung over him like a dark cloud.

None of which he wanted to think about right now. "Forget all that. What's the good news, man?"

Anthony's face erupted in a megawatt smile. "A boy," he announced proudly. "We're having a boy!"

"All right, man!" Kahari drew Anthony in a bear hug, slapping his back. "That's fantastic."

Anthony Beals, Kahari's teammate on the Oakland Raiders, had met and fallen in love with Lecia "Dr. Love" Calhoun a little over a year before. Their courtship had been the subject of all the media's attention after the whole prostitute incident instigated by the con artist Ginger.

It was all water under the bridge, and Anthony was happier than his friend ever remembered him being, now that he had a loving wife and a child on the way.

"Four more months," Kahari said. "Four more months and you'll be a daddy. I can hardly believe it."

"And it can't happen soon enough. That wife of mine has me running out at all hours of the night to get her sardines and butterscotch ripple ice cream."

Kahari cringed. "What?"

"Trust me, you don't want to know." Anthony's lips slowly curved in a smile. "But it's all good. In fact, it couldn't be better."

Yeah, Kahari loved seeing his friend so happy. "Damn, maybe I need to get some of what you got."

"You know you should."

Kahari rolled his eyes. "It'd be nice, but I don't want to end up with a Ginger. And ninety-nine percent of the women we meet are like Ginger. Out for the cash, and not much substance."

"They're not all packing guns, though."

"True dat. Ginger"—Kahari shook his head—"what a trip she was."

Anthony grimaced. "Do you have to mention her name?"

"I'm just thinking about how crazy all that was. I can't imagine going through a media nightmare like you did with her."

"What's all this fear about the media all of a sudden? You're a *hero*. Everyone knows it."

"Whatever."

"And you know Coach won't put up with your silent routine much longer, right? You're gonna get your ass fined."

Anthony was now referring to the fact that Kahari liked to give minimalist answers to the media after a game. They asked how he managed to catch an uncatchable ball, and he'd shrug and say something like, "Luck, I guess." He knew they wanted more from him, but he wasn't prepared to give it. The league's policy dictated that all players had to make themselves available to the media or face possible fines. Kahari did make himself available—he just didn't give them the detailed answers they wanted.

"I ain't been fined yet."

"I think you're taking what happened your second season way too seriously."

"What, you think it was all coincidence? Every time I explained a play to the media, I messed up during the next game. And when I stopped, everything changed."

"I don't know why you let them mess with your head. You've got this Samson and Delilah complex, like you think that if someone knows your strength suddenly you'll lose it. It's not about them—it's about you, your skills. And bro, you got skills."

"You of all people should understand why I'm shy where the media is concerned."

"This isn't about a scandal. It's about everyone's curiosity over how well you play this game."

Kahari turned, watching the boys on the basketball court. It wasn't as simple as Anthony was saying. But every time he tried to explain this to his teammates, they didn't understand his position. Some members of the media labeled him snooty for his unwillingness to talk to them. But it wasn't about that. It was all about his game.

And he'd do anything to protect his game.

Superstitious. That's what many people called him—including Anthony. It's not like he was alone. Many athletes were superstitious where their game was concerned. Whether they wore their mother's picture in a chain around their necks, or they always said the same prayer, many athletes had some sort of ritual or belief they were certain helped them perform at their best.

Was he crazy to feel the way he did—certain that if he talked to the media in explicit detail, revealed all his secrets, his game would be jinxed?

"How have the kids been today?" Anthony suddenly asked him.

Kahari was glad for the change in subject. "It's been a pretty good day. J'Ron's really made great strides. He's fitting in much better, working hard to be a team player."

"I knew he'd come around."

"Yeah, me too."

"It's hard to understand how a man can ignore his own flesh and blood."

"Tell me about it." J'Ron's father had been out of prison for a good year, yet he wasn't in touch with his son. Kahari didn't understand it, though he knew it happened all the time. It had happened to him. When he was four years old, his father and mother—who used to love passionately and fight passionately—had had one of their passionate fights and split for good. His father had left Texas for Seattle, where he'd been raised, and Kahari had only heard from him on a few occasions over the years. The devastating blow had come two years after his father's departure, when his mother, who had struggled as the single mother of two young children, left him and his sister in the care of their grandmother and gone off to find work in Louisiana.

His mother had come back six years later, apologetic that she hadn't been able to get her act together when he and his sister needed her most. As for his father, three months after Kahari had made the NFL, he died in a freak accident at work. And with the loss of his father went all hope of ever recapturing a real relationship with him.

"You just never know," Kahari said, "how long you have in this world. You can't take for granted the people in your life, especially your children."

"Which makes that whole Estela Rivera thing straight up crazy," Anthony commented.

Kahari cut his eyes at his friend. "Dude, you know I'm not even tryin' to hear her name."

"I hear you. But you get my point."

Kahari nodded. "I do. Like you said, though, only the *Daily Blab* ran her story, and on page five at that. So I'm feeling a lot better about the whole thing, especially since that was two months ago and there's been nothing about it since. Hell, Estela and I only kicked it once, a year ago—*before* she even got pregnant. And now she's tryin' to pass this baby off as mine? It pisses me off."

"Any more phone calls?"

"There've been a couple weird ones here, yeah. Hang-ups."

"Uh-oh."

Kahari eyed Anthony warily. "What does that mean? You know something I don't?"

Anthony half shrugged, half shook his head. "Naw."

"Come on, T. Don't hold out on me."

Anthony held up both hands. "I don't know anything, I swear. It's just—I don't trust that woman. Like you said, she's crazy. She reminds me of Ginger."

"Ginger?" Kahari all but shrieked.

"A little."

"Shit, that's the last thing I need. A gold-digging crazy woman to make my life hell the way Ginger did yours. Please tell me you don't think Estela is that crazy."

"All I know is, the woman's not right in the head."

"But she's not dangerous. I mean, not like Ginger. Ginger was a woman on a mission."

Anthony shrugged. "I don't know, dawg. Some women are completely unpredictable."

"Just not Dr. Love," Kahari said, changing the subject. Thinking about Estela and how she'd tried to defame his character always gave him a headache.

Now Anthony smiled. "No, not Dr. Love."

Kahari punched his arm. "You've gotten all soft on me, dawg."

"Whatever."

Kahari laughed. As much as he teased his friend, he was thrilled to finally see him so happy. His life had taken a serious turn for the better after marrying Lecia Calhoun, a.k.a. Dr. Love.

"Watch out for Estela," Anthony said. "I saw her car outside."

"For real?" Kahari's head whipped in all directions. Anthony started to laugh.

Kahari scowled. "Don't play with me, T."

"Ah, I couldn't resist."

"So she's not really out there?"

"You think I'd wait so long to tell you?"

Kahari studied his friend for a moment, then said, "I guess not."

Anthony slung an arm across Kahari's shoulder. "There's been no word from Estela for a while . . . Let's hope she's moved on to her next victim and you never see her again."

"I feel sorry for whoever the guy is."

"And that's what got you into this mess in the first place. The fact that you fell for Estela's sob story. 'I just want to make enough money to take care of my brothers and sisters in Mexico,' " Anthony said, feigning a Spanish accent.

"I fell for her because she was hot. What am I saying? I didn't *fall* for her. I was attracted to her, we went out a couple times, but all it took was one night in bed with her to know she had issues. What woman starts talking about your wedding when you've slept with her one time?"

"I can see the next headline right now. 'The Dirty Dog Left Me After Getting What He Wanted!' " Anthony laughed.

"Don't even joke about that. And you should stop laughing. If anyone fell for sob stories, it was you when you fell for Ginger's. Paraplegic mother? Alcoholic father? And what was the story about her brother?"

Anthony's hand shot up as his laughter immediately died. "All right, all right. I promise to never give you a hard time about Estela again."

"Good."

Beside him, Anthony blew out a loud breath. "I think I'll head up to the office."

"Actually, that photographer wants to get a shot of both of us to run in the paper."

"So I'm important too, huh?" Anthony joked.

"You know you're my right-hand man."

The two knocked fists.

"Just don't bring up any crazy women," Kahari told Anthony.

Anthony mimed pulling a zipper across his lips. "I'm done talking about Estela."

"Good." Because Kahari didn't want to hear her name again, much less think that she might be a problem down the road. He could only hope that he had seen and heard the last of Estela Rivera.

Four

I should have known better, but apparently I'm a glutton for punishment.

Last night, after finding out where Betsy had been towed, I convinced Marvin to take me there to get her. The idea of letting her go didn't sit well with me, especially considering I've had her for over seven years. Betsy is a '91 Volvo, and she's my very first car. She faithfully took me from Cleveland to Los Angeles when I finally decided to move here. So there's a lot of sentimental value attached to her, which makes it hard to walk away.

But only twelve hours after getting her back, she's acting up again. Marvin gave her a boost and she got me home okay, but now that I'm heading to work, she's stalled again.

"Dammit, Betsy. Now I'm going to be late!"

I leave Betsy at the curb, where she has conveniently broken down today. I know she'll be towed, but I don't care. I wasted two hundred bucks getting her out of the pound yesterday, but I won't be stupid enough to do that again.

However, I'm apparently stupid enough to have another empty wallet this morning, which means, like yesterday, that I have no cash to catch a cab. Letting out a sigh, I accept my fate with reasonable calm. What's the point in being stressed out? If I'm late, so be it. Phil is just going to have to get over it.

I'm still in NoHo, so there are stores and other businesses around. But wouldn't you know it—no ATM. At least not at the first three businesses I enter. I keep wandering along Lankershim, a main street in NoHo, and finally enter a variety store with an ATM. It's like yesterday is playing out in my mind like a bad movie. Sort of like how in the movie *Groundhog Day,* Bill Murray's character kept waking up to find he was cursed to relive the previous day over again.

Only today, when I turn on my cell phone, it doesn't turn on. *Dammit.* I forgot to charge it last night!

Deep breath in, deep breath out . . .

"Excuse me, sir," I say to the Middle Eastern-looking man behind the counter. "My cell phone's died, my car's broken down, and I'm gonna be late for work if I don't call a cab. So I'm wondering, can I please, please use your phone?"

"Of course." He smiles as he passes me a cordless receiver.

"Thank you!" I notice that his eyes linger on me, but I ignore him as I call for a cab. Sometimes I'm surprised that guys check me out as often as they seem to. Not that I'm not attractive, but how is it I get ogled at times I know I look my worst? Like now, with my hair all wild, and my face flushed from speed-walking for fifteen minutes, and I don't have a stitch of makeup on. I guess I should just take it as a compliment, something that's always been hard for me to do.

I return the receiver to the clerk, making minimal eye contact, then head outside. Five minutes later, I'm in a taxi heading to the LASN studio. As of right now, I'll be late in five minutes. I'm a good twenty minutes away, so there's not a damn thing I can do.

Damn, I hope Phil Kiesler's in a good mood when I see him. If he's miserable, maybe he'll do something drastic like fire me.

Between you and me, no matter how badly I bash LASN, I can't deny the fact that right now I need this job. It's been my bread and butter for the past three years, and my only shot at doing anything sports-related, even if the pay sucks and I haven't been able to buy a reliable car.

There are decent reporting jobs around—I know there are. But to get one, I have to make a name for myself with a big story. It's all I've been able to think about for the past year or so. I dream about it at night, that story that will put me on the map and launch me to superstardom.

Not that it's about being a star for me, but one wants to be as successful as possible in one's chosen career. Which in this case—being in front of the cameras—would mean that I'd naturally become a household name. Especially as the greatest female sportscaster to ever live.

I feel a bit deflated as I walk into the LASN studio, with its drab gray-carpeted floors. More often than not lately, I get depressed coming into work. That's because I'm here two years longer than I'd ever thought I would be.

It won't be much longer, I tell myself. *Soon you'll be movin' on up.*

I'm fifteen minutes late but I hope Phil won't even notice, since I don't see him around and I don't hear his booming voice. It's quite possible he's in his office, or in a meeting with someone that's kept him from checking on which staff members arrived on time.

At least, I can hope.

My stride purposeful, I head to my cubbyhole, drop off my purse, then grab my coffee mug. This way, it will look like I've been here awhile. The coffee stand is on the way to the assignment board, so after pouring myself a cup of the awful brew, I head over there to see what I'll be working on today. Some high school game, probably. Nothing exciting.

Nothing challenging.

My eyes scan the board . . . and then I clench one fist in anger when I see my assignment. Oh no. Not this. Anything but this.

"Zoë!" Phil's angry voice roars in the hallway behind me, causing me to jump. Hot coffee sloshes over the side of my mug onto my fingers. *Damn him . . .*

I turn to face him, plastering a smile on my lips. "Morning, Phil."

"You're twenty minutes late."

"Actually, I've been here five minutes," I point out cheerfully.

His forehead furrows in a deep frown. "Fifteen, twenty minutes—it doesn't matter. You're still late."

Obviously Phil isn't in the mood for wry humor, so I'd better take the conciliatory approach. "I know I'm late, and I'm sorry. My car broke down on Lankershim and I didn't have any money, so I had to walk awhile before finding an ATM and being able to call a cab. Do you believe it cost me twenty bucks to get—"

"Don't let it happen again," Phil warns me, his hard eyes saying he is unmoved by my story. And his tone is harsh enough to make it sound like he'd actually fire me.

As if! I mean, it's not like people are banging on his door to work in this hellhole. He needs me at this worthless excuse for a television network, and he damn well knows it.

However, given the way he's still glaring at me, I think it's wise to refrain from pointing that out.

Phil turns and stomps off, and I'm instantly relieved. But then I remember my assignment. I place my coffee cup on a counter and hustle after him. "Phil, wait."

"What is it?" he asks, planting his hands on his thick hips as he spins around to face me.

Damn, he's testy today. I can't help withering under his fierce look. But after a moment I force myself to keep my back tall and continue. "It's my assignment," I say. "I wanted to clarify it."

"It's on the board, where it always is," he quips, looking down his nose at me.

"I saw what was on the board." I chuckle, expecting Phil to at least crack a smile. When he doesn't, I ask, "Pig wrestling?"

Still, no reaction from Phil. I've got to hand it to him. He'd be great at poker. "Come on, Phil," I say after a moment. "That doesn't really exist, does it? That's just my punishment, right? So I won't be late again?" My voice ends on a hopeful note.

Phil's cold gaze answers my question and I swallow hard.

"The pig rodeo takes place this weekend," he tells me. "You'll cover the day's events on Friday. Start doing your homework *now.*"

Oh my God. This can't be true. Some pig rodeo in Acton? Of all the rotten assignments . . .

Phil heads off again, in the direction of his office. "Phil," I call out desperately, scampering behind him, "just last week you promised me that you'd give me . . . other kinds of assignments." I scoot in front of him, blocking his path. "More high-profile." How can I expect to get ahead with pig-wrestling clips on my video reel?

"Do you know how many people out there would be thrilled to cover a pig rodeo?"

He doesn't really believe that, does he? Honestly, I don't think that *anyone* would be "thrilled" to cover a pig rodeo.

"It's just that . . . What about that semipro basketball game this weekend?"

"Ken's covering that one."

Ken covers *all* the big stories. "Maybe I could help him," I suggest. "Since I have nothing else this week."

"You have the pig rodeo. I want this to be a big story, Zoë. Give me all you've got on this one."

How about five minutes. There are the pigs. There are the morons rolling around in the mud with them. Whoop-de-do.

"There's got to be something else this week, Phil. A high school football game . . . ?"

"Are you telling me you have a problem doing your job?"

Dammit, I don't like Phil's tone. "No, of course not. But—"

"Good. Then get to work. You won't have time for anything else this week."

This time when Phil walks away, I don't bother to follow him. I don't bother to say a word.

Phil is obviously in a pissy mood today. Maybe his wife has left him again. I wouldn't be surprised. He's been so hard to get along with ever since he started losing his hair.

Whatever the case, I am obviously stuck covering some ridiculous pig rodeo, and Ken Parks is probably going to keep getting the big assignments. I don't think Phil has any intention of truly giving me the better assignments he promised me. Maybe it's because I don't have a penis.

Chauvinist pig. You'd be right at home in a mud pit, wrestling with all your relatives . . .

I sulk all the way to my desk. Really, I can't stay here much longer. My sanity depends on it.

My self-esteem depends on it.

I need a big break like I need a cup of Starbucks coffee right now.

"Hey," I say to Pam, who's in the cubbyhole next to me. It's obvious from my tone that I'm not in the mood to talk. I slink into my seat, then bury my face in my hands.

I feel that Migraine from Hell coming on . . .

Three minutes later, I unbury my face and sit up straight. I won't let Phil, or this job, get me down.

What I will do is take matters into my own hands.

If Phil won't keep his word, I'm going to have to find a big break for myself.

Five

Hey, baby," I whisper into the phone when Marvin answers his cell. "I've been sitting here thinking about you, missing you."

"Zoë, I can't talk right now."

"Oh." The rejection stings like a slap in the face.

"It's been a crappy day here. Rachel Dawson came to work high, and she keeps messing up her lines. So we're shooting longer than we should be."

Rachel Dawson, one of the show's stars, has been steadily going downhill since last year. They'll no doubt have to replace her soon, but the producers have held off doing that since her fans will probably send all kinds of hate letters to the show.

"I won't be long," I tell Marvin. "I was calling because I need you to pick me up when you're finished."

"You can't get a ride with someone else?"

"No, I can't." Maybe I could, but I don't feel like asking anyone. I'm in that kind of mood.

"I'm gonna be late. Like an hour."

"That's all right. I've got more research to do anyway."

"All right then."

"Call me when you're outside."

Marvin disconnects without saying good-bye.

Sighing, I turn back to my computer. Phil has e-mailed me everything about this assignment, including links to various articles on pig wrestling. I've spoken to Daniel Buckley, the guy in charge of the rodeo, and gotten basic information from him. There are other people I'm supposed to interview so I can know what to expect on Friday, but I couldn't reach them today. I'll have to do that either tomorrow or Thursday.

I sip stale coffee as I go over the notes I've made. Surprisingly, pig wrestling is actually really big with some crowds—not that I'm any happier about having to cover this "sporting" event. But I do take it seriously, and think of various questions to ask.

The moment my cell phone rings and I see Marvin's number, I jump out of my chair. I grab my purse and dash for the door.

Outside, I smile at the sight of Marvin's white Honda, and I walk quickly toward it. "Hi, sweetheart," I say as I open the door.

"Hey," he grumbles.

My happy mood fizzles. Marvin looks miserable. He doesn't meet my gaze as I climb into the passenger seat.

Was his day on-set that awful?

I buckle myself in. "You had a really bad day, huh?"

"Yep."

"What's gonna happen with Rachel Dawson?"

"Who knows?"

Great, so he's doing the one- and two-word answer thing.

Marvin is dark-skinned, six feet tall, and quite attractive. Except when he broods. And right now he's brooding.

I can't stand pulling teeth to get a conversation going, so

as Marvin starts to drive out of the lot, I decide to talk about my day. "I had a bitch of a day, too. You'll never believe what Phil has me covering this weekend."

"What?"

"Pig wrestling!" I announce. "I didn't even know it existed. But apparently it does. Not in the city, of course, but in farming communities it's pretty big."

"Hmm."

Damn, I hate when Marvin gets like this. The thing is, I'm not sure why he's upset. Is it his day at work, is it me, or is it something else? And when he does his one- and two-word answers routine, he never volunteers anything—even if he is angry with me. It's like he expects me to be a mind reader.

Or maybe he just wants to make me suffer for some crime I committed, though I don't know what that crime is.

Leaning my head against the headrest, I stare out the window. We pass one industrial building after another along Wilshire as we head toward home. The scenery outside is drab and boring—kind of like the company inside the car.

We don't speak for several minutes, and Marvin turns on the radio. He scans past station after station, and finally stops when the raspy sound of Depraved Dave's voice fills the car.

"What do you think, guys? If your woman loves you, shouldn't she be willing to do *anything* to please you?"

"Ugh," I can't help saying. Depraved Dave is exactly what his name implies—a man with exactly zero values. At least not values that women can relate to. I can't stand the guy.

Unfortunately, he's a very popular radio host in the Los Angeles area, spewing his vile opinions for anyone who will listen.

"This is WXJY, All Talk Radio, and you're listening to *Get Real with Dave*. Guys, call me and tell me your raunchiest fantasies, and how you'd like your woman to make it a reality for you."

As the show goes to a commercial, Marvin doesn't change the station. I face him, saying, "Please tell me you're not about to listen to that crap."

"What's the big deal?"

"The big deal is I don't want to hear about all the perverted, noncommitted men in Los Angeles who want their girlfriends to do all kinds of kinky shit to please them." *And please, tell me you're not one of those guys . . .*

"Fine," Marvin huffs. He changes the station, and this time stops on 102.3 FM, a station that plays a mix of jazz, smooth R&B, and old school.

Whitney Houston is singing "Didn't We Almost Have It All." A love song, and it doesn't exactly suit the mood in the car right now.

Or does it? I can't help feeling like my relationship with Marvin is sinking faster than the *Titanic*. That we almost had it all, but for some unknown reason our relationship is about to end.

Still, I'm not about to give up. "Marvin, sweetie," I say when we turn onto Lankershim, "can you please stop at Starbucks before we go home? I'd really love a decent cup of coffee today."

Marvin not only sighs loudly, he mutters something indistinguishable under his breath. This I can't ignore. I don't like when he's testy like this, because it makes me insecure about us. About me. And it makes me hesitant to say anything to him for fear it'll be the wrong thing and make him even more upset.

But I need to know what's bothering him, and how I can make it right. So I ask, "Marvin, what's wrong?"

"Nuthin'."

We drive for a while longer, strained silence filling the car. He pulls into the parking lot of a Starbucks and stares straight ahead.

Well, obviously he's lying through his teeth. Something is wrong. Awfully wrong. But I say nothing because one—I don't know what to say. And two—I need a decent cup of coffee if I'm going to deal with Marvin's foul mood for the rest of the night.

Leaving Marvin in the car, I head into Starbucks, order a cappuccino, and then turn to leave. But on second thought I decide to head back to the cashier and order Marvin a cup of tea, his normal order when we come here.

Both items in hand, I make my way back to the car. Marvin is listening to Snoop Dogg loudly, and thrumming his fingers against the steering wheel. Even though my hands are full, he makes no effort to lean across the front seat and open my door for me.

I rest the cup tray on the roof of the car and, rolling my eyes, open the door. I'll do my best to be nice to Marvin, since I'm figuring he's had a pretty bad day or something, but I'm starting to get a bit upset myself.

"I got you some tea," I tell him as I settle back into my seat.

"Thanks," he all but grumbles.

You're friggin' welcome. I turn my gaze to the window as Marvin starts driving once again.

"We don't have to go pick up your piece-of-shit car again, do we?"

My head whips around, and I gape at him. "No."

"Good."

And that's all he says to me until we get home, and even then he doesn't say a word to me. He walks a few feet ahead of me as we cross the building's parking lot, but he's nice enough to hold the apartment's door open for me. *Gee, you shouldn't have gone to the trouble. I can't believe how good you are to me. You're the best boyfriend ever!*

Why am I still with Marvin? We're at the point in our relationship where he's making me feel worse about myself, compared to in the beginning when he used to make me feel pretty darn good about myself. I know from past experience that this is the time to get out.

But I'm not quite ready to give up. On him. On us.

On another relationship.

Marvin heads straight for the living room and I linger in the foyer, sipping my cappuccino. I'm not enjoying it nearly as much as I should be.

I debate what to do as I slip out of my shoes. After several moments, I know that I need to confront whatever the problem is head-on.

I make my way to the living room, where Marvin is already channel-surfing. "Are you pissed because you had to come and get me?"

He ignores me. In fact, he walks away from me. I tail him as he goes into the kitchen and I watch him place the tea I bought for him on the counter. Then he opens the fridge and pulls out a can of beer.

Now *that* makes me angry. I stalk toward him, getting between him and the fridge. "Marvin, are you gonna answer me? Or are you gonna ignore me all damn day?"

"Fine, you want an answer?" He glares at me. "Then yeah, I'm pissed off. You've always got some crisis or other going on, and after a long day, it's the last thing I want to deal with."

"My car broke down," I protest. "What'd you want me to do?"

"Last night I told you that giving it a boost would be like putting a Band-Aid on a knife wound. But did you listen to me? Noooo."

"I have a *job*. I need to drive to get to that job so I can make some money."

"You've got a job." Marvin chuckles mockingly. "Now that's funny."

"Why are you doing this? Picking a fight with me for no good reason?"

"Because you won't listen to me. I've told you forever that you need to get a *real* job. Hell, even working as a bit-part actress would give you more money than you make being a reporter."

He says "reporter" in the most sarcastic tone possible. Like he's rolling in the dough as a *production assistant*. Sure, he makes a fairly decent living, enough to pay his bills at least, but it's not like he's happy doing what he does. Which is why he's so miserable when he finishes work every day, if you ask me.

Marvin's big dream is to direct. I understand that dream, and I thought he understood mine.

In case he doesn't, I remind him. "You know why I'm at LASN. It's the only place that gave me a chance to work in sports. I can't get to the top without working my way up from the bottom."

Marvin mumbles something that sounds like, "You could sleep your way there."

"What did you say?"

"Come on, Zoë. Stop acting so self-righteous. You wouldn't be the first woman to use her sexuality to her advantage."

This floors me. That Marvin would even suggest I was the type to prostitute myself to succeed. "You know what—I'm going to ignore that."

I start for the bedroom, and Marvin doesn't follow me. Even though I'm relieved, I feel the sting of tears. Tears of frustration. Marvin and I just aren't on the same page anymore. We're fighting most of the time now, and I don't even know why.

At least if I knew . . .

I slam the bedroom door shut.

But does it matter why? Isn't the point that if we're no longer happy together, I shouldn't be with him? I can't deny the fact that it's been a long time since I've felt good being around him.

Nowadays, we seem to simply coexist, and often awkwardly.

As I plop myself onto the bed, I know what I should do. End the relationship. Tell him it's over, pack my bags, and move out.

And go where?

This is exactly why I've stayed. Because I can't afford to leave. As pitiable as that sounds, I just don't have the money to move out on my own.

It's not like I don't want my relationship with Marvin to work, because I do. But I'm certainly aware that if it doesn't work, I have no place to go. I'll have to go back to working part-time as a waitress, which was a hellish existence. And if I'm holding down a part-time job, how will I be able to put every effort into advancing as a sportscaster?

Do you see my dilemma? As long as I'm with Marvin, I'll have a roof over my head and the energy to put into my career.

I drag a pillow over my face. God, I'm so depressed.

"Screw you, Marvin," I say, sitting up. "I'm not going to let you ruin my evening."

I hop off the bed and go to the shelf above the television, where we have a variety of DVDs. I pick out *Sex and the City,* season four. I'll spend the evening dealing with Carrie Bradshaw's woes instead of my own.

I turn on the television and pop in the DVD, wondering

all the while if Marvin is going to come into the room and make up with me. "Ugh," I groan, realizing that there's something I need to ask him. I forgot to ask him if I can borrow his car to get to Acton for the pig-wrestling event Friday.

When will I get my big break?

Why don't you just sleep your way to the top?

Forget making up with Marvin tonight. He can sleep on the couch for all I care.

I mean really. He actually thinks I should sleep my way to success? He's supposed to be so insanely in love with me that the thought of another man looking at me will make him crazy with jealousy.

I return to the bed with the remote control. I'm about to change the channel when a blond anchorwoman catches my eye. She looks very smart. And pretty. No, gorgeous. Did she sleep her way to the top?

I extend my hand to the night table, reaching for the pack of cigarettes I used to keep there. The pack isn't there anymore because I gave up smoking a year ago. But old habits die hard, and every time I get anxious, I think about having a cigarette. And damn, I could use one right about now.

"And coming up, Jeff Colgate will tell us what's happening with Kahari Brown. He caught up with him today to talk to him about his Hero of the Year nomination."

"He's having a sensational year with the Raiders, isn't he?" the male newscaster comments.

"He sure is," the woman says. "I can't wait for the game against Buffalo this weekend."

Kahari Brown. I can't help perking up. Despite all reason, I've had a bit of a crush on him for at least two years now. He's a wide receiver with the Oakland Raiders, and has a mansion in Beverly Park, which is an exclusive area of Beverly Hills. I know he'd make a great story—the kind of story that could mean a big break for me, if ever I got the opportunity to interview him.

But back to this crush I have on him. I say despite all reason because he's a football player, and I have this fundamental thing against football players. There's a very simple and complex reason for it, the kind that's hard to ignore no matter how you try. My father was a star in the NFL. A quarterback, not a wide receiver, but a football player nonetheless. He met my mother when he was on the road, and they fell fast and hard for each other. The affair actually lasted over a year, and he was there when I was born. But shortly after that, he told her he couldn't commit, that he couldn't be a father because he was concentrating on his career. And then he left her. Left us. And I didn't hear from him again until my nineteenth birthday.

So I know firsthand that for professional athletes, their jobs come first. Because of their star status, their egos are huge and hard to compete with. Not to mention the likelihood that they'll screw around on you when they're traveling from city to city. Dating an athlete is like playing Russian roulette with a gun to your temple.

Do you want to take that chance? No thank you.

I grew up hating my father for abandoning me. Hating him and missing him at the same time. Until I became a teenager, when I no longer missed him but resented him. What kind of man ignores his own flesh and blood?

You would think I'd hate the game of football, because it took my father away, but my mother watched the sport all the time, and I found myself watching it beside her. She would proudly point out my father when we watched the Dallas games. That's when I missed him the most, when she would talk about him with pride and love, even though he wasn't in our lives. Even when I grew older and my father was no longer playing, I continued to watch football every weekend. I suppose I wanted to understand the game that had lured him away from my mother and me.

And I grew to love it, strangely enough. To understand my father's passion for it. How he could get caught up in the excitement and the glory.

But that doesn't mean I have to forgive him his weakness and negligence.

The first time I saw Kahari play, I felt there was something special about him. Like something about him reached through the television and touched me in a profound way. Not only is he extremely talented, but he's got these kind eyes—the sort, I suppose, I wished my father had. The kind that make you think he's really a nice guy despite his fame. It's easy to get caught up in fantasy where he's concerned.

The fantasy that my father could have been a man like that?

I push that thought from my mind and pop a stick of peppermint gum into my mouth as I watch the mindless commercials for dishwashing detergent, car insurance, and then plastic surgery. I've pretty much forgotten about *Sex and the City*. I want to see this news about Kahari. Maybe there's something useful in this story, some angle I can use to find a way to make my big break happen.

There's some playful banter between the news anchors when the news comes back on, and I imagine myself sitting there, in the blonde's role. And then I turn up the volume when Jeff Colgate's face appears on the screen.

"I'm here outside the Rita Brown Community Center, where just a short while ago I had the chance to talk to Kahari Brown. As I reported a couple days ago, he's been nominated for a Hero of the Year award from the Pass on the Dream Foundation for saving a young boy from a knife attack. It was no surprise to me that he didn't consider himself a hero. He's not only one of the best wide receivers in the league, he's incredibly down-to-earth. You'll see what I mean when you watch this clip."

The clip that plays shows Jeff Colgate inside the community center with Kahari. While he interviews Kahari, kids are playing in the background. I can't help smiling because Kahari does come off as down-to-earth. And concerned about the less fortunate. How bad can the guy be if he founded a community center for inner-city kids?

I feel warm inside, the way only a crush can make you feel.

When the clip ends, Jeff continues. "The awards ceremony will take place right here in Los Angeles two months from now. As far as I'm concerned, he's a shoo-in. Now, on to NCAA football . . . "

So Kahari's been nominated for a hero award? Very impressive. The only thing I'd heard about him recently was an allegation that he fathered some woman's baby but was denying paternity.

It kind of broke my heart, because it's hard to have a crush on a guy who'd do to a child what my father did to me, but I also know that lots of women are gold diggers and will make up this kind of story. So it's quite possibly a vicious lie.

Which is what I want to believe, by the way. Because this crush is nice, and I don't want anything to mar it.

My body energizes, and I've all but forgotten about the fight with Marvin. Right now I'm thinking about Kahari, that with his award nomination it's a great time to try and do a story on him. I'm not sure Phil would okay it, or even if he could swing it. But there's got to be a way.

Surely I can figure out how.

Yes, this is it. This is the key to my big break. I know it. I feel it.

Six

Kahari dropped the copy of the *L.A. Times* onto the marble counter when the phone rang. Still looking at the picture of himself gracing the front page of the sports section, he snatched up the receiver. "Hello?"

"Kahari Brown?"

He leaned against the counter. "Who's calling?"

"This is Stephen Walker with the *L.A. Weekly News*. Congratulations on your Hero of the Year nomination."

"Thank you," Kahari said warily. He was always on guard when reporters called him at home. "Listen, if you want an interview, contact my manager, Graham Elliott. He can set something up."

"No need. I won't be long. I'd just like to know if you'd care to comment on the allegation made by Estela Rivera that you fathered—"

"You're calling me about *what*?" Anger shot through Kahari's veins. "Look, I've got no comment. And lose this number!" He slammed the receiver back on its cradle. "Lord have mercy," he muttered. "Don't tell me this is gonna get worse."

"What's gonna get worse?"

Kahari spun around to see his sister, LaTonya, standing behind him in the kitchen. Wearing black Lycra shorts and a matching tank top, she had a towel slung around her neck. Her body was covered with a thick sheen of sweat, indicating that she'd just worked out.

"That was a call from some reporter," Kahari told her. "I thought he was calling about the nomination, but he asked about Estela."

Making a face, LaTonya groaned. "That hussy's still trying to get some attention?"

"Uh-huh," Kahari answered, but he was distracted. Why was LaTonya still here? And more importantly, why was she dressed in workout attire?

"Don't worry about that psycho Estela. People will catch on to her game real quick." LaTonya opened the fridge and took out a bottle of water. "I had a *great* workout today. I love that new cardio machine you got. It's really helping me tone my glutes."

"Thanks," Kahari said wryly.

"You have such an impressive gym. It's a shame you hardly use it."

Kahari crossed his arms over his chest. "LaTonya, I thought you were out. Looking for a job."

"Oh." She wrinkled her nose. "I was gonna head out this morning, but by the time I got ready it was later than I expected. So I figured I'd go out tomorrow. Although maybe what I should do is look at today's classifieds, and spend tomorrow and Friday making some calls, then hit the city first thing Monday morning."

Kahari had to hand it to his sister—she had every excuse in the book. "LaTonya, we talked about this. Last night you told me you were heading out bright and early *this* morning."

"I just explained why I decided against it." LaTonya tipped her head back and drank some water.

"Oh, LaTonya LaTonya." Kahari shook his head.

"What?"

"Come on, sis. You do this every week. Somehow time slips by and you don't end up looking for a job as you promised you would."

"Well." She smiled sweetly at him. "I guess I'm trying to find myself."

"Why don't you find yourself down at the community center more often? You know I could use you there." As it was, he could barely get her there once a week to help out with paperwork.

"And you know I was meant to do more than be a glorified secretary."

"A glorified secretary?"

"Shuffling papers. Filing. Typing. Isn't that what secretaries do?"

"Your point is?"

"How will that look to everyone?"

"Who's looking?"

She playfully rolled her eyes. "You're a big star. I'm your little sister. I can't be a . . . a secretary." She walked toward him, tipped on her toes, and gave him a kiss on the cheek. "Don't worry. I'll figure out what I was really meant to do. These things take time."

Kahari softened as LaTonya flashed him one of her charming smiles. He'd grown up protecting his little sister, and it was hard not to give in to her.

"All right, fine," Kahari said. "You've got until Monday to figure out your *path in life*."

"Thanks, bro." She walked across the kitchen, opened a cupboard, and put her empty water bottle in the recycling bin. "Now I'm gonna have a swim since it's such a nice afternoon. Why don't you join me?"

"I can't. I've gotta roll."

"But you just came in."

"I know. I have to run a couple errands before I leave for Oakland."

"Oh, that's right. You leave today."

And not a moment too soon. As much as Kahari looked forward to coming home every Monday after his weekend game, after a day here with LaTonya, he started itching to leave again.

It's not that he didn't enjoy seeing his sister. He did. But she tended to follow him around the house when he was here, and yak his ear off almost nonstop. Why? Because she didn't have anything else to occupy her time.

Like a job.

LaTonya spent more time at the house than he did these days because his football schedule had him spending most of the week in Oakland. So in many ways, it was like the house was hers.

Kahari loved his sister completely, but a year ago she had come here to "visit" for a few weeks, and she simply hadn't left. He craved his space.

Wrapping his arms around LaTonya, he kissed her on the forehead. "I'll see you on Monday."

"The house is so quiet when you're gone." LaTonya sighed.

"More reason for you to get out and find something to do."

Her lips twisted in a lopsided grin. "Be patient with me, okay?"

Kahari knew he would have to be. In the back of his mind was the reality that his mother had gone off into the world on her own to make a living, leaving her kids behind even, but that she'd had such a tough time with it. He would never kick his sister out onto the street, but he didn't want her thinking she could live off of him indefinitely.

"I'd better get ready," he said.

"Time to roll out the private jet."

"Yep." Every Wednesday afternoon, Kahari and Anthony took the hour-long flight to Oakland on a private jet. They practiced and prepared for the weekend game, then returned either Sunday night or Monday.

He hated the back-and-forth, but he wasn't about to give up his home in Beverly Hills. And at least his best friend was here with him, so he didn't feel like he was completely isolated from the team.

"When do I get to fly on the private jet with you?" LaTonya asked.

"You know Oakland is all about business. No one but me and T fly on that jet before a game." Call Kahari superstitious—and many people did—but he had a specific routine before a game and he didn't like to mess with it. Changing things invited disaster.

"Then why does Dr. Love get to go with you sometimes?"

"That's different." She *doesn't invade my space*. "But she's pregnant right now, so she's not going anywhere."

LaTonya sighed. "It was worth a try. Say hi to Anthony for me."

"Will do."

"And listen . . . If there are any of your boys on the team who are looking to settle down . . . "

"I know, I know," Kahari said. But fat chance if he was going to try and set her up with anyone on the team. For one, LaTonya needed to figure out what she was going to do with her life besides just trying to find a sugar daddy. Two, with the exception of T, he didn't trust most of the guys on the team to do right by his sister. Most of them were the stereotypical ballplayers, out for easy pussy where they could get it.

As Kahari headed out of the kitchen, he called over his shoulder, "You know the deal . . . If any reporters call, don't talk to them!"

"Okay!"

He went upstairs to get his bag, hoping he could trust his sister to keep her word. Two months ago she'd gotten into a shouting match with a reporter from the *Daily Blab* who'd called, trying to defend his honor. That wasn't the kind of thing that helped him, because it only encouraged the media even more. And, of course, the *Daily Blab* used his sister's belligerence in the story to make *him* sound like some evil person.

In general, Kahari had a strict "no comment" policy when it came to intrusive media questions. Some things simply weren't any of their business.

Like his personal life.

He had seen how the media had practically destroyed his best friend's reputation, and he'd be damned if he let that happen to him.

Estela Rivera, however, apparently had other plans.

Twenty minutes later, Kahari was downstairs in his garage with his bag. Of his four cars, he decided on the convertible black Viper.

Damn, he hoped this Estela Rivera bullshit wasn't starting up again. He had been cautious in letting his guard down, but he'd been hopeful since he'd heard nothing else from any other media.

And now this call.

Damn you, Estela.

He backed the Viper out of the garage and started down the long driveway to his gate. If Estela was going to become a bigger problem, there was only one thing he could do. Continue to ignore the press, not give them any answers, and hopefully this case would fade from public interest.

It had worked so far. He prayed that it still would.

Her eyes closed, Estela Rivera held her rosary beads clasped in both palms, her lips pressed against her hands. She was on her knees in front of the altar in her small apartment. Front and center was a statue of the Virgin Mary, which was surrounded by burning candles. Christ's picture hung on the wall above the Virgin.

In Spanish, Estela prayed. She prayed to the Virgin Mary for strength. Strength to get through the trying months ahead. Strength to be strong for her baby who so desperately needed her.

She also prayed for patience, because she knew she would need it. And she prayed that her faith wouldn't waver—the faith that Kahari would one day realize the true love for her that he had in his heart.

Because she knew he loved her. No man could spend such a passionate night with a woman and not love her.

Out of that love, a baby had been conceived, and Estela loved her son with all her heart. But her love was not enough. Her son also needed a father.

He needed Kahari.

Estela made the sign of the cross over her heart and head, then got up from her knees. Thinking about the way Kahari had rejected her after their affair, she couldn't help feeling sad. Her friends said she should get angry, that she was taking his rejection too lightly, but Estela did not want things to get ugly. She still loved Kahari completely, and more than anything, she wanted their relationship to work out.

So far she had been patient, and she was prepared to welcome Kahari with open arms the moment he came back to her.

But she would not be a fool. She would not wait forever.

She kissed her rosary beads once more, hoping that her prayer would be answered sooner rather than later.

Because one day she, Kahari, and Kahari Junior would be a family. Estela knew it in her heart.

Seven

Acton is a small farming community in Los Angeles County, and it's where I've spent the better part of the day covering the sporting event from hell.

Pig wrestling is . . . well, it's dirty. It's pretty nasty too, if you ask me, all those smelly pigs in mud and people jumping all over them as if it's the best thing in the world. It's the kind of sport that just doesn't make sense, the same way diving into icy cold waters on New Year's Day doesn't make sense. Or how lighting yourself on fire to protest injustice doesn't make sense. That said, I have a newfound appreciation for the fact that pig wrestling is actually a sport some people are crazy about.

Still, if I never see another pig again for the rest of my life, I'll be a very happy woman.

Norm didn't seem to mind, though. He's one of the LASN cameramen, and tends to work with me more times than not. He got a kick out of the whole thing, especially watching the women who got down and dirty in the mud with the pigs. I expect no less of Norm. He's six feet tall, three hundred pounds, and his best hope of getting laid on the weekend is with a blow-up doll.

"That was disgusting," I say now that we're in the parking lot. With a moan of sadness, I kick off my filthy sandals and dump them in the trunk of Marvin's car. I wasn't even thinking about the mud factor when I got dressed for this job, and I'm so disappointed I can't even begin to tell you. I spent three hundred dollars I didn't have on those Jimmy Choo sling-backs, and now they're practically ruined. I hope to hell that I can clean them up, because I love those sandals and I'd like to continue wearing them.

"How can you say that was disgusting?" Norm asks me. "I thought it was kind of fun."

I cut my eyes at him. "You would."

"Come on—hot girls in mud? I'm gonna have to make myself a copy of this tape!" Norm laughs, and his large belly shakes.

"Whatever!" I walk around to the driver's side of my car, brushing off my clothes all the way there. I know I've been splashed with some mud, and I'm sure I smell disgusting—not exactly the way I want to head home to my man.

First, Marvin was none too pleased when I told him that I needed his car, and I can see him getting really pissed off if I get it dirty. Second, I'm hoping that I'll be presentable enough and smell decent enough to seduce him. I can't stand that we haven't been getting along, and I'd like to change that.

And it has nothing to do with me needing a place to live. I do love Marvin. I love what we had in the beginning, and I'd like to get that back.

Norm whistles as he packs the camera equipment in the company's van. He's just so happy doing this job. So blissfully unambitious. Oh, he talks a good game about wanting to be a motion picture cinematographer, but I think that's all talk.

I hesitate before getting into the car. I've been debating asking him something. I want to, but I'm not sure if I should. I want to go to Oakland on Sunday to cover the Raiders game. It's at least a five-hour drive away, so it'd be against company policy since it's not an event Phil would have us cover. But if I'm ever going to move ahead in this field, I have to take my career into my own hands, don't I? I can't sit around and take pathetic assignment after pathetic assignment that will get me exactly nowhere.

Just do it. I blow out a shaky breath. "Norm?"

He stops whistling and looks at me. "Yeah?"

"What are you doing this weekend?"

His eyes light up and he wiggles his eyebrows, like he thinks I've propositioned him. "Anything you want, baby."

"Good. Cuz I'm gonna need you."

Norm claps his hands together. "Your place or mine?"

"Get serious, Norm."

"Hell, I am serious."

I'm sure you are. "I want to go to Oakland on Sunday. To cover the Raiders game."

"Oakland?"

"Yes, Oakland. I know it's far, but I'm still gonna go. And I'd like you to go with me."

"What—"

"And I don't want you to go back to the station tonight. It's Friday evening, so what's it gonna hurt if you keep the van till Monday? Phil's not around on the weekend, and you already said you don't have any other assignments. This way, we can head to Oakland bright and early Sunday—"

"Whoa, whoa, whoa." Norm is shaking his head. "I can't do that."

"Norm, please. I do *not* want to be stuck in this dead-end job forever. And I know you don't, either. Every day you tell me you want to be a cinematographer, don't you? Work in film and have a real career."

"Well, yeah—"

"Then it's time you take your destiny in your own hands. Put yourself out there in a really big way."

"How big are you thinking?"

"I want to get an interview with Kahari Brown."

"Oakland's wide receiver?" Norm asks disbelievingly.

I nod.

Norm's face twists with doubt. "I don't know about that. The guy's notorious for not really speaking to the media."

"But someone's got to be able to crack him, dontcha think? Why not me?"

"Kiesler's gonna have a heart attack if he finds out."

"Or, he's going to be kissing the ground we walk on if this works out the way I think it will, and I get an exclusive. Imagine it, Norm. An exclusive interview with one of the league's best players."

Norm still looks doubtful. "I don't know . . . "

"I do. And this is gonna work." I whirl around and grab a pen and piece of paper from inside the car. I scribble my numbers down and pass the paper to Norm. "Now, what's your number?"

"What about the next Lakers game? Why can't we try something there?"

"Because Ken will be there. It can't be the Lakers, Norm. It's got to be the Raiders. Kahari Brown is having a kick-ass year, and everyone wants to know what makes him tick. I want to be the one to find that out." Marvin's comment about me sleeping my way to the top pops into my head, and I find myself stepping closer to Norm. I place my hand delicately on his chest. "Come on, Norm," I say, all soft and whispery. "I need you."

"Oh, hell."

I smile, because I know I'm getting to him. And then I

pull my hand back, because I don't want him to think I'd do anything as crazy as actually get naked with him.

"You better not get me fired, Zoë."

"If this is a bust, no one's gotta know. That's the genius of this plan. It's a win-win situation."

Norm seems wary, but he says, "All right."

"Your numbers," I remind him, sticking the pen and paper pad in the palm of his hand.

I smile as he writes down his information. This is going to work. It has to.

"Marvin," I say as I open the apartment door. I peek my head in, holding my shoes behind my back.

There's no answer, and the apartment is quiet. It's late, though, after seven, and Marvin should be home by now.

In a way I'm glad, because this gives me the opportunity to clean up first. I can take a shower, light some scented candles, and slip into something sexy.

I creep into the apartment, dump my shoes near the door, then head into the bedroom to check the answering machine. It's flashing, so I press the play button.

"Hey, babe." It's Marvin's voice. "I'm going out with the guys from work tonight, so I'll be home late. See you later."

My mouth falls open in disappointment. He's going out? Damn it. Why couldn't he have told me this before? It's a Friday evening, and we always spend Friday evenings together.

There go my plans for seduction.

I contemplate taking a shower and ordering a pizza, but then I reconsider. It's a Friday night, and if Marvin is out on the town, why should I be home alone?

I know just what I'll do.

So half an hour later, freshly showered and wearing this hip black top I bought, Calvin Klein jeans, and strappy Gucci sandals, I grab my purse and head out the door.

* * *

I don't go anywhere fancy. There's a cool deli-shop-slash-coffeehouse-slash-lounge down the street from where I live that's really trendy, where everyone who wants to be anyone in NoHo hangs out. You have your "serious" actor types, your writers, your wannabe directors. Musicians. It's a haven for the artsy farts around here, and guaranteed not to be dull any day of the week.

Hopefully there's a poetry reading tonight, or an up-and-coming jazz band.

When I step inside Atmosphere, the lights are dimmed. There's this cool red velvet on the walls in the area where artists perform, which gives it a club lounge feel. But the other side of the place is your classic deli shop and coffeehouse. This side has brighter lights, and is filled with people who want to chat and hang out and not take part in whatever performance might be happening.

I don't immediately see anyone I know as I walk through this area, so I head straight back to the deli counter. Rocco, one of the owners, gives me a bright smile.

"Hey, Rocco." I return his smile as I step up to the counter. I feel better already. It's nice to be able to come in here and sit down at a table near the fireplace, drink some strong coffee and read the paper. Or listen to musicians who'll likely soon be signed to contracts. And Rocco makes the best deli sandwiches I've ever tasted anywhere, period.

"Zoë, you are looking radiant today."

My face warms, and I glance downward for a moment. Rocco says this to me every time I come into the shop. "Thank you, Rocco."

"What can I get for you today?"

Rocco's a tall, dark Italian cutie—and a sweetheart. I don't mind his flirtation. "Rocco, babe. The first thing I need is a caramel cappuccino."

"Need?"

"You'd better believe it."

Rocco chuckles. "One caramel cappuccino coming right up."

I watch as Rocco heads to the cappuccino machine and does his thing. "Lots of caramel," I tell him.

"I know," he chimes.

When he passes me my drink, I inhale the delectable aroma. And when I take a sip, I'm in caffeine heaven.

Rocco shakes his head as he looks in the direction of my collarbone. "You're still not eating enough, are you?"

Rocco's the kind of guy who likes a woman with meat on her bones. At least that's the sense I get because of the fact that he's always trying to feed me, and he's always telling me how thin I am.

"You'll be happy to know that I'm hungry, Rocco. Hungry enough to eat—"

"A cow?"

"Ha ha ha. Very funny. I was going to say half a dozen Krispy Kreme doughnuts. But you know what I'll have. The regular."

"Aw, live a little. Let me make you something special." Rocco pauses. "You trust me?"

The gleam in his eyes makes me wonder if I should. But I tell him, "You know I trust you." As Rocco turns and slips on a pair of plastic gloves, I quickly add, "Just make sure you don't try to give me tofu-flavored beef."

He chuckles. "I wouldn't do that to you."

Rocco knows I'm a vegetarian. He teases me all the time about not eating beef, saying that's the reason I'm so thin. I was real gawky as a kid, and picked on for it too, but I've come to accept that I'm the type who won't put on weight—at least not where I'd like it. I'd love a bigger chest and curvier hips, but that's not in the cards for me.

"Here you go," Rocco says a couple minutes later. "And before you ask, that stuff that looks like meat is actually meatless turkey. I ordered it specifically for you, and surprisingly, it's not all that bad."

"Thank you," I say sweetly.

"Anything for you, doll. Anything."

I can never figure out if Rocco is seriously flirting with me, or if it's harmless. Given that he's married and has two small children, I can only hope he's not a pig.

"Anything interesting going on here tonight?" I ask him.

"Some band named Lost Tribe will be heading out in about twenty minutes."

"Sounds interesting."

Rocco shrugs. "We'll see."

Overall, Rocco's really laid-back, and what I like about him is that he provides a space for artists to showcase their talent. I've heard that he plays the guitar himself, though he never pursued it professionally.

My items paid for, I take my tray of food and head toward the fireplace. I'm preoccupied with my search for a decent spot to sit when I hear what sounds like my name.

I turn toward the window but don't see anyone I recognize.

"Zoë?"

I turn to the left. And then I see him. Colby Stone.

That's not his real name, of course, but the "stage name" he's chosen, hoping it will help him become a Hollywood superstar. If Dr. Phil were to ask him, "How's that working for you?" he'd have to admit, "Not very well."

"Hey, Colby." I smile brightly at him. When I first came to L.A., I met Colby at a few acting workshops. I took them not because I wanted to become an actor, but because I wanted to become more comfortable in front of a camera.

"Sit with me," he offers.

I do a quick glance around but don't see anyone else I know. And Colby *does* have a coveted table near the fireplace.

I head toward him, and he gets up to greet me. That's very old-fashioned, isn't it—a man standing up when a woman is going to join him at a table. Maybe it's not old-fashioned at all, but I'm just not used to that treatment.

In any case, I appreciate the gesture.

"Will work for shoes." Colby chuckles as he reads my shirt. "Love it."

Colby is around five feet eleven, which makes him only slightly taller than me. His dirty-brown hair is highlighted with streaks of blond, and he wears it in an unkempt way. Think Brad Pitt when he wears his hair to his shoulders.

However, he's no Brad Pitt.

"How're you doing?" I ask him.

He shrugs. "Could be better."

"Oh? What happened with that big audition you had? Did you get the part?"

Colby frowns. "No. Two callbacks, and nothing! I swear, sometimes I want to give up and move back to Oklahoma."

"No! Don't say that. Then you'll go home with your tail between your legs and have to admit to your family you couldn't make it. Didn't you say that's the last thing you'd ever want to do?"

"Yeah, but how many times can I get this close"—he holds a thumb and forefinger close together—"only to fail? And you remember that film I got the audition for a couple months ago, the one I was so excited about?"

"Yeah. Whatever happened with that? You never said anything."

"I didn't give you any details because I was too embarrassed."

"I don't understand."

Colby glances around, then leans forward and whispers, "It was a porno flick!"

"What?" I exclaim.

He bulges his eyes as a hint for me to lower my voice.

"Sorry," I say. "Porn? Why? Don't you have a reputable agent?"

"Yeah, but I'd heard about this audition from someone else."

"Oh."

"It's true what they say. That if it sounds too good to be true, it is."

Colby sounds so . . . despondent. "I know it's frustrating, Colby, but you can't give up. *We* can't give up. I covered a pig rodeo today—"

"A pig rodeo? I thought they only had those back in Oklahoma."

"Well, apparently it's big in Acton. And let me tell you, it nearly drove me *insane.* I kept thinking, I can't do this forever. I can't keep working at LASN. These shit assignments will get me nowhere."

"I hear you."

"And then I get depressed if I think this is all I'll ever do. Which makes me want the dream even more."

"And don't you wonder why it's not happening for you but it's happening for others? Sometimes I feel like putting a gun to my head."

I sip my cappuccino. "I keep hoping for my big break, same as you, and though it's hard to stay positive at times, we have to believe in the dream." I pause, letting the thought of giving up actually wash over me. My stomach twists in a painful knot. "Dammit, Colby. We can't let this town eat us alive. We're good at what we do. Don't we deserve a chance just like anyone else?"

I'm a little surprised at how much I'm opening up to Colby, but my own recent audition disaster has me really bummed out. That and the fact that Marvin thinks I should sell out and sleep my way to the top.

I still can't believe he said that to me.

"I'm not giving up on the dream," Colby says, "but I ain't getting any younger."

Nor any better-looking . . . Okay, that was a mean thought. But Colby is just . . . average. He's a great actor, though. I've seen him perform in a few community theater plays, and I know he'd be great as a character actor. Look at Billy Bob Thornton's fabulous career. He's not the cutest guy on the block.

"Guys just get better with age. Not like women." God, will I *ever* make it?

Thankfully, Colby changes the subject. He starts talking about some acting class he recently took and how he met a young guy fresh out of film school who seems interested in giving him a break if he can get a studio interested in his film. I don't tell him that I was so big a moron I arrived late to the one great audition opportunity I've had since I've been here.

"See," I say, "your big break is lurking right around the corner."

"From your lips to God's ears."

Colby finishes the last of his iced tea and looks me dead in the eye. "Hey—how's Marvin?"

"Marvin is great," I reply without hesitation. "Busy, but great." I'm lying, of course. Because Marvin is still distant. Like he's mad at me for some reason and won't tell me why. But that's not the kind of information I'm gonna share with Colby. I'm not sure why, but the thought makes me uneasy.

Maybe because I'm pretty sure Colby's got a crush on me.

Maybe it's not me so much as it's the fact that I'm a black woman. Colby's into black women. At least, that's what I'm guessing, considering he's made a point of telling me that all his girlfriends have been black.

In that way, I guess he's like my father. He met my mother and lusted after her right away. Kept telling her how much he loved her dark skin, and that he felt he had been a black man in a previous life. My mother fell for all that sweet talk, and the rest is history.

Whatever the case is with Colby, he tends to give me these forlorn looks, and always wants to chat with me longer than I feel comfortable. I can only handle so much of Colby. He can get really intense at times.

By the time I finish off the last of my sandwich, I'm itching to leave. I push my chair back and stand. "Colby, as always, it was nice seeing you."

"Leaving already?"

"Yeah. I have to go home. Marvin and I are gonna see a movie."

"Oh." His tone is slightly disappointed. "That's nice."

The thing is, I want to stay and listen to the band since I have no man waiting for me at home, but that means I'll have to hang with Colby, and I don't want to do that. So I have to lie.

"You know how it is," I say. "He's so busy, anytime he's got a moment to spare, I take advantage of it."

"So things are good with Marvin, then? He's treating you okay?"

"Oh yeah. He's so sweet. You should have heard him on the phone. He kept apologizing that he was running late for our date night—it was so cute. He told me to go get myself something to eat until he got home. Which is why I'm here. But I've got to head home now. I don't want to keep him waiting."

Lies, lies, lies. I almost want to gag at the sound of my own syrupy voice.

I don't even know if my relationship with Marvin will last another week, much less another night.

That thought depresses me as I make my way home.

Eight

On Sunday I drive to Oakland with Norm, silently praying all the way there. *Please let them let us in. Please let them let us in.* In my quest for the story that will change my career, I haven't considered how Norm and I will get into the stadium with all our equipment. I can only hope that my LASN press badge will do the trick. And I've dressed the part in a black Prada dress that comes above my knees and a black blazer that I'll slip over it.

"I'm not sure this is a good idea," Norm says as we exit onto I-580 West, heading toward San Francisco.

"Why don't we try thinking positively? We're already on our way."

"We can always turn back."

"We've been on the road for four hours, Norm," I say, staring at his profile as he drives. "We can't turn back, so don't even say that."

"It's just . . . how are we gonna get in?"

"The way every other member of the press gets in."

"We're not like other members of the press."

"Listen," I say. "I'll do all the talking, okay? You just stay quiet and follow me in."

I don't bother to confide in Norm that I'm having my own doubts, fueled by my conversation in bed with Marvin this morning. He doesn't think that my driving all the way to Oakland is a good idea. He thinks it's a "friggin' waste of time" and that I'll only end up disappointed. In fact, we had such a fight about it that I told Marvin not to expect me home tonight, that I'd be staying with my friend Rose.

Well, Marvin's lack of faith in me has only helped make me even more determined, and I'm not about to take no for an answer from anyone.

Still, despite my resolve, I know that my press badge is about as good as toilet paper for an event like this. Hopefully I'll get some dimwitted moron who will cave under a flurry of eyelash-batting.

I drift off, and when I wake up we're no longer on the highway. We're downtown, I can tell that much. I look for a street sign and see that we're on Broadway.

"Norm, where's I-880?"

"Behind us."

I dig the map I printed off MapQuest.com out of my purse. After a moment I tell him, "We have to turn around. We were supposed to take I-580 until we hit I-880, so we need to go back on I-880 and head south, then get off at Hegenberger Road and go left. We take another left at Coliseum Way, and then it's on to McAfee Coliseum and the Raiders."

Butterflies dance in my stomach at the realization that we're almost there. Just minutes away from this opportunity I'm creating for myself.

Suddenly I'm not quite as brave.

Just do it. You'll be fine.

I'm not even sure what I'll ask Kahari yet, I guess because

that depends on the game he plays against New England. I hope he's super, and that he's fired up and ready to answer some questions.

Fifteen minutes later, Norm and I are in front of the coliseum, and Norm is unloading the van. When he's finished, I'm going to drive around the area and find a place to park. My hands are sweating, and it doesn't help that I see Jeff Colgate and his impressive film crew at the press entrance. Oh, and there's Austin Minter from ESPN. Howland Gray from TSN.

Is it my imagination or are they looking our way, wondering who the hell Norm and I are?

"You have everything?" I ask Norm.

"Yep."

"Okay, I'll find a place to park. Or do you want me to stay here with the equipment?"

"Actually, why don't you watch all this stuff and I'll park the van."

"Sure."

I'm wearing my sunglasses so as I look around, no one can see my eyes. They're definitely curious, which is cool as far as I'm concerned. Let them wonder who this new, smartly dressed chick is. And when I'm the one who gets Kahari to talk, they'll certainly remember my name.

Inside, I'm trembling, despite my thought. I keep looking around for Norm to round a corner. The minutes that tick by seem like hours.

Finally, there he is. I blow out a relieved breath.

I check the time on my watch. "We have an hour till game time, Norm. Time to rock and roll."

"Let's do it."

I try my best to look nonchalant as I wander up to the press entrance. The big boys have already gone in. Someone

I don't recognize, probably from a local station, is now making his way in with his camera crew.

Once he's through, I lift my press pass with a quick flash and start walking in behind the latest news team. But the woman who's standing at the gate quickly puts a hand down in front of me.

The woman, Hispanic-looking and as wide as a linebacker, glares at me. "Let me see that pass."

Of course, when you need a cute guy, there never is one.

I extend the pass to her.

"LASN?" the woman asked.

"L.A. Sports Network," I reply confidently.

The woman's brown eyes narrow. "I've never heard of it."

I chuckle nervously. "You *haven't*?"

She shakes her head. "Naw."

Oh, great! Please don't let me have gotten all the way here only to be turned away!

"It's based in L.A. You know, where most of the major studios are. It's huge. I mean, one of the biggest sports networks in the Los Angeles area. I don't know why you've never heard of it."

"You're not on the list."

"I'm not?" I ask disbelievingly. "Obviously there's been some kind of mistake. Granted, we don't always cover the Raiders games, but this is a big one, with the excitement high over the rematch with New England."

The linebacker doesn't look impressed.

"We really need to get in," I continue.

"You're not on the list."

No, please no.

I'm contemplating what to do next when Norm steps forward. "Hey, sugar," he says. "It's all right if I call you sugar, isn't it?"

Oh, great. Just what I need. For this woman to lodge a complaint against Norm for sexual harassment.

But she surprises me when she says, "Sugar, hmm?" and doesn't sound outraged.

"I call it like I see it, and you are sweet."

The woman actually giggles, and blushes like a schoolgirl.

"What *is* that fragrance you're wearing?" Norm asks her.

I want to tell him to cut back on all the corny lines, that surely they're not going to help. But again, the woman seems flattered.

"It's new," she explains. "Something with a French name. My ex got it for me," she adds with a snort. "I almost didn't wear it."

"Your ex?" Norm asks, his eyes narrowing. "What man in his right mind would walk away from you?"

"I walked away from him. He was cheating on me."

"No," Norm says in a horrified whisper.

"Imagine my shock. I found him with some bitch in *our* bed."

I'm amazed as I watch this scene play out in front of me. Like a cat, I quietly step backward and let Norm take center stage.

"If he was dumb enough to cheat on you," Norm goes on, "then you deserve much better."

"Oh, I know it. But it still hurts."

"Of course."

Now Norm places his hand on the woman's. "I'm not from around here, but I come to the Bay Area a lot. What's the chance that I can give you a call when I'm back in town."

Work it, Norm. I can't believe the woman's lapping up his corny lines.

"I suppose so. That'd be nice."

They're quiet for a moment, and when I look their way I

see the woman is writing her number on Norm's hand. Then he must tickle her palm or something, because she starts laughing.

When they both stop chuckling, Norm looks at his watch. "Oh, man. Look at the time. People are starting to arrive for the game, and we've got to get in there. Are you sure we're not on the list?"

The woman steps back. "You go on ahead."

"Thank you kindly, Louisa."

Louisa actually grins at me as I follow Norm into the stadium. When we're safely several feet away, I gape at him. "How'd you do that?"

"Never underestimate my charm, Zoë," Norm says with a wriggle of his eyebrows.

"I certainly won't," I say, meaning it. I've always thought Norm laughably cheesy. Who knew some women liked cheesy?

"Where to?" Norm asks.

Yes, where to? "Where the big boys have gone. Which I suspect is to the locker room, for pregame footage and interviews."

I lead the way, my gait strong. I see the bigwigs standing at the far end of the stadium, their cameras set up, some rolling as the various sportscasters are speaking.

As we get closer, I recognize Brian Cox, who's the huge sportscaster in the Bay Area. And I hear his deep voice. " . . . with much talk today on New England's part about evening the score. But Russ Edmonds says his team is prepared and pumped, and that the Raiders *will* walk away with another win today."

Austin Minter is saying, " . . . the way they're playing, I'm betting that the Oakland Raiders go all the way to the Super Bowl."

Man, I'm nervous. I'm standing here among legends.

There's no way I'm going to set up camera beside these guys.

"Norm, let's try to move behind the crowd. Then I need you to look busy with your equipment while I try to get into the locker room."

"You're the boss."

I edge my way to the double doors, behind which I can hear voices. *This is it.*

Easing the door open, I peer inside. I see several of the team's players. Bobby Smith. Clark Gooden. Ooh, and there is the legendary Anthony Beals. He'd also be great for a story, but around a year and a half ago all anyone in Los Angeles could talk about was Anthony Beals when his five-month marriage to some piece of work had ended in public scandal.

So everyone knows all there is to know about Anthony Beals. And when it comes to his games, he talks willingly about the plays and why a certain strategy works.

It's Kahari who gives these generic answers that mean nothing. Answers like, "I was lucky," or "I couldn't have done it without the rest of my team." He's the one I have to break.

I continue to scan the room from the crack in the door's opening. And then I spot him.

My breath catches in my throat at the sight of him as he's walking toward the rest of the guys. It's that whole crush thing, and I have to say, in person, he looks larger than life. He's got these broad shoulders, and a huge chest. He wears his hair closely cropped, and has warm, caramel-colored skin. Honestly, his body is as close to perfection as I've ever seen on a man.

He glances my way, and I quickly release the door and jump backward.

"Damn," I mutter. "I did *not* come here all this way to wimp out."

But I'm also not sure what the protocol is. Can I even try to get an interview before the game? None of the other sportscasters are.

I open the door again, and now all the players are huddled in a circle, their heads bowed. Someone is saying a prayer.

"What's happening?"

I jump at the sound of Norm's voice. Then I turn to face him. "I'm not sure this is a good time. The team's praying. And no one else is over here trying to get an exclusive. I don't want to ruin any pregame ritual."

"You just want to stand here?"

"Well . . . yeah. When they start filing out, we can get some footage of that. And I can try and get Kahari's attention."

"You sure you know what you're doing?"

"Of course." *We'll see . . .*

And so we wait. And wait. The crowd is getting louder as the stadium fills.

Finally, there is movement. "Okay," I say to Norm. "The guys are starting to file out. Start rolling."

Norm hoists the camera onto his shoulder and I grab the microphone. Seconds later, the door swings open and the guys spill out of the locker room. The cheerleaders have formed two lines at the entryway to the field, marking a path for the players. The guys also form a line, and one by one the star players are being announced before they head onto the field.

"There's Kahari, Norm. Number 81. You see him?"

"Yep."

"Let's get closer." My heart is beating a mile a minute as I edge as close to Kahari as I dare. He's jumping on the spot, pumped. Suddenly I realize this isn't the time to disturb him. But I'm already here, and I have to take a chance.

He glances my way, and I'm instantly second-guessing myself. I can't do this now. Can I? In fact, the big-name reporters have disappeared. Shouldn't I be trying to get to a press box or something?

Over the loudspeakers I hear, "Kahari Brown, wide receiver. Number *81*!"

The crowd roars with applause, and Kahari jogs onto the field.

I stand there stupidly, my fingers numb on the microphone.

"That went well," Norm comments wryly.

I turn to face him. "Shut up, Norm."

"I asked you if you had a game plan. Didn't I ask if you had a game plan? And you just stand there—"

"Please"—I wave my hand angrily—"I'm trying to think."

The thundering sound of running feet draws my attention. The rest of the team is jogging onto the field, and the crowd is screaming its delight.

"Don't look at me like that, Norm. This wasn't the time. We'll have to get him after the game, in the pressroom with everyone else."

"All right," Norm says in a singsong voice as he lowers the camera. But I hear what he doesn't say just as loudly.

You know this is pointless, so why are you even bothering?

"I really need you to be positive, Norm. That's the only way this is going to work."

"I'm not saying anything."

"That's the problem. You could try and help me figure this out too, you know."

"Zoë, this was *your* plan."

I groan and start to walk off, then draw up short as I see someone. My eyes instantly lower from his face to the press badge he's wearing on a chain around his neck.

This brotha is fine as hell—and probably going to get us kicked out of here.

"Come on, Norm." I head off with determination, feeling the man's eyes on me as I pass him. I round a corner to the left, then stop and look to the right. Where am I going, anyway?

"Excuse me?" I hear.

Damn. Should I ignore him? There's no way I'm about to get kicked out of here, so I start walking again. "Hurry, Norm," I whisper.

But I don't get more than a few steps before the man says, "Hold it, miss. Wait right there."

Nine

Sighing in defeat, I halt, then slowly turn. The man is already heading toward me and Norm.

Damn, the jig is up.

Still, I offer him a smile as he nears me. "Um . . . hello."

"You look lost," he comments.

"Well . . . not really."

"Aren't you heading for the press box?"

"Yes. Yes, we are."

"Then you're going the wrong way."

"Oh." I force a chuckle. "Of course. I was going to get some water . . . first."

Grinning, the man steps right up to me. "I'm Alex Crawford. *Oakland Tribune*. And you are . . . "

"Zoë Andrews." I extend a hand, and he shakes it firmly. "And this is my cameraman, Norm."

He nods toward Norm before turning back to me. "How come I haven't seen you before?"

"Norm and I are from L.A. We're with the L.A. Sports Network."

"L.A. Sports Network," he says thoughtfully. "Hmm. Never heard of it."

"You haven't? I'm so surprised." I can't think of anything smarter to say.

"I'm heading to the press box now. Why don't you come with me? There's plenty of water there."

Yes! "Oh. Sure."

"It's this way," he says, nodding to the right.

"Right. Each stadium is different."

Alex flashes another soft smile, then places a gentle hand on my elbow. Suddenly it hits me. The warm looks, this subtle touch. He's interested.

Marvin's voice sounds in my head. *You wouldn't be the first woman to use her sexuality to her advantage.*

Maybe Marvin is right.

"I do appreciate this," I tell Alex. "You had me pegged right. I was lost."

"You're in good hands now."

Norm lags behind us, and I give him a look over my shoulder. He winks at me, which I take to mean he thinks I should use Alex's interest to my advantage.

I wink back, letting him know that I'm on it.

The box is filled with journalists who sit in bleacher-style desks typing away into computers as each play of the game is made. You would think that with all the work they're doing, there's not time to have a good time, but the box is well stocked with beer, wine, and coolers.

"Here," Alex says, handing me a glass of wine.

"Oh, I'm fine, thank you." I want to settle in to watch the game.

"No, please."

Since he won't take no for an answer, I accept the glass.

But I don't make eye contact with him. I stare down at the field, letting him know I'm interested in seeing the game.

Play after play, Kahari is simply spectacular. I can't help jumping to my feet and cheering when he makes a one-handed catch in the end zone.

"The guy's amazing, isn't he?" Alex asks me.

"I don't think there's a better wide receiver in the league," I respond confidently. And I really mean it. Kahari's got such dexterity that time after time he catches balls you'd expect him to miss.

I wonder how he puts that athletic body of his to use in the bedroom . . .

At half time, the score is 10-7 in Oakland's favor. Not a huge lead, and I find I'm a little anxious. I want Oakland to win this game. It'll be so much better for the interview.

Over the half-time break, I stay in the box with Norm and Alex, passing the time by having a couple drinks and munching on a turkey sandwich. Alex hangs close to me, making me a bit uncomfortable. I know there's no way I could ever be the type to sleep my way to the top.

I'm relieved when the game starts again, and almost immediately, New England scores. Now they're ahead by four points, and you can feel the tension in the crowd.

I sit on the edge of my seat, my eyes glued to the field. Kahari continues to impress throughout the third quarter, but New England is still ahead when the fourth quarter begins.

New England loses the ball to an interception, and the crowd goes wild. Oakland has momentum back, and the first pass that Anthony Beals throws is a long one into Kahari's hands. Kahari, a couple feet away from New England's corner, takes off down the field.

Hopeful, I start to rise, but now New England's safety is gaining on Kahari . . .

Kahari dives into the end zone, and everyone in the box roars with excitement at another touchdown.

New England next executes a flawless offense, resulting in a touchdown. They're four points ahead with twenty-one points. I glance at the clock. Five minutes and two seconds left.

My stomach churns as I anxiously wonder how this game will ultimately play out. I'm also a bit nervous over the fact that we'll soon be heading downstairs. My big moment is about to arrive, and I can only hope that my plan to interview Kahari works.

"You look worried," Alex says to me.

I realize then that I'm gnawing on a fingernail. "A bit," I confess.

"Oakland's got this one," he assures me.

I'm not so sure. "It's a four point difference and there's five minutes left. What if Oakland only scores a field goal? They'll lose by one point."

"Have a little faith, will ya?"

"I'll try."

As Alex eases onto the sofa beside me, I look across the room. Norm is at the food table, eating a handful of Doritos. He's spent pretty much all his time over there.

"What are you doing after the game?" Alex asks me.

I glance at the hand Alex has placed on my knee. The thin gold band is clearly visible.

"We have to hit the road. It's a long drive back to Los Angeles."

He leans close to me and asks, "You've got no time to hang out? Get something to eat."

"I don't think so, but I could ask Norm."

"I was thinking you could ditch Norm."

The reporters in the room hoot and howl in applause. I jump to my feet, looking out the glass windows onto the field. Kahari Brown is dancing in the end zone as he holds the ball.

"Yes yes yes yes yes!" Alex yells from beside me. "Damn, that guy is on fire!"

Which is why I'm desperate to interview him. I now look at one of the three TVs in the box and watch the instant replay. Down by three points, Anthony Beals threw a Hail Mary pass straight into Kahari Brown's hands. Kahari added at least twelve yards after the catch—known as YAC in the game—and ran the ball into the end zone.

Alex turns to me, high-fiving me, but he doesn't let go of my hands. "I told you, didn't I? I called it at 21 to 17, didn't I?"

"You did." I wriggle my hands free.

I glance at the game clock as Alex heads back to his computer. One minute and eight seconds left. I bite on a finger as New England executes a hurry-up offense, but after three downs they're forced to kick the ball.

One of Oakland's punt returners takes the ball to the Oakland thirty-yard line. The offensive line heads onto the field.

Anthony Beals's first pass is to Kahari, who easily catches it. He makes the sport look like child's play, that's how talented he is.

"And that's it, folks," the announcer says. "Oakland is going to run out the clock . . . "

I turn to Norm. "We've got to go downstairs. Maybe get on the field. No, we'll head straight to the pressroom and try to get a good spot."

Alex is suddenly beside me again. "Let me take you downstairs."

I'm a little wary of spending any more time with the touchy-feely Alex, but I do need him to ensure that I get into the pressroom.

So Norm and I follow him downstairs, where he takes us back in the direction of the locker room. There's already a throng of other reporters who are waiting to get into the room.

"Stay close to me, Norm. I'm gonna try and get up nice and close."

It doesn't take long before the line starts to move and the reporters are heading into the pressroom. Alex shows his pass to the person manning the door and says to him, "They're with me."

As easy as that, we're in.

I can feel the excitement in the room, and my body is buzzing with energy. My chance is almost here. My moment to shine.

"Closer, Norm," I say as I weave my way through the crowd for a better position.

We're as close as we're going to get to the long table covered with royal blue material that's set up at the front of the room. I guesstimate that we're about twenty feet from the front.

Five minutes pass before a side door opens and Russ Edmonds, the head coach, enters the room followed by Kahari Brown. They sit side by side behind the table.

"Kahari! Kahari!" The shouts start, with each reporter trying to be heard.

"Kahari Brown—Ryan Townsend with Channel 4 Sports. Amazing game. How'd you pull off that one-handed catch?"

Kahari shrugs. "Luck."

"Kahari—Alex Crawford with the *Oakland Tribune.* I've heard a rumor that you pulled a hamstring after last week's game—"

"Negative," Kahari says.

"Kahari is in perfectly good health," the coach states.

I watch and I wait for the perfect moment to form my own question. And when there's a pause in the room, I speak.

"Kahari Brown, I'm Zoë Andrews from LASN." My heart is pounding out of control. "What I want to know is how you do it. Week after week, all these incredible catches."

He gives a little smile as he shrugs, as if guarding the secret of his success with his life. "It's a team effort," he replies. "When we gel, we gel, and produce results."

When we gel, we gel? Surely he could give a better answer than that.

I'm about to ask that when the coach says, "Last question."

Another reporter interjects before I can. "Kahari, can you speak to the rumors that you and Paul Dixon have an ongoing rivalry?"

"I don't know where y'all get your information, but I get along with everyone on my team."

"That's all for now, folks," the coach announces as he stands. Kahari scans the room as he gets to his feet, his gaze connecting with mine. Then he holds up his hand in a goodbye wave.

No! He can't leave. I have to get him to talk. I have to do *something.*

He is almost at the door when I blurt out "Wait!" as if my life depends on it. My frantic-sounding outburst gets his attention—and everyone else's in the room.

"I . . . I was wondering . . . " I can't think of something to ask that hasn't been asked. "Well, wondering if—"

"I'm sorry, sweetheart," he says with an easy shrug of his shoulders. "My time's up."

Sweetheart? What is that—some kind of sexist brushoff? Because I'm a woman, am I to be taken less seriously?

I feel slighted.

I open my mouth and ask the first question that pops into

my mind. "Is it true that you got Stella Rivera pregnant but you're denying your child?"

Now Kahari's head whips around. As his eyes land on me, his face contorts with disbelief first, then anger. But he doesn't say a word. Instead, he turns and walks out of the room at a brisk pace.

The other reporters glare at me, and I can't help withering on the spot. Damn, I feel like I'm about to be the victim of a lynching.

"What was that about?" Norm whispers.

"I don't know," I respond, "but let's go."

Before I can take three steps toward the door, Alex blocks my path. I look up at him, expecting to see a friendly face, but he actually scowls at me.

"What kind of question was that?" he demands. "I thought you were a serious journalist."

At least I'm not a philandering pig, you jerk.

But while I cling to some sense of pride because I'm morally superior to him, his look of disappointment still makes me feel awful. Like I'm pond scum or something.

"Norm," I say urgently, then start pushing my way through the crowd.

There's a roomful of eyes shooting daggers in my back as I exit, and only when I'm outside of the pressroom do I allow myself to replay the question I stupidly asked Kahari.

Why did I say that? Why, why did I say that? What was I *thinking*? And the way Kahari looked at me, not to mention everyone else in the room—I don't know if I'll ever get over the sick feeling of humiliation that has taken root in my stomach.

I've had some really shitty days, but this one has got to be the worst one ever.

Ten

As the recap of the game played on ESPN, Kahari and Anthony watched it from their respective beds in their hotel room.

"Another fantastic game for Anthony Beals, who was last year's MVP, and Kahari Brown, who I'm betting will be this year's MVP," Tom Evans said. Retired from the game of football, he had played at quarterback for many years.

"You got that right," Matthew Collins agreed. Only recently retired, he was one of the greatest running backs to ever play the game. "I don't care that he missed that ball in the second quarter. He redeemed himself at the end of the game with that amazing one-handed catch."

"Speaking of amazing—or should I say bizarre—what was with that one reporter at the end of the game?"

"That came out of left field, didn't it?"

"And this isn't even baseball."

Both sportscasters chuckled.

"I've said it once, I've said it a million times," Tom said, his blond hair bobbing as he shook his head, "female reporters just aren't as focused as men when it comes to sports."

"Come on, Tom."

"What—you think that's sexist? Take a look at this clip."

The television screen filled with a scene from earlier that day, in the locker room, with Kahari and the coach heading to the door. Kahari sucked in a breath, knowing what was coming next.

"Is it true that you got Stella Rivera pregnant but you're denying your child?"

The ESPN camera that had been filming Kahari and the coach quickly whipped around to catch a shot of Zoë Andrews, the woman who'd asked the question. Then the camera went back to Kahari, catching the scowl on his face before he stalked out of the room.

"Unbelievable," Matthew said, "but I think Kahari did the right thing when he didn't dignify that question with an answer."

"I think that lady ought to stick to watching soap operas and eating bonbons," Tom said, then laughed.

Kahari hit the mute button. "You see that?" he asked Anthony. "It's as bad as I told you, right?"

"Not quite. They're totally dissing her. That's a good sign."

Anthony's answer failing to mollify him, Kahari got up and started to pace. "Who the hell was that woman, anyway? I've never seen her here before."

"Smooth, calm down."

"You think she was a real reporter?"

"Who knows?"

"This was a football game. A sports event. Our eighth win in a row. Why the hell would she ask me about *Estela*?"

Anthony shrugged. "I dunno, dude."

"You think Estela put her up to it?"

Anthony got off the bed and walked toward Kahari.

"Maybe she did. But most likely, that reporter had an ulterior motive. Looking for her fifteen minutes of fame, probably. And it backfired on her."

"This time. But what about the next time?"

Anthony threw his hands up.

"I'm not even sure what Estela wants, but I figure it's gotta be money. So why hasn't she gone to a lawyer?"

"Because she knows she's got nothing to give a lawyer." Anthony placed a hand on Kahari's shoulder. "Listen, she's not the first woman to claim she's been knocked up by a football player. She won't be the last. But it's pretty obvious that no one believes her, or the press would be all over her story."

Kahari let out a deep breath. "You're probably right."

"Give Estela a few more weeks before she disappears altogether. And think of the bright side."

"The bright side?"

"Yeah," Anthony said, squeezing Kahari's shoulder. "You didn't marry her."

Kahari cracked a smile. "You know that's right. Can you imagine?" Anthony had gone through enough hell by marrying the wrong woman that Kahari never wanted to experience anything even close to that.

"That's why me"—Kahari pointed to himself—"I'm staying single."

"It's all about the right woman," Anthony said, starting for the door. "Come on. Let's go get a bite to eat. Coach wants us up bright and early to go over the tape from the game, and I'm already ready to hit that pillow."

Kahari followed Anthony across the room to the hotel door. They'd get a bite to eat, have a beer . . . and he would forget about Estela Rivera.

Is it true that you got Stella Rivera pregnant but you're denying your child?

Damn, who was that woman? Initially Kahari had found her attractive when his gaze had landed on her. Until he heard the ugly words that had come out of her mouth.

"Whoa, wait," Kahari said when Anthony's hand was on the doorknob. "You can't just open the door like that. Look through the peephole. See if there's anyone out there."

Anthony did as instructed, then quickly jumped back.

"What?" Kahari asked, panicked.

"It's Estela."

"Oh, shit," Kahari whispered.

Anthony started laughing, and Kahari realized that his friend was lying. "Don't play me, dawg."

"I couldn't resist."

Kahari punched Anthony's arm. "That shit ain't funny. You know that woman's got me all stressed."

Anthony winced as he opened the door. "Point taken, Slugger. You don't have to beat my ass."

"You've just gotten soft ever since becoming a married man."

"Ha!" Anthony chuckled as he peered into the hallway, looking both left and right. "The coast is clear, but let's take the stairs just in case. Wanna avoid all those groupies in the lobby."

"You think I'm being paranoid?" Kahari asked.

"I don't know," Anthony said as he got to the stairwell door. "Maybe just a little."

"Maybe I am," Kahari acknowledged. "But can you blame me?"

Anthony opened the door, took a step, then drew up short. "Hey, Estela. What are you doing here?"

Kahari rolled his eyes. He wasn't about to fall for that again. "Stop your playin', dawg."

But as Kahari stepped forward, Anthony stepped to the side and Estela appeared.

Hell no!

She looked up at him and smiled. "Kahari."

"What are you doing here?" he asked.

"You didn't return my calls."

"And you know why."

"You can't run from me forever, Kahari. What about our son?"

Kahari had long ago lost patience with Estela, even if he did feel a bit of pity for her. The woman had to be nuts to continue hounding him the way she was. And that was too bad, considering she was extremely beautiful and could probably make some guy happy if she wasn't a nutcase.

Anthony glanced at Kahari over Estela's head, his eyes questioning. Kahari gave him a hard stare, letting him know he did not want to be left alone with her.

"I'll give you two a moment," Anthony said anyway, "but then we've got to roll, Kahari. The reservation's for eight, remember?"

"Yeah, I know." Blowing out a frazzled breath, Kahari took Estela by the shoulder and led her into the hotel hallway. "Estela, you've got to stop following me around. You've got to stop talking about our baby, because we both know that you got pregnant *after* we stopped dating."

Her eyes filled with horror. "How can you say that? You know this baby is yours!"

Why had Kahari expected her to simply disappear? "Estela, please."

Looking crushed, she asked him, "Why are you doing this to me?"

"*Me* doing this to *you*?" Kahari shook his head. "You're the one telling the media all kinds of lies. And I don't appreciate you getting that reporter to ask me about us today, right after my game. That was completely inappropriate."

"I don't know what you're talking about."

"And it was embarrassing, too." He paused. "You act like you care about me—"

"I do. Kahari, you know I do."

"Then stop trying to make me look like some kind of villain in the media. It's obvious they don't believe you, anyway, since no one credible is milking your story."

"No one is 'milking' my story because I've asked them not to. Out of respect for you."

Kahari's eyes narrowed in confusion.

"After that first time, I haven't gone to the media again. No, I did go to them—to ask them not to pursue the story I originally told them."

"What?"

"Yes, Kahari. It's true. I've been caring about your feelings in all of this, protecting you. Because of our son." She paused as her brown eyes narrowed. "But I won't be so nice in the future if you continue to deny me and your child."

"What's that supposed to mean?" Kahari asked.

"Do the right thing."

"Which is what? You want money—is that it?"

Estela shook her head as she stared at him. "This isn't about money."

"A college fund started for your kid?"

"This is *not* about money," she repeated.

"Then what's it about?"

Hurt streaked across her face. "How can you ask me that?" She took a step toward him, reaching for him, and Kahari moved away from her. "Baby, please . . . "

The hell of it was that Estela looked . . . sincere. Like she believed every crazy word she said. Kahari couldn't help feeling bad for her and annoyed at the same time. "If you really believe everything you're saying to me," he began slowly, "then you need help, Estela. Help I can't give you. Please—"

"I love you, Kahari."

Damn. "I've got to go."

"No, wait."

But Kahari didn't wait. He turned and ran into the stairwell. "Let's go," he said to Anthony, barely pausing before thundering down the stairs.

"What'd she say?" Anthony asked from behind him.

"She's lost her mind. The woman needs some serious help."

"Meaning what?"

"Is she coming?" Kahari asked, looking over his shoulder.

"Naw," Anthony replied. "Tell me what's going on."

"Maybe she's on crack, or she's shooting heroin or something, because she's talking like she believes that baby's mine."

"Shit."

"She also said she's been protecting me from the media. Yeah, right. I know she used that Zoë woman to get to me today. And hell, how does she always know where I am? We check in under assumed names, yet she's called me at hotel after hotel . . ."

"I think you're right. She's gotta be working a media connection."

"She needs to get help," Kahari said as he hit the first-floor landing.

"Sounds like it."

But would she get it? Or would Estela Rivera become even more of a problem?

Eleven

Is it true that you got Stella Rivera pregnant but you're denying your child?

The words haunt me—and the evil glares I got from everyone in the media room—the entire ride home with Norm. And Norm—damn, do I ever want to strangle him at times—he does a good job of reminding me of my eloquence.

"I still don't get why you said that," he'd commented about forty-five minutes ago. "Where'd you hear that story, anyway?"

"Norm, will you just *shut up*!" I'd yelled in frustration. He looked wounded afterward, but at least he stopped talking.

I close my eyes on and off during the drive, but I can't sleep. I feel too sick.

Why *did* I ask that question?

Because I had to know. It was impulsive, yes, but I wanted to see how Kahari would react to it. I wanted to know if he's a man worthy of being in my fantasies or not.

Unfortunately, I didn't get an answer to my question.

We're about an hour outside of Los Angeles when Norm turns to me, and I can tell by the expression on his face that he wants to say something.

"What?" I ask, still testy.

"Maybe it's not as bad as you think," he says.

A little sigh escapes me. "Norm, thank you for that. Really. But can we just drop this already? The trip was a bust, and I'm sorry about that, but hey, at least I tried something. I do thank you for coming with me, though. I really appreciate it."

Norm's lips lift in a faint smile. "I wasn't doing anything, anyway. And guess what—I had a good time."

"Good. So we can drop this wretched subject already?"

"God, you're tense. You want to get a drink or something when we get back?"

I grimace as I cast a sidelong glance at Norm.

"Maybe not," he quickly says, then faces the road.

I am at the point of exhaustion when we reach North Hollywood close to midnight. Not only can I not forget how badly I screwed up my chance at a great story with Kahari, but I have this sick, tense feeling in my gut regarding my relationship with Marvin. I'm almost afraid to see him after our fight this morning. I didn't really mean what I said, that I'd stay with Rose tonight. I just wanted him to realize that he has to support my dreams.

Norm pulls up to my apartment building a few minutes after midnight. I reach across the seat and squeeze his hand. "Thanks again for coming with me."

"No problem. Sorry I had to stop so many times for food. I know you wanted to get home sooner."

"Hey, we're home safe and sound. That's all that matters."

"See you at eight."

Ugh. I don't want to think about that. I am so not in the mood to go to work in the morning. At least I've convinced Norm that I'm not entirely bad news and he's going to pick me up.

As he drives away, my mind returns to the situation with Marvin. It's time to make things right with him.

I think of what I can say as I open the apartment's front door.

We have to talk about our relationship.

No, that sounds too formal, too kiss-of-death.

Marvin, we've drifted apart and I'm not sure why. I'd really like us to fix our relationship.

No, that makes it sound like our relationship is in serious trouble. Which is how it seems to me, but what if Marvin doesn't feel the same way? If he doesn't, then bringing up our problems like that could certainly put him off.

Marvin, I love you.

I don't like that either. It sounds like a "but" is going to follow it, which is never good.

Just go inside and wing it when you see him, I tell myself. I can slip into bed beside him and wake him up with a big sloppy kiss.

I slip my key into the lock and push the door open. Though it's midnight, I hear the sound of soft jazz. And I can't help smiling. Marvin is obviously feeling as badly about everything as I am and he wants to make things right between us.

God love him.

Inside, I let my knockoff Gucci tote slip to the floor and kick off my shoes. As I make my way to the bedroom, I'm already pulling off my blouse.

A smile on my face, I open the door—then stop dead in my tracks. For a moment I can't understand the scene playing out before me, though I know something is horribly wrong.

And then my brain starts to work, and even though the room is dark, I understand. God help me, I understand. Marvin is lying on his back, and I can hear his moans of ecstasy. But he's not jerking off, because there's another body, this huge hump between Marvin's legs covered by the bedsheet.

He's in the mood for romance all right. Just not with me.

With another woman.

"Holy shit!" Marvin says.

As if the doorknob has turned to fire, I release it and jump backward.

"Zoë—" Marvin and his slut are already scrambling out of the bed, grasping at clothes and the bedspread to cover themselves.

I spin around and run into the kitchen, but then think better of that and head for the front door. Before I can get there, however, Marvin is in the hallway with the bedspread wrapped around his waist like a toga, blocking my path.

"It's not what you think," he tells me.

I narrow my eyes at him, stunned by what he's just said. "Admittedly, this feels like a nightmare right now, but I'm not crazy enough to believe you *weren't in our bed having sex with another woman*!" Anger is seeping into my veins, which is good. I need anger to get through this.

"You're the one who said you weren't coming home. I thought our relationship was over."

"So you bring another woman into our bed before I've even moved out? And I never broke up with you, you jerk. Don't make excuses."

"All I'm trying to say is, it was only sex. Nothing more."

"Thanks for clearing that up," I scoff.

The other woman appears at the bedroom door, and I can't help looking her way. My stomach bottoms out when I see the face I've seen so many times before.

"Melody!"

"Oh God, Zoë." She doesn't meet my eyes. "I'm so sorry. I thought you guys were breaking up, that you weren't happy."

"How could you do this to me?" I demand. "I've had you over for dinner. We've gone shopping together. We've talked about . . . " About everything, including my dissatisfaction with Marvin lately. Melody works with Marvin on the set of *Passion's Shore.* I liked her immediately when I met her, and never thought she'd ever betray me like this.

"Marvin told me—"

"Get out," I snap.

Melody is apparently only too happy to oblige, scampering to the door like a gazelle trying to escape a lion.

"And you—" I wag a finger at Marvin.

"I know I messed up, and I'm sorry," he says.

"You're *sorry*?"

"Yes."

"Oh, I'll just bet you are. Sorry you weren't able to get off!"

Strangely, I feel like I'm only playing the part of the jilted girlfriend, because in reality something inside me starts to warm. Like a ray of sunshine providing light to a seed that's going to allow it to grow. And I know this seed is going to blossom into a beautiful flower. It's almost like my relationship with Marvin has blocked any light from getting to this seed, but in this moment I know that despite what's just happened, I'm going to be happier.

Marvin places a hand on my shoulder. "You and me—we haven't been getting along. You've been giving me the cold shoulder. Not having sex with me." He shrugs. "I'm a guy. What was I supposed to do?"

"Oh, that's right. For you, it's all about the penis. Forget a committed relationship. That doesn't matter to you. As soon as you're not getting sex—"

I stop myself. First, I was more than willing to have sex with him, and he knows this. And second, none of this really matters. The point is, I've known for a long time that I needed to end this relationship, and now I have no more excuses. I'm free.

"I know I messed up," Marvin continues, "but things have been tense between us. You hardly bring in decent money. And the thing is, all you have to do is use your father's name. Use it and you know you'll get ahead."

I stare at Marvin in horror. "You want me to use my father, a man who was barely in my life, to get ahead?"

"If it'll help, why not?"

"So this is about me not bringing in enough money?" I ask for clarification. "That's why you had your dick in another woman's mouth?"

Marvin looks down. "I blew it. And I'm sorry. I don't have an excuse." He takes a step toward me. "But we can get past this, can't we? We can move on and be happy."

"Move on?" I ask incredulously.

"Yes." Now Marvin takes another step, and when he reaches for my hand, I don't stop him. "Can you find it in your heart to forgive me?"

"Forgive you?" I snap my fingers. "Just like that?"

"Maybe . . . maybe this needed to happen."

"What?"

"Hear me out. Maybe this happened to test my feelings for you. Because the moment I saw you standing in the doorway, I knew I couldn't lose you."

Maybe Marvin has been working on *Passion's Shore* for too long.

"Please," he says, squeezing my hand, "tell me you'll forgive me and I swear I'll never hurt you again."

"You promise?"

A smile spreads on Marvin's face. "Of course, baby."

"It's good to know we at least agree on that. That you'll never hurt me again."

"I won't. I promise I won't."

"Oh, I know you won't. And you want to know why? Because I'm not giving you the chance. Marvin, it's *over*."

His jaw drops. "What?"

I pull my hand from his. "It's over. *Kaput. Finito.* From now on, there is no you and me."

Just saying the words is like a huge weight lifting off my shoulders. So huge I almost smile.

"Zoë, you're kidding, right?"

"Marvin, do me a favor and go back to bed, cuz I'm really friggin' tired and I'm about to collapse."

"Huh?"

I leave him standing in the hallway, looking confused, while I head to the living room and throw myself on the sofa. I am bone tired, and I really do need to get some sleep.

Twelve

It is one thing to have the weight of the world lifted off your shoulders. It is another thing to have no place to park your head at night.

This is something I'm distinctly aware of as I drive to the studio with Norm, so much so I'm almost tempted to ask him if he's got a spare bed.

Almost. I'm not quite that desperate.

"How'd you sleep?" Norm asks me after ten minutes of driving.

I make a face as I glance his way. I don't have the energy to do much else.

"Same here," he tells me. "I keep thinking that Kiesler's gonna know. He's gonna take one look at me and know I took the van . . . "

Now I'm compelled to speak. Which is just as well. Catching a few more minutes of sleep now will be like torture, so I might as well wake up.

"He's not gonna know unless you tell him, Norm. We won't volunteer any information unless we're asked."

"I hope you're right."

"In fact," I go on, "why don't you drop me off at the front and we'll go in separately." Which is way more than any type of precaution we need to take, given that there's no way Phil will ever even know we were in Oakland.

Twenty minutes later, Norm drops me off near the side of the building before driving toward the parking entrance at the back.

Easy as pie. Everything's cool.

As I walk through the front door, I force a smile on my face. "Hey, Jackie," I say to the receptionist. "How was your weekend?"

"Mine was fine." She pauses—a long-drawn-out, pregnant pause—then asks, "Yours?"

Okay, what was with that pause? And am I being totally paranoid here, or did she raise her eyebrows suspiciously when she asked me that question?

"My weekend was fine," I lie. "Same old, same old. Boring."

I continue on before she can ask any more questions, heading to the small kitchen on the way to my cubbyhole. I pour myself a cup of what smells like the usual putrid coffee. What the hell? It's caffeine. And this morning I need it in a serious way.

"Zoë Andrews."

I freeze at the sound of Phil's voice. And then I force a smile onto my face and turn to face him. "You always know where to find me," I say, and laugh.

"You look like hell."

"Thanks," I say wryly. "It's this new makeup I bought last week. It does wonders for my eyes."

His expression hardens. "I'm gonna need to speak with you in my office, Zoë. Right away."

"Okay, sure. Just let me get some cream—"

"Now."

Damn, this is serious. Or is it? Maybe I'm thinking the worst when Phil's actually got good news for me. Like that he'll be giving me a fifty percent raise effective immediately.

The power of positive thinking and all that, right?

"Follow me," Phil tells me.

"All right," I answer in a cheerful voice.

Phil heads out of the small kitchen, and like a puppy dog, I follow him. A million things race through my mind. *He knows we went to Oakland. But how can he know? Damn, did Norm already confess?*

I can't believe Marvin was fucking Melody!

Moments later, when I step into Phil's office and see Norm, I start to freak. Oh, I'm still looking cool and confident on the outside, but inside, I'm falling apart. This is bad. Norm probably confessed the moment he walked into the studio.

The spineless moron!

"Close the door, please," Phil instructs me.

I do, then look at Norm. He looks away.

Phil sits at his desk, and reluctantly I take a seat beside Norm. Should I blurt out an apology? Or just wait to see what Phil's going to say?

"You took the van to Oakland this weekend." It's a statement, not a question.

Again, I look at Norm. He says, "He already knew."

How? I want to scream.

"You know it's against company policy to take property unless on a company assignment."

"Phil, I'm confused. Why do you think we were in Oakland?" Okay, that's pathetic, but I want to know how he knows. Because if Norm went crying to him like a big, bloody fool—

"Cut the bullshit, Zoë. I saw you on TV."

"TV? You saw *me*?"

"On ESPN. And a couple other news stations. Making an ass of yourself."

"What?"

"Are you going to play dumb all morning, or are you going to answer my question?" Phil demands.

"I'm not playing dumb. I just don't understand."

Phil leans across his desk, his scrawny face red with anger. "Here's what I know. Somehow you and Norm here wormed your way into the Oakland stadium yesterday. Somehow you got close enough to the Raiders to ask some questions. And *you*"—he levels a glare on me—"you get the bright idea that you're working for some gossip rag or something, because you ask Kahari Brown about a baby? Some friggin' *paternity suit*?"

I slink down in my seat.

"What'd you do—pull that out of your ass?"

"No!" I say defensively. "Of course not. I did research on Kahari Brown. And I read that somewhere."

"Where?" Phil challenges me. "The *Daily Blab*?"

"I don't read the *Daily Blab*." Well, not regularly. And I'm pretty sure I didn't see the story there. At least I *think* I didn't. I only know that I read a story *somewhere* about a woman named Stella Rivera accusing Kahari Brown of fathering her baby, and him not doing right by her. Granted, I only saw the story once, but I remembered it because athletes impregnating and abandoning women is a sore spot with me, given that my father did the same thing to my mother.

"It doesn't matter," Phil says. "The point is, you made a fool of yourself with your 'insightful sports question,' " he says, making air quotes. "And you made a fool of this station.

You went there representing LASN—without permission—and you represented us in the worst possible way. And you, Norm"—Phil now glares at Norm—"I never expected this from you."

"It's not his fault," I interject. Because I'm getting the feeling that Phil's next words are going to be along the lines of "You're fired," and Norm doesn't deserve to be let go just because he was trying to help me out.

"Zoë, you don't have to—"

"Yes, Norm, I do." I sigh softly as I face my boss once more. "Phil, this was completely my idea, so if anyone's gonna suffer for this, it should be me, not him."

Phil looks from me to Norm and back to me again. "All right," he finally says. "Norm, you can go. But let me make this perfectly clear, if you ever do anything like this again—"

"I won't, sir." Norm scrambles from his seat, offers what looks like a bow, then runs from the room.

I stare at the door long after Norm is gone.

"Zoë."

I swallow hard. "Yes?"

"I just don't think you're happy here."

Oh, not this. Not that whole turning-the-tables routine. "Phil, please. Don't patronize me. If you want to fire me, just fire me."

"Okay." He sits up in his seat. "You're fired."

For a moment I am too shocked to speak. But then I ask, "What did you just say?"

"You're fired, Zoë." Phil is already rising from his desk. "Gather your things."

I climb out of the chair. "Phil, wait." Just moments ago I was brave—brave because I didn't think Phil would really call my bluff. But he has, and I can't help thinking about the fact that I no longer have a boyfriend, and thus have no place to live. This is the absolute worst time for me to lose my job. "Phil, please hear me out."

He clears his throat. "Zoë, it's been obvious for a very long time that you haven't been happy here. You've wanted bigger stories, more money—"

"I was trying to prove myself," I tell him. "I went to Oakland because I know that every great reporter takes risks. I wanted to show you that I'm the kind of reporter who can handle bigger stories. Like Ken."

"You did the opposite."

"I made a mistake. I'll learn from it."

"You've done good work for me, so I'll give you a good reference."

"Phil, please."

"Though God knows I shouldn't."

"One mistake, Phil? You're gonna fire me for one mistake?"

"Keep talking and you can kiss the good reference goodbye."

He's not even going to listen to me. He's just going to fire me, no second thought.

"We can't talk about this?"

"There's nothing more to talk about."

"Phil, you're pissed. I get that. Give me shit jobs for a while. Whatever you want. Just don't fire me."

"I'm sure you'll make out just fine."

I can't believe it. How dare he do this to me after three long years!

And now I'm angry. Angry enough to boldly walk up to his desk and look him straight in the eye. "Let me get this straight. This is a dead-end job that most people would rather jump off a bridge than accept, and you're *firing* me? For one lousy judgment call?"

"With your brain, you should be a rocket scientist."

I can't help glaring at him.

"All right," he begins in a conciliatory tone. "That was out of line."

"This isn't fair."

"Life ain't fair."

"Why don't you put me behind a desk or something?" I ask in a tone that is pretty close to groveling. But even as I say the words, I know that's something I don't want. How will I ever launch my career as the greatest female sports reporter in U.S. history if I'm filing papers at some lowly cable sports network?

The answer is simple—I won't.

The problem is, without a man, and without any source of income, I'm pretty much out of options. I don't know what I'm going to do.

Well, there is one thing. The one thing I said I'd only do if hell froze over.

And it's pretty apparent to me that hell just froze over.

Thirteen

"All in all, a fabulous game, and I'm proud of you guys," Coach Edmonds said. Standing, he had one foot resting on a chair as his eyes scanned the room. "We were down, but never for a minute did you play like we were out. And that's how games are won—by thinking like winners. If we keep playing like this, then there's no stopping us this year!" The coach raised an exuberant fist in the air.

A chorus of "yeahs!" erupted in the room as all the guys cheered in agreement.

"You really are the best bunch of guys I've had the honor of working with, and you're doing me proud. Now go home, kiss your wives and your children. And get some rest. Because you know that Denver's going to be out for blood when we play them this weekend. Thomas, you're seeing the doc after this meeting?"

"Yep."

"Good. Let's hope that ankle is in tiptop shape for this weekend."

Lamar Thomas, another of the team's wide receivers, had sprained his ankle during the game against New England. It was touch and go as to whether he'd be able to play on it this weekend, and if he couldn't, that would mean more pressure for Kahari. But he was ready for it.

"All right," the coach said. "See you all on Wednesday."

As the guys started to get up, Colin Gray, a linebacker, quickly stood and held up his hands. "Before y'all head out, I want to tell you all what we've decided for Frankie's bachelor party." Frankie, a veteran kicker, gave a bashful smile from his seat in the corner. He was marrying his longtime girlfriend, Shelley. "We're gonna do it this Thursday night—in Vegas."

"Vegas?" Anthony said to Kahari.

"It's a short flight," Colin went on, "and Coach was nice enough to agree."

"Surprising," Kahari mumbled to Anthony. But as he looked at the coach, he could see the dissatisfaction in his eyes. Kahari knew that the idea of anyone getting married during the season was a big no-no to him, because it meant an unnecessary distraction for that player. But Frankie was a longtime player, and his fiancée had put her foot down. The two had compromised by planning a small wedding now, and would wait until the season was over to go on their honeymoon.

"So what we'll do," the coach began, "is have our regular practice on Thursday, and leave on a flight to Vegas right afterward. Friday is a travel day, anyway, as we're heading to Denver, so we'll head there from Vegas instead."

"Where are we staying?" one of the guys asked.

"Bellagio," Colin answered.

"Sweet," someone called out.

Coach Edmonds glanced around the room. "This shouldn't put a kink in our schedule. But y'all need to keep your heads in Vegas, ya hear? This is one evening of fun, then it's back to business. If I didn't love you like a son, Frankie, I would never have okayed this."

"I appreciate it, Coach."

"Okay then." Coach Edmonds clapped his hands together. "See you Wednesday."

As the players started filing out of the room, the coach stepped up to Kahari. "Kahari, I want you to stay back for a minute, if you don't mind. We need to have a little chat."

"Sure, Coach." Kahari shrugged nonchalantly, though he wondered what the coach could want to talk to him about.

When the rest of the team had vacated the room, the coach finally spoke. "I haven't brought this up before, and I didn't mention it after yesterday's press conference because I wasn't sure how best to broach the subject. You can say it's none of my business, but what happens to my guys *is* my business, especially if it starts affecting your game. So tell me about this Estela woman."

"Here we go."

"I'm hearing things, Kahari. In more places than I'd like."

"This is because of that reporter."

"I was as shocked as you were to hear that question, and quite frankly a little pissed off. The press conference was *not* the forum for an issue like that."

"I know, and I wish I could tell you it won't happen again."

"Who is this woman?"

"Estela—she's crazy. That's all I can say."

"So this claim that you've fathered her baby—"

"—is total bullshit."

The coach slung an arm across Kahari's shoulder. "My job is to run a successful football team. I need you not to be distracted in any way."

"I'm not distracted."

"Are you sure? Because if you need help dealing with this situation . . . "

The coach let his statement hang in the air, but Kahari had a pretty good idea of what he was implying. In the past, the coach had been known to "influence" a woman or two that had become a problem by offering them some kind of cash settlement. At least these were the rumors Kahari had heard. He'd never asked for specifics regarding any of these instances, as those situations were none of his business.

"I'm fine, Coach."

"I hope so, Kahari. Because I want this team to go all the way to the Super Bowl this year, and you're one of my best players."

"Don't you worry about me," Kahari said, making sure to sound upbeat. He didn't want the coach to have any doubts as to whether this problem with Estela would affect his performance. And she wouldn't. For Kahari to perform to the best of his ability, he had to zone out all the negative energy around him and concentrate wholeheartedly on his game. He knew he could do it, and he would.

"On a positive note," the coach said, gripping his shoulder, "congrats on the nomination. That's exactly the kind of recognition you deserve."

"Thanks."

"And it does a lot of good for the team. It's nice to see a professional athlete celebrated for the good he's doing in his community. So many people like to concentrate on the negative, all those stories of whores and drugs."

"Tell me about it."

"But you've got your head on straight," Coach Edmonds said. "Always have."

Kahari merely nodded. He was a bit uncomfortable with all this praise that was suddenly coming his way. Yeah, he considered himself a good guy, but he was hardly perfect.

It wasn't like he hadn't made his share of mistakes, the

kinds of mistakes the media would run with if they dug into his past and discovered them.

"Coach, you have a great day."

"You too, Kahari. Again, you let me know if you need anything."

"I will."

Coach Edmonds collected his folder and started out of the room. Kahari followed him. Anthony was standing in the hallway, waiting for him.

"Ready to roll?" Anthony asked. "We've got a plane to catch."

"You bet."

Fourteen

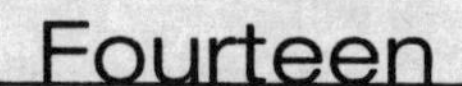

I take my time clearing out my desk—at least forty minutes. After hyperventilating for a good five minutes after leaving Phil's office, then forcing myself to calm down, I decide not to do the one thing I swear I'll only do whenever hell freezes over. I haven't spoken to my father in four years. When he called me on my nineteenth birthday, I wanted nothing to do with him, and it took me six more years to finally reach out to him. For a year after that, we tried to force a relationship. That was a huge disaster, and ultimately very painful for me. It's easy to talk about forgiveness and letting go of the past, but extremely hard to do.

Every so often he'll leave a message for me via my mother, letting me know that if I need anything, anything at all, all I have to do is call him.

What I needed was a father during my formative years. But he was never there.

I sit at my desk for a while with my head in my hands, contemplating my dismal future. Lord, please don't tell me that I'll have to tuck my tail between my legs and head back to Cleveland and live with my mother. Not because I don't love my mama—I love no one more—but because that would pretty much mean me giving up on my dream, and that's something I don't want to do. Even if I can't make it as a sportscaster, there are other opportunities in L.A.—like hosting a TV show. Or being a veejay.

And I'm not particularly keen on being in the same city with my sister, Lola, who was instrumental in breaking up a relationship with a guy I thought I'd marry.

Lola the temptress. At least that's what Quinn called her in his lame-ass defense of his wandering penis.

Katie, one of the station's research assistants, appears at the opening to my office. "How're you doing?" she asks, and sounds like she really cares.

"Oh, I've had better days."

She nods in sympathy.

We're not best friends or anything. Not even good friends, really. But I welcome her concern. Especially after practically everyone else I once worked with figures they have to avoid me. Like my getting fired is contagious and they're at risk of catching it.

"I saw you on ESPN," Katie says in a whisper.

"I didn't even watch the news last night. Was it bad? Or do I want to know?"

"It wasn't awful . . . But the sportscasters were kinda speculating on where you'd come from, and why you'd ask a question like that. One of them even said—"

I whip a hand in the air to silence Katie. "You know what? I don't want to know." Because I'm suddenly wondering if this is bad enough to tarnish my reputation. If my "brilliant" plan backfired on me in ways I never even considered.

And if it did, I don't want to know that, because if I know that, I might just be tempted to hop on the next train to Cleveland.

"Where'd you hear that, by the way?" Katie asks me. "About him getting some woman pregnant?"

Am I the only one who read this somewhere? "I read it in the paper. And don't ask me which one, because right now I don't remember."

"Weird. I never heard anything about it."

Suddenly I'm thankful that the rest of my former colleagues have decided to avoid me. If Katie's making me feel this bad, I can only imagine how much worse I'd feel if others offered to try and cheer me up.

I give Katie a faint smile. "Katie, I'm almost done clearing out my stuff. And I have a couple more phone calls to make."

"Give me a hug." She walks toward me, arms outstretched. I ease up off my chair, but don't fully stand as she hugs me. "Take care," she says as she pats my back. "And good luck with everything."

"Thanks. You take care as well."

I lift the phone's handset and place it to my ear. Katie wiggles her fingers at me, then disappears. Once I'm sure she's gone, I replace the receiver.

Who do I have to call?

My father?

No. You are not calling your father!

I should, however, call my agent, Dina. Let her know I'm now available 24/7 for all those auditions she'll now be able to send me on.

Yeah, right.

I do give her a call, and get her voice mail, so I leave her a message. "Great news," I say in a sarcastic voice. "I no longer work at LASN. So whatever you can send me out on, pleeeease do. I really need a gig, Dina."

As I end the call, I think about the fact that I suddenly have to find a new place to live. Oh, man. What am I going to do?

Gail! I can give her a call. With Bob gone, she'll probably

love the company. Oh yes yes yes! I dial her number, but she's apparently not home either because her voice mail picks up.

I end that call and thrum my fingers on my desk. I know I'm wasting time, but I'm just not sure what I'm supposed to do right now.

Who else can I call?

I think for a moment. And then it hits me. I can call Kahari Brown. To apologize.

It's not like I didn't read that story about him and some woman named Stella who claims he's abandoned their child. I *know* I did—even if no one else seems to have ever heard of it. But maybe there was nothing to the story, which is why it never made it into the mainstream media. In which case, it's no wonder I made a complete fool of myself and LASN, not to mention that I was totally out of line.

So isn't an apology in order? After all, I don't want the guy freaking out when he sees me again—when I'm working for a legitimate sports network.

Because I *will* get a job with a legitimate sports network.

I push my chair back and stand. Now I have a purpose, and this gives me a reason to stall a little longer while I figure out where I will go. Art, who works in the editing room, is a total computer nerd who knows how to find anything about anybody via the computer. That includes the private phone numbers of stars and other high-profile people.

Once he told me that he called up Sharon Stone and actually got her on the line. "What'd you say?" I asked him eagerly, amazed at his gall.

"I didn't say anything. I just listened to her voice until she hung up on me."

Art is exactly who I need right now. I hustle down the hallway toward the editing room where he works.

An apology makes everything better, and I intend to give one to Kahari on a silver platter.

Fifteen

A few hours later, Kahari walked into the foyer of his multimillion-dollar home and kicked off his Nikes. He couldn't wait to hit his bed and take a snooze for at least three hours. Even though he'd gotten to bed at a decent hour last night, he was still exhausted because he'd stayed up most of the night thinking about Estela's appearance in the stairwell and wondering exactly what he needed to do about her.

Placing his keys on the hall table, he listened for sound. He heard none.

"LaTonya?"

No answer.

Hmm . . . Had his sister taken his not-so-subtle advice? Was she out looking for a job?

He rolled his eyes. Just because he didn't hear anything didn't mean she wasn't here. The house was so large, twenty drifters could be partying in the left wing and he would never know.

For now, though, the only "drifter" he had to worry about was his sister. She claimed that she loved Southern California so much that she wanted to find work in the area, but she'd said that over nine months ago, and LaTonya seemed very content to socialize and shop and drive around Beverly Hills looking for stars rather than search for a job.

Anthony often told Kahari that he needed to get tough with her in particular and people in general because if he didn't people would try to live off of him forever.

Kahari knew his friend was right, and he'd have to take action where LaTonya was concerned sooner rather than later. For now, he didn't quite have the heart to kick his sister out.

There was only one person he would never ask to leave his home, and that was his grandmother—were she to ever live with him. She had worked so hard to give him the opportunities that had enabled him to have this career, he would be indebted to her forever.

He walked farther into the house, toward the kitchen, before he finally heard some sound. Music. He could make out the sound of Bob Marley's voice and the lyrics to "One Love."

Shaking his head, he walked to the patio door and hauled it open. The reggae beat was instantly much louder. He stepped into his vast backyard overlooking the Hollywood hills, and took in the view of the ocean off in the distance. It was a shame he didn't get to enjoy this place as much as he'd like to.

Turning, he scanned the area for LaTonya, but didn't see her. And then her head burst through the water's surface.

She drew in a gulp of air. Then, seeing him, she smiled and swam toward the pool's edge. "Hey, big brother."

"Hello, sis," Kahari replied. He paused briefly, assessing the situation. She was enjoying a leisurely swim at three in the afternoon. He had a bad feeling that LaTonya hadn't left the house today.

But still he said, "Tell me you've already been up and out looking for a job." If she hadn't been out already, she certainly wouldn't be going anywhere now.

"Kahari . . ." She gave him a sugary look to match her tone, one that practically screamed, *Why should I have to work when my brother is a multimillionaire?*

"Come on, LaTonya. We've talked about this."

"For your information, I was out earlier."

"Oh." That was a nice surprise.

"And I've been depressed ever since."

Kahari's eyebrows shot up. "Why?"

"Bright and early, I got a call to see this agent I dropped my head shot off to last week, and I was really psyched. It was like, finally—something good was gonna happen for me. But when I got there, you're not gonna believe what this agent said to me."

"What?"

"He said I had a great look, that I was voluptuous—really roped me in with all this flattery. And he told me he could probably put me to work right away."

"But in some kind of sex magazine," Kahari guessed, his stomach sinking. While L.A. was home to many legitimate show business opportunities, there were way more seedy ones, and people looking for stardom were often victimized.

"It wasn't a sex magazine, but almost as bad if you ask me. He said he could get me work as a plus-size model!" LaTonya's entire face twisted in a frown. "Do you believe that? Me? Like I'm *fat*! Granted, I used to be an eight before I came here, but I'm only a size ten now. Only in L.A. can you be a healthy size ten and considered fat."

Kahari couldn't argue that point. Women in this town were ecstatic if they were a size zero—a size Kahari had never even heard of back in Fort Worth. Nor when he'd been in college at Notre Dame, for that matter.

None of which was really the issue right now.

"LaTonya," he began cautiously, "I thought you were going to look for a real job."

"Modeling is a real job."

What the hell had gotten into his sister? Where had the sensible woman he'd known all of his life disappeared to? Before coming to visit him, she had been studying early childhood education with plans to be a grade school teacher. Now, she suddenly wanted to be a star, when that had never ever been her dream growing up.

He dragged a chair to the pool's edge and took a seat. "You know what I mean. The kind of job you actually get paid to do. Regularly. The kind of job that can cover your monthly expenses if you get your own apartment."

"Come on, Kahari."

"No, not that sweet 'Come on, Kahari' tone. Not today."

"But Kahari . . . It's not like this place isn't big enough for both of us."

And that was the real issue. Not only did she not want to work, she didn't feel she had to.

"LaTonya," Kahari began in a frank tone, "I've been very generous with you, and I'll always help you out. You know that. But you can't live here forever."

"What about until I finish my book?"

"Your what?"

"My book. Remember—I told you I was writing a mystery."

"You're writing a book," Kahari said in a deadpan voice. Hell, what would it be next?

"Well . . . I haven't actually started it. Because I'm researching," she quickly added. "But I know I want it to take place in Hollywood. Maybe someone is murdering talent agents." Her eyes lit up. "Yeah, a frustrated actor who's been rejected by everyone in town. It'll be a little grisly, cuz this person is pissed off. And I have to figure out a way to put some hot sex in there, because anything with sex in it will sell big-time."

"Oh really?"

"Uh-huh. I've got it all figured out."

Yeah, she sure did. She had every excuse in the book that would have her living with him until she was old and gray.

She should write *The Book of Excuses.* Now *that* would probably sell a million copies.

"You enjoy your swim," Kahari told her. "I'm gonna head inside and check messages."

"Oh, that reminds me. Someone from some paper called. Harold Davis, I think. He said he was hoping he could get an interview with you about your hero nomination."

"You took down his info?"

"Of course," LaTonya replied, swimming on her back.

"All right. I'll call him."

"And . . . " LaTonya swam to the edge of the pool.

"And what?"

"There was another call from some other reporter. At least I think she was a reporter. She rambled on and on, and I could hardly make sense of what she was saying. But it sounded like she was offering an apology for some out-of-line question she asked after the game on the weekend."

Kahari's eyebrows shot up. "Are you serious?"

"Why would I lie?"

"I don't know. Maybe you're pulling my leg because you saw the game and heard this woman. She made it onto ESPN and some other news networks."

"I didn't see it." LaTonya paused. "I was out."

"I'm sure you were."

"I had my book club meeting last night," she said, smiling sweetly.

Again, she had an answer for everything. She liked to enjoy his success, but she hardly ever watched any of his games.

What to do? She was still his baby sister. He still loved her with all his heart.

"Did this other reporter," he began, "leave a number?" Not that he was going to call her. He would accept her apology and leave it at that, and be thankful that no one else had tried to badger him about her claim. That had been his worst fear when Zoë Andrews had asked that question—that other reporters would have pounced on her allegation like she'd offered them gold. Thankfully, they hadn't.

"No."

You should have asked for one, he almost said, but didn't bother. How many times did he have to remind his sister that he had voice mail for a reason? In the past, he'd asked her to tell media types and others to call back and leave their messages for him, but more often than not, she forgot.

His sister needed something to do. She needed a job to occupy her time.

"I'm gonna take a snooze," Kahari said, starting to walk back toward the house.

"Okay. I'll see you in a little while. I can barbecue some chicken."

"Sure."

As Kahari made his way to the second staircase near the back of the kitchen, he was no longer thinking about his dilemma with his sister. He was thinking about Zoë Andrews and the fact that she had called.

Maybe Estela *had* put her up to the question. That could explain why she'd sought him out to offer him an apology.

Which she owed him. The woman had been completely out of line.

In his bedroom, Kahari stripped off his jeans and T-shirt and crawled under the covers. He would have to think about all of this later. Right now he needed to catch a few z's.

Sixteen

After killing as much time as I could at the studio, I did the only thing I could do after packing my things. I went back home. I know it's not home anymore, but it's where all my stuff is, and I don't have anywhere else to go. I know Marvin will be working all day, so this will give me time to pack in his absence.

Here I am, outside the door, hesitating to open it.

I no longer hesitate when I hear the sound of someone else's door opening. I quickly slip my key in the lock and hurry into the apartment.

I take a deep breath and look around. Everything looks normal. Marvin's dirty sneakers sloppily strewn about in the foyer. The kitchen, visible from where I stand, has mugs and plates littering the counter.

And then my gaze falls on two wineglasses, wine I know I didn't share with him.

Marvin and Melody.

It has a nice ring to it. Maybe they'll become a couple.

Asshole.

I should feel awful just being here, given what this place

now represents. I should be on the verge of bawling my eyes out. But the truth is, I'm not anywhere near as sad as I should be that our relationship is over, which says a lot in itself. I know a part of me is happy I'm able to move on, but why am I not drowning my sorrows in chocolate and lattes?

Maybe because I'm too tired.

I haven't really slept in nearly a day and a half now, and I'm about to collapse where I stand.

Yawning, I head to the bedroom and plop onto the bed. I think I'm asleep before my head hits the pillow.

I wake up to find Marvin standing over me. He's smiling.

Wait a minute. Maybe I'm dreaming.

"You're awake," he says.

"Oh, hell." I quickly scramble to a sitting position.

"No, no," he says, holding a hand up in a stop position. "You don't have to leave."

I slide my butt off the bed. "Yes. I do."

"Zoë, wait." Marvin's voice is uncharacteristically gentle. So is his touch on my arm as he urges me to sit down again.

"Why should I wait?" I ask.

"I don't know if this will come out right, but I hope you understand what I mean. My being with Melody—in a strange way, it helped me realize how I really feel about you."

"That you hate me?"

"No," he says, frowning slightly. Then his lips curl in a smile. "That I don't want to lose you."

Maybe I *am* dreaming. Because this is just too weird.

"Marvin, you were having sex with her in our bed." Remembering that, I quickly hop off the bed and stare at the sheets like they're covered with dog poop. I was too tired for it to matter earlier.

Seeing my gaze, he says, "I know, and I'm sorry. I'll change the sheets right away. Wash them twice."

"That won't wash away what you did."

"I'm trying to make amends."

"You're doing a really shitty job of it."

He holds up both hands in a gesture of surrender. "All right. I won't say anything else."

"Thank you."

And then there's silence. Regret swims around us. Two people who had once been lovers, and now we won't mean anything to each other anymore. I'll refer to Marvin as the ex who screwed around on me. A distinction he'll share with more than one boyfriend from my past.

"Do you have somewhere to go?" he asks.

I shake my head.

"You can stay here."

I shake my head again.

"Well, for a few days, anyway. Until you find a place to go."

"I don't know, Marvin." I glance at the bed again. "I can't sleep there anymore."

"The sofa's comfortable."

I don't answer. Instead, I start to pace. I'm wondering what the hell other options I have, considering I no longer have a job and I'm broke.

"Come on, Zoë. Are you gonna punish yourself because I was the asshole?"

Good point.

"All right," I say softly. "I'll stay here until I find a place I can go."

"I really am sorry." He sighs. "Sorry for everything."

He seems contrite, which will make staying here easier. And I'm glad there's no ugliness right now, because there's really no point to it. Our relationship is over. Why make things worse than they need to be?

"I'm going to head out," I tell Marvin. "I need something to eat."

"I can cook something," he offers.

Marvin cook? I shake my head. "That's okay, Marvin. I'll . . . be back."

He smiles at me, and that kinda creeps me out. I hope he doesn't think I'm about to forgive him.

Damn, I wish I had somewhere else to go.

When I get back from the coffee shop, I knock on Gail's door. Although Marvin told me I can stay at his place for as long as necessary, I don't feel comfortable doing that. I don't want to risk getting soft, and let his apology get to me. Because I don't want to forgive him. I just want to move on.

Gail opens the door a crack. "Oh, hi."

"Hi, Gail. I hate to ask this, but I was wondering if I could stay with you for a couple days."

"Oh." She glances behind her but doesn't open the door wider.

"It's okay," I tell her, sensing her hesitation. "It's just that . . . I caught Marvin in bed with another woman this morning, and it's over."

"Oh my God. Are you okay?"

I nod. "More than I thought I'd be. But I have to move out, and I don't really have anyplace to go."

Gail nods. But still she doesn't open the door to invite me in.

"Gail, are *you* okay?"

Now she slips into the hallway. She grins from ear to ear. "Actually, I'm great. Bob is back."

"Oh!"

"Yeah, and we're working things out. It's like you said, he was just upset and needed time to think."

Wonderful. Just wonderful. "That's great."

"I'm so sorry for going to your place like I did, breaking down like that."

"There's no need to apologize."

"Well, I still feel kind of silly. I totally overreacted."

"But things are fine now. That's what matters."

"They are." Gail sighs wistfully. "I really wish I could help you out, Zoë, but now's not a good time to stay with me. Bob and I, we're in the middle of trying to work things out and all."

"No, no, no. Of course."

"I really am sorry."

"Don't apologize."

Gail backs into her apartment. "But if you need anything . . . "

"I'll call." But I won't. I hate imposing, especially after I've already asked for help and been denied.

"See you later," Gail says. "And I'm *so* sorry to hear about Marvin. I thought he was one of the good ones."

Gail squeezes my hand, then disappears into her apartment.

What now? I think. *What now*?

Back upstairs to Marvin's apartment. Unfortunately, I don't have another option.

Seventeen

I'm in Marvin's kitchen, frying eggs. And this is the weird part. Kahari's in the kitchen with me, and we're both laughing.

"That had to be the craziest apology I ever heard," he tells me, then slips his arm around my waist. He kisses my neck. "But I love you for it."

He loves me. I sigh like a fool and turn back to the stove.

But the eggs are gone, and suddenly Kahari and I are rolling around on a beach that looks a lot like the one on the set of *Passion's Shore*.

My eyes pop open. I still smell eggs. I lift my neck and peer into the kitchen. Marvin is standing in front of the stove, completely naked.

Wait a minute. I must still be dreaming. Although the dream has turned into a nightmare.

"Hey, Zoë," he says.

Oh God. I'm definitely not dreaming. I pull the cover over my head as I ask, "What are you *doing*?"

"Making breakfast."

"Naked?"

"I'm doing laundry, too."

We've been broken up for twenty-four hours and already he has no clean clothes?

"I'm making scrambled eggs," he continues. "I've got croissants baking in the oven."

Now I sit up and pinch myself. Marvin *cooking*? The pinch hurts, and even leaves a red mark on my fair skin. No, not dreaming.

"I didn't start the coffee yet," Marvin tells me as he starts to turn. "So, do you feel in the mood for—"

"Marvin!" I throw my hands over my eyes.

"What?"

"What are you doing?"

He pauses before saying, "I thought we just went over that?"

"No, what are you doing turning around to talk to me when you're *naked*? We've *broken up*." I'm stressing my words in case he's forgotten this very major change in our relationship.

He laughs. "Come on, Zoë. How many times have you seen me naked?"

With the lights on? Not very many. "We're no longer a couple, Marvin."

Or is this his way of trying to seduce me? Strutting his stuff, making breakfast for me for the second time since I've known him. (The first time was the morning after our first date. I didn't sleep with him, but I did spend the night since we watched a couple movies and then it was late and I was tired.)

"What kind of coffee, Zoë?"

"Can you please put something on?"

"Now you can't stand the sight of me?"

That's not the issue, but I find myself saying, "No. Not after seeing your naked ass with Melody."

"Oh, fuck. Here I am trying to be nice—"

"I didn't ask you to be nice."

"Are you so perfect, huh? You've never made a mistake ever in your life?"

Now I take my hands down from my face, because it's silly to argue with my eyes covered. "This isn't about *me* never making a mistake in my life. This is about *you* screwing around on me."

Marvin grabs the hot skillet, and visions of domestic violence flash through my head. But he throws it loudly into the sink, cursing as he does.

I scramble to my feet. "All right. This was a bad idea. I'm gonna get my stuff, and I'm gonna leave."

"Why don't we do this?" Marvin says, stalking out of the kitchen. "I'm gonna get dressed for work, because I really need to get out of here right now. Then you can pack your shit and leave. Slip the key under the door on your way out."

Ulterior motives. Every guy freakin' has them when they're playing sweet and nice. "You got it," I yell at him.

"Good!" He slams the door after entering the bedroom.

Oh, shit. I knew this was too good to be true.

Who do I call, who do I call, who do I call? Because I have to call someone. I'm suddenly homeless.

An idea hits me. *Rose.*

Yes, Rose. I haven't seen her in over four months, but we e-mail regularly and I still consider her a good friend. She's a newlywed now, and I know I'll be imposing if I ask to stay with her, but it's not like I have any other choice. This is the problem when your life revolves around your career and your man—you don't make the kind of strong female friendships you should. There are a couple other people I know living in this building, but I don't want to be anywhere near here for fear of seeing Marvin again in this lifetime.

Inspired, I pull up Rose's cell phone number on my cell and call her, figuring the ringer is turned off this early. I don't want to call her house, because she and J.P. are still honeymooning, after all, and I'm not that self-centered.

"Rose, this is your long-lost friend," I say with my hand making a cave over my mouth and the phone. "I hate to ask you this, but I've got no place to go. Long story, but Marvin and I broke up, and I don't have anyone else to turn to right now. When you get this message, please call me back. And Rose, you know I wouldn't ask if I weren't totally desperate."

And then I end the call. If it's not Rose's place tonight, then I'll be sleeping in some dive that calls itself a motel.

Please, Rose. Please be in town. And please don't turn your back on me when I need you.

All I can do now is hope for the best.

What do you do when you have nowhere else to go?

You shop, of course.

In my case, I window-shop along Lankershim, going into the quaint boutiques and checking out all the items I'd love to buy. After a while I get depressed, so I pick out a cute crocheted blouse and a pair of faded jeans and take them to the dressing room. I'll just try them on, make myself feel better.

Inside the dressing room, my cell phone rings. I pull it out of my purse and look at the display. My agent Dina's number.

I feel a moment of excitement—then caution clouds the moment. With the way my day is going, she could be calling to say she's no longer representing me.

I hit the talk button and put the cell phone to my ear. "Hello, Dina."

"Zoë. I'm so glad I finally caught you."

"You called before?" It's not even ten-thirty yet.

"I left you three messages on your house phone."

"Oh. Well, that explains why I didn't get your messages. I don't live there anymore."

"Ah," Dina says. "You can tell me about that later. Right now I'm calling with some great news."

This isn't the first time Dina has called me with "great" news. She gets excited about every audition she sends me on. She's not a big-name agent, but she was willing to take me on with no acting experience, and I admire her spunk—but I lack the eternally hopeful quality she seems to possess.

"What's the audition for?" I ask nonchalantly.

"True Story," she answers, her voice bubbling with excitement.

I think for a moment. "You mean the television show *True Story*?"

"The one and only," she answers in a singsong voice.

The show is total tabloid TV. Lots of scandalous Hollywood gossip. Who's sleeping with whom, what actor's been caught doing drugs, what starlet is screwing her director.

It's completely *not* the kind of show I want to be a part of.

"They called me specifically asking for you," Dina continues. I can picture Dina bouncing on her seat, that's how happy she sounds.

"Dina, I know I said I was desperate in my message, but I'm not that desperate. I can't do a show like that."

"Zoë, don't be crazy. This is *True Story*. They're huge."

"Huge, yes. Scrupulous, no."

"Ah, you don't know that. Think of the exposure."

There's no doubt about it, the exposure would be great. But it's not my cup of tea. "I can't do it, Dina."

"Zoë, do you need money?"

"Yes."

"Do you need a career?"

"Yes."

"Do you know how hard it is to get a break like this in this town?"

I sigh wearily. "I know . . . But *True Story* concentrates

on more dirt than anything positive. My love is sports. How will this show help further my career?"

"Are you kidding me? This will completely help your career."

"Dina—"

"No, listen. I have a feeling that this is it, Zoë. Really it. Do you know what that will mean for you? Financial independence. Exposure. People across the nation and the world will see how dynamic and fantastic you are. And before you protest, I know you want to be a sportscaster. Which is exactly why you need to do this—so we can build a great tape of you that I'll send out to all the sports shows. With a great tape, it's only a matter of time before you're hired doing the job of your dreams."

Dina's got a point. A good one.

"Zoë?"

"I hate it when you're right."

"You know you love it," she replies, and I can hear the smile in her voice.

"I'll go to the audition, but don't get your hopes up. I'm hardly the beautiful airhead type I've seen on that show."

"Will you trust me already? I have a feeling."

Dina and her feelings. I sigh softly. "All right. I'll keep my fingers crossed. What time's the audition and where am I going?"

A minute later, I have all the details scribbled on an ATM receipt I located in my purse.

"First thing tomorrow morning," Dina tells me. "Don't mess this up!"

"Don't worry. I'll borrow a reliable car for this one, or even rent one if I have to."

"I'm keeping my fingers crossed, but I don't think you need that. Zoë, this job is yours."

"Dina, I wish you wouldn't say that. I'll try my best to wow them, of course, but in this business you just never know."

"*I* know. Will you trust me for once? Zoë, I have a feeling. The kind I'd bet my life on."

Eighteen

"Rose, you're a total sweetheart. Have I told you that lately?"

"Only about fourteen times since you got here," she replies, laughing.

Rose, my dear friend, has just brought pillows, and blankets, and a thick down comforter to me on the sofa. She's an absolute sweetheart, the kind of person you can depend on whenever you really need her. And she never judges me—she accepts me for who I am and loves me all the same.

Why can't I meet a man like her?

"Is there anything else you need?" she asks.

"Are you kidding? I'm stuffed." I pat my belly. "You make the best eggplant casserole I've ever tasted."

She flashes me a mock scowl and says, "J.P. hates it."

"Eggplant is an acquired taste."

"No, he'd eat it if there were meatballs in it, or deep-fried chicken wings. Some kind of meat. He doesn't believe in vegetarianism."

"Which makes me appreciate all the more the fact that you'd make an entire dish just for me."

"Anything for you," Rose tells me.

"Speaking of which . . . "

"Uh-oh."

"I'm gonna need a car tomorrow for that audition I was telling you about. And this way I can pick up the rest of my stuff from Marvin's apartment. So is there any way—"

"Don't say another word. You can borrow the car."

"Rose." I leap from the sofa and wrap my arms around her. "You're the best, you know that?"

"I know."

In a lot of ways, Rose is like me. She's biracial, though it's her father who is black, and her mother is Italian. And I have to say, Rose makes the best Italian dishes. Before falling for J. P., she had a string of bad boyfriends, and we used to commiserate over the lack of decent men. Rose also has a sister she doesn't get along with that well, though for different reasons.

"Hey," she says, pulling away from me. "I'm gonna head off, okay? J.P. wants us to watch a movie."

"He's gonna hate me being here, isn't he? I've taken over your living room."

"Are you kidding? J.P.'s favorite thing to do is watch a movie in bed with me."

"Let me guess. You don't quite make it to the end."

Rose winks. "What can I say? We're still honeymooning."

"Tell me about it. I can't believe J.P.'s taking you to Jamaica again. It's a good thing Marvin screwed around on me this week, because if it had been next week, I wouldn't have reached you."

"That man knows how to spoil a woman."

"And you deserve it. Go on." I give her a gentle push. "You go enjoy . . . your movie."

She grins at me before hurrying to the bedroom.

It's nice, seeing Rose so happy. For a long time she felt she'd never get married, that her Mr. Right had probably died as a child.

But then she met J.P., and the rest is history. He's a great guy. Italian, like her mother, and he treats her like a queen.

If only I could be so lucky.

You have to believe, right? That's the only way it'll ever happen.

I curl up on the sofa, wondering if there's a soul mate for me out in this world. Knowing my luck, he's alive on the other side of the planet, searching for me too, but we'll never find each other.

Forget all that, I tell myself. *You're barely out of one relationship, and you're already on the hunt for someone else?*

That's almost as bad as Gail.

No, I tell myself as I close my eyes. *You're through with men. It's time to concentrate on your career.*

The next morning, I arrive at the *True Story* studio half an hour earlier than my scheduled time. Thank God for Rose and her late-model Acura.

I'm hopeful, but past experience with auditions has made me jaded. For that reason, I don't bother to get all dolled up for this one. Of course, since most of my clothes are still at Marvin's, I didn't have much choice.

But I think I look okay. I'm wearing the outfit I bought yesterday—the crocheted top and faded jeans, and my favorite pair of ankle-high boots with a three-inch heel. The outfit says hip and funky, and if the people at *True Story* don't like it, then screw them.

I head to the front door and pull it open, and instantly I'm impressed. Now *this* is a studio. Everything is modern, and looks very expensive. I'm a bit surprised because I didn't think the show was worth that kind of money, but then again, it's the dirt that sells best in this town.

I walk up to the reception desk, which in itself looks like a work of art. Sculpted completely from beveled glass, it's simply stunning.

A pretty brunette smiles up at me. "Good morning. How may I help you?"

"I'm here for the audition."

"Audition?" she asks, a hint of confusion in her striking blue eyes. They've got to be contacts.

"Mmm-hmm." But as I glance around, I don't see anyone else hanging in the hallway, going over sides—the pages of script for the audition. The only people I see appear to be working here. The casting area must be down the hall.

"I'm not seeing any audition scheduled." She looks up from the calendar on her desk. "Who are you here to see?"

"Eva Raines."

"Oh, okay." She nods her understanding. "And your name?"

"Zoë Andrews."

"Right. There you are. If you go to the left, you'll see the waiting area. Have a seat and I'll let Ms. Raines know you're here."

Turning, I start for the waiting area. It's large and lavish, boasting black leather sofas and glass coffee tables. The walls are adorned with photos of stars posing with various *True Story* hosts.

That's impressive, but even more impressive is what I see at the far end of the room. A counter with a coffeemaker and two fancy-looking coffeepots, beside which is a basket full of fruit.

I leap toward the coffee. There are real mugs on a shelf above the coffeemaker—no cheap Styrofoam here.

I pour myself a cup and load it with real cream and some

sugar. And when I taste it, I know that if nothing else, I'll at least have come away from this place with a decent cup of java.

Maybe this is a good sign.

By the time I sit down and pick up a copy of *People* magazine, the receptionist appears in the doorway. "Zoë?"

"Yes?" I toss the magazine onto the coffee table.

"Ms. Raines is ready to see you now. If you'll follow me."

I follow the receptionist through a series of corridors until we finally arrive at double doors at the end of a hallway. There is a name embossed in gold on the door that reads EVA RAINES, EXECUTIVE PRODUCER.

"Good luck," the receptionist tells me.

"Thanks," I say, and draw in a nervous breath. I wait at least five seconds before I reach for the door's brass handle.

The woman I see has dirty-blond hair and a full, round face. Seeing me, she grins from ear to ear and pushes herself back from her massive mahogany desk. As I walk toward the desk, she heads toward me. She's plump, pleasantly so if you ask me, and looks extremely classy. From the top of her professionally styled hair to her plaid Burberry dress to her Kate Spade flats, she exudes confidence and success.

"Zoë Andrews." She takes my hand and pumps it. "It is so good to meet you."

It is? "Thank you, Ms. Raines. The pleasure's all mine, I assure you."

"Please, take a seat."

She gestures to a white leather chair. I practically sink into it, that's how soft it is.

I wait until Eva is back in her own chair before speaking again. "I've got a head shot for you." I open the folder I've brought with me. "And a résumé. Most recently I've been working for—"

"LASN. As a reporter."

"So you know I have a sports background."

"I know you have great instincts."

I hesitate, confused. "I'm sorry. Have you actually seen some of my work for LASN? I didn't realize my agent had sent you a tape."

Eve shakes her head. "She didn't. I saw you on ESPN."

My stomach bottoms out. *Oh, help me.* "That"—I clear my throat—"well, I wouldn't exactly call it my shining moment."

"What I want to know—what the world wants to know—is why you asked Kahari Brown that question."

My breath leaves me in a rush, as though I've just been punched in the gut with a sledgehammer. *Please don't tell me you've brought me here to humiliate me.* Could this woman be a diehard Raiders fan using the ruse of an audition to get me in here? Angry as hell, and she wants to let me know it?

No, that doesn't make sense. Does it? No, of course not. That's pretty extreme, even for a diehard fanatic.

"I . . . " I hedge, not sure what to say. "I guess, in hindsight, that wasn't the smartest thing to ask."

"Are you *kidding*?"

At first I think Eva is definitely upset with me. But then I see her eyes, wide with excitement, and I realize she's actually happy.

"That kind of hard-nosed question," she says, wagging a finger, "is exactly the kind of thing we here at *True Story* believe in asking. Forget the sports. Who cares about all those completed passes? Who cares about who ran for how many yards? What matters is the story behind the story. In this case, the story behind the seemingly successful ballplayer."

"You mean the dirt," I comment, and somehow I don't

roll my eyes. Why are they so hell-bent on the scandalous angle?

Eva grins as she leans back in her chair. "Exactly. But make no mistake about it, we help people. By exposing the truth, we save a helpless person from being a future victim."

"I guess so," I say to be polite.

"Let me be frank with you, Zoë. You're in my office today because I'm the head of *True Story,* and I know what I want when I see it. We can use someone with your distinct talents around here."

My brain works to make sense of all she is saying. She thinks I've got talent. She's the head and knows what she wants . . .

"Are you saying . . . " I narrow my eyes with speculation. "Are you saying you're offering me a job?"

"Can you start tomorrow?"

"Holy shit." Of all the intelligent and respectful things to say! "I'm sorry. It's just—"

Eva laughs. "You work in this business as long as I have, and 'Holy shit' is about as pleasant as 'Have a nice day'—but a whole lot more genuine."

I don't believe this. How can I believe this? For three years I've plugged away in this town hoping for a break, and not one has ever come my way. Now I'm supposed to believe I'm being handed one on a silver platter?

"Zoë?"

I shift in my seat, straightening my shoulders. "Yes?"

"I asked if that was okay with you—starting tomorrow?"

Make that a platinum platter. "Uh, sure. I can do that." *And if you want me to start right now, I'm okay with that too!*

My happiness at finally landing a gig like this dampens when I remember this isn't my dream job. It's tabloid TV.

It's exposure, I tell myself. *Exposure that you need. It's a stepping-stone to a better career.*

"Now, we'll need to take care of the paperwork. It's standard here to sign you to a one-year contract at a salary of one hundred thousand."

One hundred thousand! The words sound in my head like an explosion.

"I trust that that's satisfactory?" she asks, her voice rising on a hopeful note.

"I suppose I should speak to my agent first—"

"After a year, we are very generous with salary increases and stock options."

Me, stock options? Someone pinch me. My entire body is tingling with excitement and my head is getting light. Who cares if this is tabloid TV? *One hundred thousand dollars!*

"Zoë?"

I groan softly, because I want to say yes right now but know I can't. "It sounds really fantastic, and I want to say yes, but I should call Dina."

"Let's call her right now."

Eva turns the phone to me, and I dial Dina's number. Thank God, she answers on the first ring.

"Dina Beckham."

"Dina, it's Zoë."

"Zoë! How did it go?"

"I'm in Eva Raines' office right now. She's just offered me a position."

"Hot damn! Didn't I tell you? When I have a feeling, I'm rarely wrong."

"Dina, she offered me a salary of one hundred thousand." I say this as calmly as I can. "Naturally, I told her I had to speak with you first."

"Put her on the phone."

I extend the receiver to Eva. "My agent wants to talk to you."

"Dina, hi," Eva says in a singsong voice. "I think Zoë's

fabulous. Yes. Only for the first year. We'll negotiate a new contract at that time, plus give her stock options. Of course. I'll fax you the contract for you to look over before she signs it. What's your fax number? Great. Okay, here she is."

Eva hands the phone back to me. "Hi again."

"Zoë, this is freaking fantastic. Don't act too excited, though. I'm going to try and see if I can't get another twenty-five percent out of her. I'll be happy with ten."

"So what do I do now?"

"Say yes. We'll work out the contract details by the end of the day."

Oh my God. Is this really happening?

"Thanks, Dina. I'll talk to you later."

As I hang up the phone, Eva looks at me expectantly. "Well?"

"I guess I can start tomorrow."

"Excellent!" Eva practically leaps across her desk to shake my hand. "And guess what—you're heading to Vegas on Thursday."

"I . . . am?"

"Yes. You have your first assignment!"

An assignment. Beneath the desk, I pinch my leg. Hard. Sweet Jesus, this isn't a dream.

"Wow, Vegas. I love that town. What will I be doing? Covering some swanky star party?" Maybe this job won't be so bad after all. Getting up close to all the hottest Hollywood stars . . .

"Even better. You're going there to do a story on Kahari Brown."

"K-Kahari Brown?"

"*True Story* has learned that he'll be attending a bachelor party that night with some of his teammates, and I want you there."

Me. Vegas. Kahari Brown. I swallow. "Be there and . . . ?"

"And see what happens. See if he's up to something scandalous."

"You mean . . . find dirt?"

"No, not find dirt. Uncover it. That's what a good investigative journalist does."

There's a twinge of something inside me. Guilt maybe. At least a bit of a stab at my conscience. I'm not exactly thrilled at the idea of tailing Kahari Brown, not after what happened in Oakland on the weekend.

Then again, Eva Raines has offered me a job paying a hundred thousand dollars a year. I'd have to be out of my mind to turn down such a fabulous opportunity.

I put a smile on my face and say the only thing I can. "I can't wait."

"Fantastic. I'll fax your agent the contract, and when you come in tomorrow you can sign it. Then we'll get right to work. I'll show you the studio, introduce you to the staff, and get you ready for Thursday."

"Sure," I say. And then I remember that I don't have a car. "Um, what time tomorrow?"

"I sense a problem?"

"No, no problem. Well, maybe a little one. My car died, and I'm going to need to lease one ASAP. Perhaps if you write some sort of letter, proof that you've offered me a job—"

"Not necessary. Go to the Mercedes dealership on Beverly Boulevard. Ask for Peter. Tell him I sent you. He'll set you up with something nice."

"Really?"

"Really. I'll call him the moment you leave."

And now I know it's true what they say—that when a door closes, a window opens. Because a window has opened for me, and in an instant my life has changed for the better.

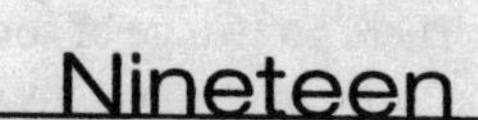

Nineteen

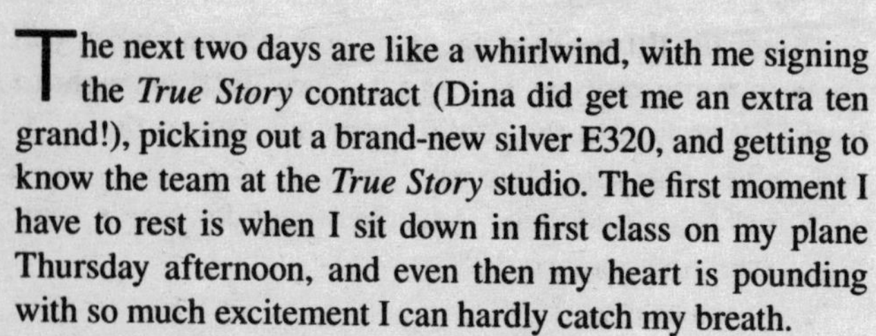

The next two days are like a whirlwind, with me signing the *True Story* contract (Dina did get me an extra ten grand!), picking out a brand-new silver E320, and getting to know the team at the *True Story* studio. The first moment I have to rest is when I sit down in first class on my plane Thursday afternoon, and even then my heart is pounding with so much excitement I can hardly catch my breath.

Zoë Andrews, reporting for True Story . . .

Can you friggin' believe it?

I know—I wasn't thrilled about this when Dina called, but obviously I wasn't seeing the big picture. I'll be on national TV on one of the most popular shows. And if I'm uncovering dirt, as Eva said, should I feel guilty? Shouldn't the star behaving badly be the one who feels bad about his or her behavior?

I haven't even called my mother yet, everything's happened so fast. But I'll call her when I get to Vegas and check into the Bellagio hotel.

"Something to drink?" the flight attendant asks me.

I suddenly remember—drinks in first class are free. "You have vodka cranberry?"

"We sure do."

I am loving this. Zoë Andrews, real reporter.

It's about damn time!

It's been nearly five years since I've been to Vegas, and there are even more lights and stunning-looking hotels now than the last time I was here. I feel a rush of excitement as I take the private car from the airport to the Bellagio. Being in Vegas is like sampling many great cities in the world—New York, Paris, Rome.

"Here we are," the driver announces.

Wow. The first time I came to Vegas, I stayed in a small hotel off the strip. The Bellagio by comparison . . . well, there is no comparison. This place is large and majestic and oozes the image of money.

"Thank you so much," I tell the driver, and I give him a generous tip. Two weeks ago, I would have cringed while doing it, but now it's par for the course. This is my new life. Fancy hotels, fancy cars, and lots of great shoes I can actually afford.

I'm nervous as I check in, but I don't know why. I guess I don't want Kahari to accidentally bump into me. There's no chance of that happening right now, of course, because he's off in one of the hotel's restaurants for a dinner with the team. After that, they'll be partying in the bar for high rollers. Later, I'm sure, there'll be skanky naked women, but that much Eva wasn't able to find out.

Minutes later, I open the door to my room and reach for the light switch. "Holy shit." This is a suite, and from first glance it's huge, and elegantly decorated.

As I walk into the room, I notice the gigantic floral arrangement on the dining table. There's an envelope on the table in front of the bouquet.

I quickly snatch it up and tear it open. The card inside reads, "Welcome to the *True Story* team! Here's to a great future with us. Eva."

Oh my God, how sweet is that? I feel like I'm part of something big here, like I'm valued. And it's a damn nice feeling, given what I'm used to.

I dump my belongings and head for the phone. I dial Eva's cell number.

"Eva Raines."

"Hello, Eva. It's Zoë. I'm here. All checked in. And the room is fabulous."

"I'm glad you like it."

"I do. I really do."

"Good. Now, according to my source, the team is meeting for dinner right about now. That'll probably be boring, so rest up if you like. But at eight-thirty the party starts in the bar. You need to be there, Zoë. Like I told you before, I've set you up with a camera crew from an affiliate station, and they'll be ready to head to the hotel whenever you make the call. But in the meantime, don't forget your watch."

"I'm wearing it. And it's lovely, if I do say so myself."

Eva gave me the neatest little camera. It's hidden in the face of a watch, and will be perfect for catching footage of scandalous behavior if I don't have time to call the camera crew.

"Are you ready for this?" she asks me.

I hope so. But I tell her, "Yes. Definitely."

"Tell me what you're supposed to do."

"I'm going to hang out in the bar, watch the guys in general and Kahari in particular. If I see him engaged in any type of disgraceful behavior, I'll catch it on my hidden camera. Then, having that evidence, I'll try to force an interview with him, at which point I'll call Ray Ficco and his camera team to come to the hotel."

"Good, good."

"Of course, he could just tell me to get lost, that he's not going to talk to me regardless of what I've caught him doing."

"That's why I have a Plan B. You always need a Plan B."

"Plan B?"

"Mmm-hmm." She pauses, then adds in an excited whisper, "I got you in, Zoë."

"In? In where?"

"In his room."

"H-how?" I stammer.

"We're *True Story*. We can do anything."

"You're not kidding."

"One thing you'll learn about me, I never kid about anything as serious as business."

Wow, wow, wow. She wants me to go into his room? Ambush him?

"What you're going to do is this: If he's on his best behavior tonight, you're going to go to his room and wait for him. And when he gets there, you're going to try and convince him to give you an exclusive about this woman he knocked up. You'll figure out a nicer way to say it, of course."

"Of course." *What have I gotten myself into?*

"Is that brilliant, or what?"

"It's . . . brilliant." What else can I say? "But tell me again—why will he want to talk to me?"

"I trust you to think of something. That's why I hired you, Zoë. Because you've got great instincts. Now, go downstairs and ask for Miguel Sanchez. Tell him you're Zoë Brown, and he'll take care of you."

"Zoë *Brown*?"

"He has a sister," Eva explains. "One who is supposedly

on her way to see Kahari. So, act sisterly. I've worked it all out with Miguel."

Act sisterly? My stomach is in knots. I know I need this job, but suddenly I'm not sure about this. The word entrapment is dancing in my head.

"Call me whenever there's a development."

"Yes, I will."

"Don't forget to have fun," Eva says.

"Right. Right, of course." But I wonder, what does she mean by that? Something along the lines of what Marvin said to me about using sex to get ahead?

I push that thought from my mind and say, "I'll talk to you later. I've got work to do."

Eva laughs hoarsely. "Call me at any hour if anything breaks. I don't care how late."

"Got it."

A moment later, I hang up, close my eyes, and silently pray for courage.

I hop off the bed. If I don't do this now, I may never do it.

"Here I come, front desk. Zoë Brown, here for my room key."

This night could get interesting indeed.

NFL players certainly know how to have a good time.

This upscale bar in the hotel is filled with barely dressed women in stiletto shoes and thigh-high boots. If you ask me, they look like hookers. They're hanging all over the players, laughing and flirting like their only goal in the world is to please them, as if they don't have any brains and ambitions of their own.

Which wouldn't surprise me.

I am doing my best to fit in with the wallpaper, sitting at a corner table away from the rowdy group and holding a newspaper up to my face. Not very original, but it was the only thing I could think of. My hair is pulled back in a ponytail, because my wild mane is pretty distinctive.

At least there are some other non-football-player guests in the part of the bar where I'm sitting.

I hide a yawn with the newspaper, then glance around the room again. To Kahari's credit, he doesn't seem to be lapping up the female attention, though he's chatting with some of the women.

Flicking my wrist forward, I glance at my camera watch. It's twenty-five minutes after nine. I've been here for half an hour, and nothing really crazy has happened. At least not with Kahari. Some of the players have disappeared into the bathroom with the women, maybe to do drugs or get a blow job, but Kahari hasn't done any of that.

Since nothing's happened here yet, I probably ought to head upstairs.

I down the last of my vodka cranberry and creep toward the door on the far side of the bar so none of the players can see me.

But before I step out the door, I see a flash of movement. A body?

I rush into the hallway in time to see long, dark hair flowing about a woman's shoulders as she's running.

"Wait!" I cry out.

The woman throws a quick glance at me before running to a stairwell.

I recognize her instantly from the *Daily Blab* article, and a heady feeling of excitement starts to spread through my body.

I *knew* I'd read about her somewhere. I *knew* I wasn't crazy. This is a bona fide lead. Because the woman is none other than Stella Rivera.

Ooh, this is big news. I know it is. As I search for my phone in my purse, adrenaline is pumping through my body like zaps of electricity.

I call Eva's cell.

She picks up right away. "Eva Raines."

"Eva," I say in a frantic whisper, "it's Zoë Andrews. I think I'm onto something. Something big."

"What is it?"

"That woman—the one who claims Kahari fathered her baby—she's here. In Vegas."

"With Kahari?"

"No, she's not with him. She just ran from the bar when I was leaving. It's like she's stalking him or something, which would definitely be news."

"Where's the camera crew?"

"Ready to act at a moment's notice."

"Get to Stella. Get her somewhere and tape her side of the story."

"I'm going to try, but she took off when she saw me."

"*Find her.* If you have to search every hotel in the city, find her."

"I will," I assure Eva. I quickly look behind me, half expecting to see Kahari there, or even Stella. But neither is. I'm alone in the hallway.

"Great work," Eva tells me. I can hear her ear-to-ear smile in her voice. "Zoë, this is fabulous."

"More later," I tell her, then end the call.

I whirl around, wondering where to go, what to do.

The lobby?

It's as good an idea as any. I'll take an elevator down, and hopefully I'll meet up with Stella at the stairwell before she makes it all the way down.

Pleased with myself, I run to the elevators.

Twenty

Kahari stared at the dark-skinned beauty and tried his best not to yawn.

"Come on," she said, trailing a finger in circles over the top of his hand. "I'll make it worth your while . . . "

Lord have mercy, these women were all the same. The heated gazes, the touchy-feely routine, the promises that they'd rock his world.

"Look," he said, pulling his hand from hers. "I've enjoyed talking to you, but I'm going upstairs alone."

"Oh no no no." Courtney—at least Kahari thought that was her name—shook her head and tsked softly. "I'm not letting you get away that easily."

"I'm really tired."

"I've heard that you like playing hard to get."

"Hard to get? I have to be on a plane tomorrow morning."

"So do all these guys, and I don't see them rushing anywhere." She lowered her lids in what Kahari figured was supposed to be a sexy look. "If you don't want to go upstairs, why don't you let me take you to the bathroom. Give me five minutes, baby. You'll be begging for more."

Same old, same old. What Courtney didn't realize was that Kahari heard this spiel all the time. Oh, it varied somewhat, but the core was the same. The women wanted sex, figuring it would give them a way to cash in on his earnings.

The groupies who followed the team around did all kinds of crazy things, like slip their panties into his pocket or pass him their hotel room keys. He could be the world's biggest jerk for all they knew or have ten different diseases, yet they were eager to sleep with him nonetheless.

"Five minutes, baby," she said, and reached for his crotch.

Kahari quickly grabbed her wrist and pulled her hand back. "I'm gonna give you the benefit of the doubt and say that's the alcohol making you act like this. Because I'm sure your mama raised you to have better respect for yourself."

"Let's leave my mama out of this, shall we?" Courtney leaned forward, exposing even more of her already exposed cleavage in the tight lacy top she was wearing. "I'm not too drunk to know what I want . . . and to go after it."

"Then that makes this easy."

Her smile was victorious. "Good."

"Easy to say good-bye. I'm not trying to meet another woman who wants me to be her meal ticket."

Courtney stared at Kahari in confusion. "What?"

"Hey, if you're really looking to get laid by some ballplayer, why not check out Steve Emmett." Kahari nodded in the direction of the man at a table with a group of near-naked women. "He's always more than happy to sleep with groupies."

Courtney's eyes flashed fire as she glared at him. "Asshole."

"Tramp," he muttered, then shook his head.

Damn, he had had enough of this.

He made his way through the bar to where Anthony was sitting at a table with a couple of the married guys who didn't cheat on their wives. Out of all the men on the team, Kahari only knew three that were decent.

"Hey, Smooth," Anthony said. "Sit down, bro."

Kahari pulled out a chair and slumped into it. "I swear, these women."

Anthony laughed. "They don't realize how bored we get of all the T&A they like to flash."

"Where the hell is Frankie, anyway?" Kahari asked, looking around.

"Last I saw him," Jefferson said, "he was heading into the bathroom with two women."

"Why the hell's he getting married?"

"Because Shelley's breathing down his neck," Murray replied.

"Whatever," Kahari commented. "It's none of my business."

The sound of a loud crash drew everyone's attention. Kahari looked behind him to see Wayne, one of the team's rookies, on top of a woman on a table. His face was buried in her chest. Apparently he'd put the woman onto the table without removing the glasses first, so they'd all crashed onto the floor.

Clyde, one of the team's middle linebackers, howled as he grabbed Wayne off the woman. "Come on, man. No time for that."

"Jesus," Murray muttered.

Clyde made a funnel over his mouth with his hands and yelled, "Come on, y'all. We've gotta roll! It's off to the strip club."

"That's my cue to bow out," Anthony said, then sucked back the dregs of his beer.

"Mine too," Kahari said.

"Hey," Anthony said, "you're not married."

"So that means I need to have strange pussy up in my face?"

"I'm starting to worry about you," Anthony said with a smile.

"At least I'm not about to run off and marry a Ginger."

"Ooh, that was low."

Kahari shrugged nonchalantly, though he was smiling. In reality, he knew that Anthony had had the best of intentions when he'd married that gold-digging bitch.

"You all going with these guys?" Kahari asked Jefferson and Murray.

"Are you kidding? My wife would have my ass on a platter if I went to the strip club," Jefferson chimed. "I guess I'll head upstairs. Or maybe hit the slots."

"I'll go with you," Murray offered.

Kahari and Anthony sat for a moment longer, watching the rest of the intoxicated players start to gather together. "Let's wait till they all leave," Kahari said. "Then we'll head out."

"You want to play some blackjack?" Anthony suggested.

"I dunno, dawg. I'm kinda tired."

"It's only ten o'clock."

"Yeah, but . . . "

"But what?"

"What if Estela's hiding out somewhere?"

"You're not serious."

"Just last week the psycho was hiding outside the hotel room. Hell yeah, I'm serious."

Anthony clamped a hand on Kahari's shoulder as he stood. "Don't let Estela ruin your fun. Let's go win some money."

* * *

Unfortunately, I didn't end up seeing Stella in the lobby, and I waited a good fifteen minutes. I'm still pumped, though, raring to go, so I decide to head upstairs to Kahari's room. Just to be certain he was still in the bar, I went up there first to check, and I spotted him quickly, chatting with a dark-skinned bimbo.

I have to admit, I felt a twinge of something as I watched them. A feeling of unpleasantness in the pit of my stomach.

Jealousy, maybe? Or perhaps disgust. I so want to believe he's one of the good ones, if only for the sake of my silly crush.

In any case, I have a job to do, so I head to Kahari's room. And that's where I am now, standing outside his door.

I may be pumped, but I'm also scared out of my mind at the prospect of actually going inside. What is he going to think when he comes up here and finds me?

Probably that I'm like every other groupie he's encountered tonight—out to seduce him.

Sucking in a shaky breath, I glance up and down the hallway before slipping my electronic key into the lock. Like magic, the green light comes on.

Do it do it do it, I urge myself. How hard can it be to go inside? I know Kahari's in the bar, so it's not like he'll pull a gun on me or anything for breaking in.

That thought hardly eases my conscience, and my stomach is in such awful knots as I slip into the room that I wonder if I won't throw up. Maybe I'm not cut out for this after all.

Nonsense! You can do this, and you will.

I flip on the light switch, and am a bit taken aback by what I see. The room is large and elegant—no surprise there—but it's also unexpectedly neat. I'm not sure why that surprises me, but I suppose I expected to see jeans tossed carelessly onto the furniture, or open beer cans on the coffee table. *Something.* Instead, the place is so neat that even Kahari's suitcase is closed and in one corner of the room.

I shouldn't be doing this, shouldn't be snooping like I'm some sort of pervert, but here I am, putting one foot in front of the other and walking straight toward what must be the bedroom door.

I swing it open with force, as though I am ready to yell "Gotcha!" But no, the bedroom is also painfully clean. One pair of neatly pressed black slacks is laid out on an armchair, and on the night table beside the bed there is a glass of water.

I've come this far, why stop now? I keep walking, heading straight into the bathroom. Is Kahari always this neat? He's got a closed travel case on one side of the counter, and two bottles of cologne beside that. I lift Obsession for Men and sniff. Mmm, I like.

My eyes wander to the toilet, which is a few feet away in this large bathroom. And at last I feel a moment of victory. The toilet seat is up.

It's almost like an indictment of guilt. See, he's not perfect. Of course he'd get a woman pregnant and abandon his child!

Okay, enough already. The last thing I want is for the guy to show up and see me rifling through his things.

I head back into the living room area and sit on the sofa.

And then I wait. And wait.

Twenty-one

As soon as Kahari and Anthony hit the casino floor, heads started to turn. As they walked through the slot area, eyes narrowed with speculation before widening in recognition.

It had started. Any second, the fans would begin approaching.

No sooner did that thought come into Kahari's mind than a guy in an Oakland Raiders jersey that boasted Anthony's last name practically threw himself in their path.

"Oh my God. Anthony Beals! Kahari Brown!"

"What's up?" Kahari and Anthony said at the same time.

"What's *up*?" the guy asked in disbelief. "I totally love you guys. You, Beals, you've got to be the best quarterback ever. And Kahari Brown? Oh my God, there's never been a better wide receiver on the team."

Anthony shook the guy's hand. "Thanks, man. Appreciate it."

"That's right," Kahari agreed.

"Holy shit, I can't believe I'm meeting you! What are you doing here? Aren't you playing Denver on Sunday?"

"We're in town for the night," Kahari explained. "For a bachelor party."

"Cool."

"And speaking of which," Anthony said.

The fan held out two hands, as if to keep Kahari and Anthony from moving. "Look, I know you guys are busy and all, but can you take a moment to sign my jersey? Damn, my friend Matt's gonna be so pissed that he didn't come on this trip with me!"

"No problem," Kahari told the guy. Then he leaned toward an older gentleman sitting at a neighboring slot machine. "Excuse me, sir. Do you have a pen?"

"I'm sure I do."

The man rifled his pockets for a pen, and within seconds passed one to Kahari. The fan hunched his back over to make it easier for Kahari and Anthony to sign.

"There you go," Anthony said, the second of the two to sign their John Hancocks.

"Oh, man. Thanks so much!"

Anthony passed the pen back to the older man. A moment later, he and Kahari were off again.

They ended up at a blackjack table with a minimum bet of two hundred and fifty dollars.

Before they could even start to play, a small crowd began to form around them. Women and men, mostly in their twenties and thirties. Kahari was used to this, and he knew Anthony was as well. Most places he went, even the grocery store, at least one person recognized him. With the numerous commercials and print ads he did, it was hard for him to go unnoticed.

"You playing?" Anthony asked him.

"Yeah, I'll play." Kahari glanced at the crowd, smiled a quick greeting, then counted out two thousand dollars from his wallet. He passed the money to the dealer, who gave him a stack of one hundred and fifty-dollar chips.

"Big money, big money," Anthony said, knocking fists with Kahari.

Three rounds later, Anthony was down fifteen hundred dollars and Kahari was up five hundred. But at least the crowd was entertained. Win or lose, the crowd applauded and cheered.

"How the heck do you always have all the luck?" Anthony asked, shaking his head.

"They don't call me Smooth for nuthin'."

"Ha! You got me there, my man."

Kahari watched as a woman with long red hair slipped through the crowd and next to Anthony. He had to have noticed her, but his friend paid the woman no attention. After years of this kind of attention, you got used to tuning it out.

"I can't go out like a punk," Anthony said, and reached for his wallet. As he peeled out more bills, a movement beyond the dealer's shoulder caught Kahari's eye. A sense of dread hit him in the gut like a linebacker's helmet.

"Aw, shit," he whispered.

"What?" Anthony asked.

"I think I just saw Estela."

Anthony whipped his head around. "Where?"

Kahari surveyed the area beyond the dealer, but could no longer see the woman who'd made him think of Estela.

"I don't know . . . I thought she was . . . "

"Dawg, you're letting that woman drive you crazy."

"Gentlemen," the dealer said, "are you in?"

Kahari collected his chips and got to his feet. "I'm out."

"You're leaving me?" Anthony asked.

"Yeah, and you should probably head upstairs, too. Before you lose even more. I don't want your wife getting on my case for not keeping you in line," Kahari added with a smile.

"That's why I've got to win back what I've lost."

"Famous last words." Kahari shook his head. "See you in the morning."

Kahari started to walk away, but stopped abruptly when the hairs on his nape stood on end. His gaze swept the casino area, but again, he didn't see anyone.

"Damn, Estela," he muttered, then continued to the cashier.

A short while later, Kahari blew out a sigh of relief when he opened the door to his hotel room and stepped inside. He reached for the light switch and flipped it up.

"Holy *shit*!" he cried out, seeing the body on the armchair.

At the sound of his voice, the woman's eyes popped open. She scrambled to a sitting position.

"How the hell did you get in here?" Kahari demanded.

"Oh, hi there." The woman got to her feet.

"Hi there? Are you out of your mind?"

"Um . . . good evening?" she offered instead.

Scowling, Kahari advanced, and the woman withered backward, stopping when she hit the wall.

"You answer me, and you answer me right now. How did you get in my r—"

Kahari stopped abruptly as he suddenly recognized the woman. Her hair was pulled back, unlike the way she had worn it on Sunday, which is why it had taken him so long.

"Oh God. I know who you are," he said with a sinking sense of dread. "And you can stay right there, because I'm calling the—"

The woman leapt at him like a corner from an opposing team coming at him for the tackle. But where he was normally grace under fire on the football field, here, in unfamiliar territory, he was too stunned even to move.

He was even more stunned when she threw her arms around his neck and kissed him.

Twenty-two

Not one of my smoothest moments, certainly, but I didn't know what else to do. So I kiss him, kiss him like I'm a woman starved for affection.

And call me stupid—perhaps *really* stupid—but I like this kiss. Maybe it's the rebound factor, but Kahari's lips seem extra velvety soft, and he smells so delectable I almost want to sink my teeth into his neck.

Or maybe it's the crush factor—I'm finally kissing a guy I've lusted after for so long.

Whatever the case, now I understand what Gail meant when she talked about needing a palate cleanser, and how the first guy you kiss after your ex helps to erase the memory of the Big Jerk from your mind.

Ooh, kiss me, baby . . .

But then I feel the splash of cold reality, because Kahari is pushing me away. And not only has he just pushed me away, he's glaring at me like I'm worse than a piece of scum on the bottom of his shoe.

Which pretty much shoots the whole palate cleanser fantasy straight to hell.

"What are you doing?" he demands.

"Please don't call the cops."

"That's why you kissed me?"

"Well . . ." *Not entirely. I've always fantasized about kissing you. God only knows why . . .*

"Fine. I won't call the cops. Just go."

"No, wait."

His eyes narrow again. "Wait?"

I raise both hands in a gesture I hope he'll see as non-offensive. "Don't freak out."

"It's too late for that. How did you get in here?"

"I just want to talk to you, Kahari."

"I *don't* want to talk to you."

My stomach tightens painfully. I know I shouldn't take it personally, but I don't like the way he's said that.

"You're that reporter. The one who asked me about Estela on Sunday."

"*E*stela—with an *E* in front? I always thought it was Stella, without the—"

"Please stop the rambling and leave my room."

"Listen to me, please. I work for *True Story.* You've heard of the show, right?" When he doesn't respond, I continue. "I want to interview you, Kahari. About Estela. About her claim that you fathered her baby."

"I know you didn't just say that to me."

"Why not? The world wants to know your side of the story."

"And you think I'm just going to sit down and talk to you?"

"Well. Yeah."

"Then you're crazy, because I don't want to be in the same room with you, much less give you an interview."

"Ouch."

"You call Estela and tell her the plan backfired."

"What?"

"Don't play dumb."

I look at him in confusion. "What are you talking about?"

"Is Estela here?"

"Um . . . " Should I tell him I saw her?

"Are you investigating me? Is that why she keeps showing up where I am?"

"Whoa, slow down, cowboy. You've totally lost me."

"All right," Kahari says, his face twisting in a scowl. "I'm not playing this game anymore."

"Good, no more games. Let's set up a time for your interview."

"I don't want to talk to you."

"You've made that point clear. Do you *have* to drive the knife farther into my heart?"

"What?"

Oh, lovely. I said that out loud.

"I'll give you five seconds."

Damn, what would Barbara Walters do? I ask myself, scrambling to figure out a way to fix this situation.

Marvin's comment about me using sex to get ahead pops into my mind. Why have I been so self-righteous about the subject? Sex sells, and a girl's gotta do what a girl's gotta do.

So I extend my hand and run a finger down his chest. I'm pretty sure Barbara would *not* do this, by the way, but what can I say? I'm desperate, and if I know one thing, it's that athletes like sex. I'm not planning to seduce him, but I'll soften him a little.

"I just want to get a little closer to you," I tell him in a tone that sounds a lot like a purr.

He knocks my hand away. "Are you *crazy*? You need to stay as far away from me as possible."

I gulp a little. Why do I keep taking his words personally? It's not me he hates. He hates what I did to him.

Wait a minute . . . what exactly did I do to him? Ask him a question? Was that so wrong? I mean, really. Spurred on by this, I ask him, "What exactly do you have to hide?"

Kahari holds up both hands. "I've had about enough of this."

"No, really. Do you have some deep, dark secret or something? Because all I did was ask you a question. If you've got nothing to hide, why can't you answer it?"

"You are exactly the reason I don't like talking to the media. You find an angle, and go for the jugular, whether or not it's true. And you don't care about what happens to people in the process."

"Then why don't you tell me your story? A one-on-one interview so you can set the record straight?"

"You don't give up, do you?"

If you only knew how my knees were shaking . . .

"We can do it wherever you want—wherever you're most comfortable."

"That's it. Your time here is up."

Kahari takes hold of my arm. His strong hand wrapped around my forearm actually feels good. So good, a surge of heat shoots through my body.

I hate guys like him. Guys who spread their sperm around for sport. Guys who father babies and deny them.

So why am I so friggin' attracted to him?

I know what this is. Subconsciously, I have a love-hate relationship with football players. On one hand, I have so much resentment for my father, you'd think I would want to become a missionary instead of a sportscaster. But then there's my heart, and I suppose in a way, I must be looking for some type of love and affection from a ballplayer to make up for my father abandoning me. It's one messed-up cycle, with the abandoned child seeking acceptance in all the wrong places.

I wonder what Dr. Phil would think of my psychoanalysis.

The cold reality that I've blown my chance at a story hits me when I hear the doorknob turn. Eva is going to fire me.

"Don't do this, Kahari. Please."

But suddenly I'm in the hallway, and the door is closing in my face.

Tell me that didn't just happen.

A young couple stares at me in alarm as they stroll hand in hand in my direction. I grin sheepishly and say, "Lovers' quarrel, you know. He's so passionate about everything. But you should see when we make up . . . "

My voice trails off as the couple hurries past me, like they think I'm some crazy person or something.

Damn, maybe I am. Why else am I tempted to knock on Kahari's door again and beg him to see reason?

Sanity prevails and I decide not to make a bigger fool of myself than I already have. My heart heavy, I head toward the elevators. I've blown this, really blown this, and I can only imagine what Eva will say.

Good-bye hundred-thousand-dollar salary.

I should have known it was too good to be true.

Twenty-three

Kahari sat slumped on one of the suite's armchairs long after Zoë Andrews had left. His heart was racing like he'd run down the field for a touchdown, but he in no way felt the same kind of joy. Instead, he felt odd. Winded and shocked.

How the hell had that woman gotten into his room?

And why on earth had she kissed him?

Was she simply after a story, or had she been hoping to seduce him?

It had to be the story she wanted, and she was willing to do anything to achieve her goal. Damn reporters. They couldn't be trusted as far as you could throw them.

Letting out a loud groan, Kahari finally stood. He marched to the door and peered through the peephole. He didn't see anyone out there, but bolted the door nonetheless for good measure. In his haste to get her out of the room, he hadn't thought to see if she'd gained access with a key.

Damn woman. What do you want?

And why had she kissed him? Try as he might, Kahari couldn't quite get past that one.

He had accused her of being crazy, but maybe he was the crazy one. Because instead of feeling outraged as he remembered the kiss, he felt something else. A twinge of excitement. The same twinge he'd felt when she'd planted her lips on his.

Maybe it was time he found a woman to sleep with, because apparently it had been too long.

Kahari made his way to the bathroom, where he turned on the faucet and splashed cold water on his face.

Tomorrow was another day. With any luck, he'd been harsh enough with Miss Zoë Andrews that she'd know better than to bother him again. As for Estela, he could only hope she would realize that all her crazy tricks weren't working, but he wasn't about to bank on it.

"I don't care how hard it is," Eva tells me the next morning. "Do it."

I've just explained to her that last night's mission was a bust. I also added that I'm not sure Kahari will ever want to talk to me again.

"Don't give him a choice, Zoë. You hear me?"

"I hear you." I hear her so well I can hold the phone away from my ear and make out every word she's saying.

"Okay," she continues in a softer tone. "I don't mean to be hard on you. I know you're new at this. But take it from me—you can't give up without a fight. You keep on him, Zoë. Break down his resolve. And it'll work out. I promise you."

I roll my eyes and sigh softly. Whatever I tell Eva, it's not going to matter. She wants Kahari's guts on a platter, and she probably wouldn't care if I had to burn down the casino to achieve that.

"All right," I grudgingly agree, thinking of the rent I'll have to pay when I get my own apartment, and the fact that without this job, I'll be in serious trouble. There's no doubt about it, I *need* this job like I need a hit of caffeine right now.

Eva's words still ringing in my mind, I head to the bathroom and put on my makeup, spritz myself with delicate perfume, and decide that sexy attire is the only way I'm going to get through the door. I know, I tried the whole sex appeal thing last night and it didn't work, but he wasn't ready for me then. Today I'll knock, and when he comes to the door I'll smile sweetly. He won't be able to resist me.

God, I hope not.

I leave my hair out so the thick curls are wild and sexy. I like this look. It says I'm confident in my own skin, and I sense that's the attitude Kahari will like.

And off I go. Amazon warrior, out to get her man.

Five minutes later, the elevator pings softly and the doors open. Despite what I told myself just a short while ago, my stomach is suddenly in serious knots.

"I know we got off on the wrong foot," I say softly as I walk into the elevator. "You're a fascinating guy—can I buy you a drink?"

Wrong, wrong, wrong.

"Kahari, hi. Me again. About last night . . ."

The elevator doors open, and I hesitate before stepping out. I should have had a shot of alcohol for my nerves.

I force myself to get off the elevator before the door closes. No sooner than I do, I see a familiar face down the hall near Kahari's room.

Estela Rivera!

She's hanging near his door, as if waiting for him to come out, and I hustle down the hallway. Finally, she lifts her head in my direction, and her eyes widen in alarm. She quickly turns and starts walking toward the stairwell.

"Estela Rivera!" I call out to her.

She halts, as though shocked that I know her name. But then she's moving again.

"Estela, wait. Please. I think I can help you."

Though she is at the stairwell door, she stops. This time she turns and eyes me curiously.

"I can help you," I repeat.

"Who are you?" she asks.

I walk toward her, slowly at first, until I'm sure she's not heading anywhere. "My name is Zoë Andrews, and I work for *True Story*."

"You mean you're not . . . involved with Kahari?"

"Me? God no. You're Estela Rivera, right?"

"Yes." Her voice has a distinctive Spanish accent, so "yes" sounds like "jes" when she says it.

"I'm here because I heard about your story, and I've been trying to interview him about it."

"But he won't talk to you, right?"

"Right."

She grunts her disgust.

"Kahari Brown is the father of your baby, but he won't acknowledge that—right?"

"Yes, that's right."

I reach into my Louis Vuitton Papillon handbag—my first extravagant purchase after landing this gig—and extract a business card. "As I said, I work for *True Story*. Our show is seen internationally on a daily basis. Have you heard of it?"

"Yes, of course."

"I can help you, Estela. Tell your story to us, to the world. I think that's exactly what you need to help force the situation in your favor."

Estela continues to eye me warily as she extends her hand to accept the card. She looks down at it, then back up at me.

"You'll interview me on television?"

"Yes. It'll be great exposure. I think I only saw one story about you somewhere, but nothing else. And as far as I'm concerned, your story should be heard."

"The *Daily Blab* ran the story, but then Kahari was so angry with me."

"Of course he was angry. Because he doesn't want the truth to get out. Estela, I understand where you're coming from. No one really knows this about me, but my father . . . he was an NFL player. Very successful thirty years ago. And much like Kahari, he got my mother pregnant and then walked away from her. From us."

"So you do understand."

"Yes. More than I'd like to. And that's why I know it's important to get the word out. Guys like my father and Kahari can't just take advantage of women and not take responsibility for their actions."

There's a part of me that feels bad about what I'm saying, because I don't know Kahari's side of this story. But what can I do? I've got to get Estela to talk to me. And where there's smoke, there's fire, right? At the very least, I have to do everything in my power to keep this job I've landed. An interview with Estela will go a long way in terms of job security.

"Your father never claimed you?" Estela asks.

"Not until eleven years ago, after I was already an adult." And it's something I'll never forgive him for, no matter how much he wants me to. How can you excuse away nineteen years?

"Men," Estela huffs, shaking her head. "They're such pigs."

"Tell me about it." I pause, then say, "I know you might want some time to think about this."

"Yes, I think that's a smart idea."

"What room are you in? I can call you later."

"304."

"I'm in room 811. Call me anytime if you have any questions."

Estela nods at me, her expression grim. I reach for her shoulder and squeeze it gently as a sign of support. "It's going to be okay."

She glances down, like she doesn't want to meet my eyes, and I realize that there's something else on her mind.

"What is it?" I ask. "Is there something else going on?"

She starts to cry softly. "I don't want you to think that I'm crazy or something. Some kind of stalker. It's just that I had to do something. When I found out he was going to be here, I came hoping he would talk to me. I'm not a rich woman. I begged a friend to lend me the money to fly here, and to stay at this hotel. I'm doing this for our son. Kahari Junior."

"Of *course*. If I didn't understand that, I wouldn't be offering to help you."

"Thank you," Estela says in a soft and vulnerable voice, then, clutching her purse under her arm, she starts down the hallway toward the elevator. As I watch her go, I'm reaching into my purse. Eva Raines is going to be thrilled.

"Eva Raines," she answers in the gruff, urgent-sounding voice she always uses.

"Oh my God, Eva," I say excitedly.

"You got Kahari to talk?"

"No, but I think I've got something better. I just had a chat with Estela Rivera."

"You tracked her down?"

"Uh-huh. And I'm pretty sure she's going to give us a television exclusive. I told her to think about it, because I didn't want to scare her. But I've got her room number, and I'll call her later today."

"Excellent!" Eva says. Then, "Did she say she wants to get paid?"

"Nope. She didn't mention that at all." I didn't even consider that she might want to get paid for her story, though now that I think about it, many people probably do. If Estela doesn't want money, that makes her more legit, doesn't it?

"Zoë, I *love* you! You are a genius."

"I don't think she's out for cash. She wants everyone to know the truth. But I get the impression she's not well off. She said a friend lent her the money to get here."

"I'll call the hotel immediately and book the best suite available for her."

"Oh, that's a great idea."

"That should help loosen her tongue."

I frown a little. For a moment I thought Eva was being nice. "I don't think she'll have a problem talking. She wants him to do right by her son."

"Great work," Eva tells me. "Didn't I tell you that you have great instincts?"

"You did." I can't help it, I'm feeling proud right now.

But once I end the call, my feeling of pride wavers a bit. It's marred by guilt as the realization dawns on me that while I'll be helping Estela, I'll be hurting Kahari.

But he had his chance, didn't he? I offered him the opportunity to share his side.

That argument doesn't exactly alleviate my conscience, but what can I do? I need this job. I have to do this interview.

Which means that I have to put Kahari and how this will affect him out of mind.

Twenty-four

The interview takes place the next morning, in the suite the show has rented for this occasion. It is quite an elaborate suite, probably the best one in the Bellagio. To say it is massive is an understatement. Two walls that meet at a ninety-degree angle boast floor-to-ceiling windows with a lethally gorgeous view. I say lethal because I'm afraid of heights, and every time I get near those windows, I imagine myself breaking through the glass and tumbling to my very tragic death.

"Zoë?"

The sound of Estela's voice nearly sends me crashing into the glass, but I quickly recover from my fright and turn around to face her. Smiling, I say, "Yes?"

"Why are you being so nice to me?"

"What do you mean?"

"This," she says, gesturing to the suite. "The room you surprised me with last night was spectacular, and now this. This one is like a palace! The bathroom here alone is bigger than my apartment!"

My former apartment too, but I don't tell her that.

"Why rent another room for the interview when the suite you gave me is already so beautiful?"

Because True Story *has money to burn?* "Well, because this way, you had some privacy getting ready this morning. You wouldn't want the camera crew and caterers in your room, invading your space."

"Ah," Estela chimes, understanding. "I'm simply not used to this kind of treatment. I feel a little like royalty."

"Good," I tell her, rubbing her shoulder.

"And the spread of food. My God, it could feed a football team. How can this all be for me?"

I walk toward the six-foot-long table. It is covered with fresh croissants and bagels, an assortment of jams, every kind of fruit imaginable, as well as a selection of deli meat slices. There are silver coffeepots with regular and decaf options, as well as hot water. And there are hot food options as well. Scrambled eggs and bacon and pancakes are warming in separate pans.

I pop a piece of pineapple into my mouth and savor its sweetness. "Well," I begin, facing Estela, "*some* of this food is for me."

Estela chuckles nervously, her anxiety seemingly eased somewhat. I don't tell her that Eva was so elated to learn she wouldn't have to pay for Estela's story that she sprang for the room without any hesitation.

"Are you ready?" I ask Estela. I should be one hundred percent into this interview, my first big story. But I'm distracted. I keep thinking about how Kahari will react to it. And, if I'm completely honest, I'm thinking about that kiss we shared.

He pushed me away, but not right away. I'm pretty sure it wasn't right away. All night I obsessed about what that must mean.

"You want more coffee?" I ask Estela. "Some scrambled eggs?"

"No, I'm fine. I'd like to get started before my nerves get to me and I sprint toward one of those windows."

"Aren't they freaky?" I say, almost with relief. Thank God I'm not the only crazy one.

Only crazy enough to kiss Kahari Brown senseless.

"Ray," I say to the cameraman. "And Paul." He's the soundman. "We're ready."

I conduct the interview, surprising myself at how easily I get into a flow. Dammit, I *knew* I was born to do this.

I only half pay attention to the specifics. It's a typical story. Ballplayer can't keep his pants up, sleeps with a groupie and gets her pregnant, then doesn't want to take responsibility for his child.

Where have I heard this story before?

I swallow as an unexpected lump forms in my throat. I'm surprised I feel anything. I could easily substitute Sean Andrews' name for Kahari Brown's, but I am over that. Aren't I? Of course I am. I've been over my father since I was five and my mother tracked him down for my sake but he didn't have more than a few words to say to me.

When Estela finishes telling the story of how she and Kahari met and fell for each other, her eyes are filled with tears.

"This was hard for you," I comment.

"Yes." She wipes at her tears.

"Some people might think you're trying to be vindictive by telling this story. Are you?"

"No, no. Oh God, no. I love Kahari. I'm doing this because I want him to know that I still care for him, and that I need him. Our son needs him."

"Thank you, Estela. I appreciate you sharing your story with us."

"No, I thank you."

I reach across the sofa and squeeze her hand. After Ray has captured this moment, I look to him. "How was it?"

"Great. Paul, any problem with the sound?"

"Nope. The sound was good."

"Excellent." I get to my feet. There's no doubt this will be a compelling segment on the show. Ray will tape me doing my opening and closing spiel later, since the key this morning was to get Estela's story, and to make sure she was comfortable on camera.

Estela also stands. "Is that it?"

"Yes. We'll go over the video, make sure everything's okay. If something's wrong, we'll give you a call."

"Oh. When?"

"Within a couple hours."

"I see."

"So if you don't hear from us by then, you're free to hit the slots." I flash a wide grin.

Estela frowns slightly as she crosses her arms over her chest.

"Hey"—I place an arm around her shoulders—"how are you feeling?"

"I'm okay."

"No regrets?"

"Not really, no."

"I'm glad to hear that." Because she's already signed the waiver, and I'm not sure Eva would let her off the hook at this point.

Estela sighs softly. "Sometimes I'm so mad at him that I want to hurt him. I know people will think that's why I came forward, and yes, there's a part of me that's angry with him. But I want him to realize that I'll do anything for our family."

"I can't believe he's ignoring you. After you dated for six

months . . . " I have to admit, that part of the story was the hardest for me to stomach. I know I shouldn't be personally involved in any way, and so what if I've had a crush on Kahari Brown for quite some time now. It's not like I ever had a chance of being with him.

So why did Estela's words feel like a stab in my heart?

"I can leave now?" Estela asks me.

"Uh-huh. You go back to your suite, and like I said, if you don't hear from us in a couple hours, you can enjoy the rest of your stay here. The show will air tonight."

"Tonight?"

"Yes. Everyone's really excited about it."

"Wow."

"Have you decided when you're heading back to Los Angeles? Remember, the show will cover the cost of upgrading your ticket to first class."

"You have all been so nice to me." Estela's lips lift in a soft smile.

If you only knew, I think. But I say, "Whatever you need, you call me anytime. You still have my card, right?"

"Yes."

"Don't lose it. Because I meant what I said. Anything you need . . . "

"Thank you so much." Estela shakes my hand firmly. "On behalf of my son, I thank you."

"You're welcome. I hope . . . I hope everything works out for you."

I walk Estela to the door, where, once in the hallway, she waves at me over her shoulder.

I close the door and turn back to the massive suite. Now it's time for my big moment.

Showtime.

Twenty-five

"Hey, don't sweat it." Colin clamped a hand on Kahari's shoulder and gave it a supportive squeeze. "Everyone has a bad game."

"Yeah," Kahari grumbled. "Sure."

Another player walked by and squeezed his shoulder, but Kahari didn't bother looking up to see who it was. He sat slumped on a bench in the locker room, his head hanging in shame. What a bitch of a game he'd played. He wasn't sure he'd get over it, especially with all his teammates offering their sympathy.

"Hey." Anthony now took a seat beside him. "Don't beat yourself up."

"Don't beat myself up? I'm the reason our winning streak is over."

"That's not true. We just didn't play our best."

"I had that ball, dammit," Kahari said, shaking his head. "But somehow I dropped it, and the cocky Sam Peterson took it all the way back for a touchdown. The touchdown that won the game for them."

Anthony sighed softly. "It happens. Football can be unpredictable."

"It doesn't happen to me."

"Look, Smooth, you've got a lot on your mind."

Exactly. And normally Kahari could block out all the bullshit. But seeing Estela Rivera on TV Friday night, crying the blues about how he had done wrong by her, still had him feeling sick to his stomach.

"When we get back to Oakland," Kahari began, "I'm not gonna stick around for the meeting in the morning. I want to head home right away."

"Which means you want me to skip the meeting, too. Since we *do* fly together."

"I'll pay your fine," Kahari told him. Anytime a player missed a mandatory meeting they were fined a thousand dollars. Right now Kahari didn't care. He couldn't stand the idea of having to face everyone in the morning after the abysmal game he'd played.

"Smooth, you sure?"

"Yeah, I am."

Anthony paused. "All right then. We'll leave when we get back to Oakland. It's not like I don't want to see my lady, anyway."

"See?" Kahari forced a smile. "It's all good."

If only Kahari believed what he was saying. But he didn't. Because things were far from good. They were downright bad.

Less than twenty-four hours later, Kahari and Anthony sat on their private plane, Kahari staring at a copy of the *Oakland Tribune* in horror.

"How can they do this?" he asked in frustration.

"With all their bullshit 'anonymous sources,' " Anthony

replied, "that's how. That way, they never have to take the heat for any of the crap they come up with."

Kahari had made the front page. The fucking front page. There was a picture of Estela beneath the headline "Kahari Brown's Jilted Lover?" The only thing missing was the friggin' halo, she was wearing such an innocent I'd-never-hurt-a-fly-much-less-lie-about-my-baby's-paternity expression.

"I'm as surprised as you are," Anthony said. "I never thought anything would come of Estela's lame-ass story."

"How soon before my life completely goes to hell? My manager's called, wondering what the hell is going on. LaTonya said family's calling from Texas because they saw that damn TV spot." Kahari rolled the newspaper in his hands. "I can't deal with this."

"What you ought to do is file a lawsuit. The paper shouldn't print stuff like that without getting your side of the story. Even if nothing comes of it, a lawsuit will be enough to get people's attention. I don't want to see your chance at your hero award jeopardized because of crap like this."

"I don't think the award's in the cards for me. But hey, at least I was nominated."

"You deserve this," Anthony insisted. "You shouldn't lose out because of Estela. And while you're at it, sue her ass as well."

"I'd rather see her committed."

"And sue *True Story*."

"Sue everybody, hmm?" Kahari asked, chuckling probably for the first time since the *True Story* segment had aired.

"Hell yeah."

"You're probably right about *True Story*. If they hadn't run Estela's interview, the papers wouldn't be picking up the story. I can't believe that Zoë Andrews." One minute she'd been trying to get him to tell his story, the next thing he knew, Estela was pouring out her lies on national television. Everyone in America would think he was the biggest prick around, and it was all that woman's fault. She hadn't stopped until she'd drawn blood.

"You were right about that reporter, Smooth. She's got an agenda. Whether she's working for Estela or she figures she's gonna make a name for herself, who knows?"

Kahari wondered if the people at *True Story* knew about Miss Andrews' tactics. That she'd thrown herself at him in an attempt to get him to talk. How kindly would they take to that?

Most likely they wouldn't care—as long as the woman produced results.

"As soon as we hit L.A.," Kahari began, "I'm gonna find the number for *True Story.* And I'm gonna call them and give them a piece of my mind. Especially that damn reporter."

With that thought, Kahari laid his head against the headrest and closed his eyes. He would make sure that Zoë Andrews regretted the day she had ever come into his life.

With Eva in my office at the *True Story* studio, I retrieve the scathing message Kahari left on my voice mail and place the phone to Eva's ear. As Eva listens, she winces more than once.

"Yikes," she comments, then replaces the receiver.

"As bad as I said, right?"

Eva nods her agreement as she pushes her butt off the edge of my desk. She walks toward the window in my office—which has a fantastic view of the parking lot—then turns to face me again.

"So what do I do now?" I ask her. "He's threatening to sue."

Eva grins. "This is exactly what we want."

I look at her in confusion. "It is?"

"Once people start threatening to sue, it's almost a given that they'll tell their side of the story."

"It is?"

"People bitch and moan all the time. Say we painted them in an ugly light. And it's music to my ears. Because then we offer them the chance to tell their side of the story. If we didn't, then, sure, they could probably have a leg to stand on legally. But for one thing, we're not responsible for what Estela alleged happened—something that's stated in the release she signed—and two, once we give Kahari his chance to clear up any bogus facts, he can't sue us for slander."

"Oh," I say thoughtfully as I cross one leg over the other behind my desk, "I didn't think of it that way."

"And we at *True Story* get what we want." She pauses as she starts walking toward me. "Kahari is pissed right now. Ripe for the picking. All you have to do is talk to him and convince him to give us his side of the story. Then we'll have Estela's version, his version . . . and somewhere in the middle will be the True Story." Eva grins like she's the cleverest person in the world.

"You want me to talk to him again?" I have to say, the thought of an enema is more appealing. I'm pretty sure the guy hates me.

"Zoë, are you listening to a word I'm saying?"

"I heard you. It's just . . . well, maybe I should let him cool off for a while."

"The ratings for Friday night's show were through the roof. And it's all because of this story. We'll replay clips of it all week—until Kahari tells us his side."

I'm about to ask why, but I stop myself. I know why. It's all about the ratings, and Eva will milk the story to death if she has to.

"I've got some calls to make," Eva tells me, starting for the office door.

"Wait."

She turns. "What?"

"So . . . just call him?"

"Or go see him. But whatever you do, get him to talk."

That's all? She has no tricks up her sleeve she wants to share for dealing with super-irate football players?

When she's at the office door, she adds over her shoulder, "I expect to hear something favorable later today, or tomorrow at the latest."

"Of course," I reply with a smile.

But as soon as Eva is gone, I drop my head on the desk. God help me, getting Kahari to talk to me is going to be the hardest thing I've ever had to do.

Kahari had just finished an intense game of racquetball and was heading out of his gym when the phone rang. He snatched the receiver off the wall. "Hello?" he practically barked into the phone.

"Kahari?"

"Who is this?"

"Don't hang up."

Don't hang up? Kahari scowled.

"This is Zoë Andrews."

"Buh-bye."

"No!" she cried out. "Kahari, please. I got your message. I wanted to talk about it."

"What's there to talk about?"

"It's pretty obvious you're pissed."

"You think?"

"Let's arrange a meeting. We can sit down face-to-face and talk."

"I think you've done enough damage. Last week I was an

upstanding citizen. Now I'm a contender for the biggest jerk in America. All thanks to you."

"Are you denying Estela's claims?"

"I don't have to answer to you."

"No, but what about answering to America?"

"What?"

"It's obvious you feel you've been slandered—"

"Feel? I more than feel I've been slandered, lady."

"If that's the case, then I sincerely apologize. But give me the chance to make it right. Set the record straight by sharing your side of the story, Kahari. We at *True Story*—"

"Slander me, make me look like a first-class asshole, and then offer me the chance to tell my side of the story?"

"If you'll remember, I offered you the chance to tell your side of the story first—but you turned me down."

"Oh, that's priceless. I'm hanging up now."

"No, wait!"

Kahari slammed down the receiver back on its cradle, amazed at Zoë's gall. Was the woman out of her mind?

She had to be. After the colorful message he'd left her, he figured he'd never hear from her again. And yet here she was, calling him again.

Maybe she wasn't so much crazy as she was calculating and manipulative. How nice of her to offer him the chance to set the record straight—after she'd all but backed him into a corner! She damn well knew he wasn't interested in talking to any tabloid television show, but she'd caused even more damage by talking to Estela instead.

Kahari grabbed a water bottle off the nearby counter and splashed water onto his face. The phone rang again. He didn't answer it.

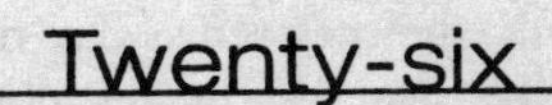

Twenty-six

Here I am. Outside the front door of the Rita Brown Community Center. I'm either the bravest person around or the craziest.

Right now, I'm thinking crazy.

But Eva was very explicit in her chat with me earlier. She told me that I *need* to get Kahari to talk, and it's pretty obvious I can't do that if he won't take my calls.

I know Kahari hates me, but I'm up for the challenge. I'm already committed to this story one way or another. And if I want to ensure my career at *True Story* is a long one, I know I have to get Kahari to talk.

I take a deep breath and enter the building. It's huge, and sort of looks like an indoor sports complex. There's a basketball court to the right and even bleachers. On the left, there is a massive rock-climbing wall. There's also weight equipment in the room, and stationary bikes. There are other smaller rooms off this main one, and in one of them I can see a row of computers.

I'd say there are at least fifty kids in here enjoying the facilities, ranging in age from five to eighteen. The adults working with them don't seem much older—probably in their early to mid-twenties. I continue to glance around the vast area, but I don't see Kahari.

At the far right of the room, behind the basketball court, is a staircase that leads to a second level. The second level only stretches across that right wall, from what I can see. Other than that, the rest of the building has a high ceiling, and the kids' laughter bounces off of it.

Pushing my sunglasses into my hair, I turn to the right. Here, there's a large area covered with mats on which sit a huge dollhouse and other colorful toys for toddlers. A girl who looks to be about eighteen is sitting on the mats with an infant who is pressing buttons on a table that light up and make music.

The girl sees me heading her way and smiles. "Hello," I say. "I'm wondering—is Kahari Brown here?"

She shakes her head. "I'm not sure. You might want to check upstairs, though. That's where the offices are."

"Thanks."

When I reach the back wall, I turn left, heading for the stairwell. I'm halfway there when a basketball suddenly rolls into my feet. Following the ball is a young male who is charging toward me like a bat out of hell.

"Whoa, whoa," I say, thrusting out both arms to brace myself for a collision.

His sneakers squeak as he comes to an abrupt stop. As he collides with me, he giggles.

"Sorry, miss."

We bend to scoop up the ball at the same time, and this time bump heads. Stunned, we look at each other for a moment, and then start to laugh.

I snatch up the ball. "Here you go."

"Thanks." He gives me a quick, assessing look. "You here from the Pass on the Dream Foundation?"

"Um . . . not really, but I am here because I'm doing a story about Kahari."

"Cool."

"J'Ron!" someone yells. "Are you comin' back or what?"

"Here." He throws the ball back to the court.

"J'Ron?" I ask.

"Uh-huh. What's your name?"

"I'm Zoë." I extend my hand, and he shakes it.

"Can I be in your story?" he asks.

"Oh. Hmm. I'm pretty much doing an in-depth story on Kahari Brown, hoping to get Kahari's perspective on . . . things."

"I think it's cool he's been nominated for this award."

I fold my arms over my chest. "Have you been coming here for a long time?"

"Since this place opened a year ago. And I gots ta say, Kahari—he been like a father to me."

"He has?"

"Uh-huh. The father I ain't never had. He's real cool, ya know? He really cares."

I can't help smiling as I look down at this young guy. He's probably twelve or thirteen, his hair braided in cornrows, and wearing baggy sweats. I wonder what his life is like. Without a father, has he gotten into trouble, acted out in school?

"I didn't have a father around either when I was growing up," I confide in him. "And you know what—that's not your fault. It doesn't make you less of a person."

"Yeah, I know."

I smile softly. "I'm glad. You seem like you've got your head on straight."

"I do. Most o' the time." He grins devilishly.

"J'Ron—you comin' back or what?"

"Coming!" he yells, then rolls his eyes.

"You'd better get back to your game," I tell him. "But thank you for talking to me, J'Ron."

He surprises me by giving me a hug. Then he starts to run off. His grin is as wide as the state of California as he says, "Put me in your story, Zoë. Please!"

The little charmer.

I sigh happily as I watch him. And then I nearly jump out of my skin when I feel a strong hand wrap around my upper arm.

I whip my head to the right to see Kahari glaring down at me.

"What the hell are you doing here?"

Kahari stared into the stunned face of Zoë Andrews, anger mounting inside him with each passing second. It was one thing to try and get to him, another entirely to exploit any of the kids who came to this center.

She pulled her arm free. "You won't take my calls."

"Which should be a huge clue that I don't want to talk to you."

Hurt flashed in her eyes. "Are you always so mean?"

"Are you always so persistent?" When she didn't answer, he went on. "And what are you doing talking to the kids who come here? Because if you were even thinking of trying to get any of them to talk on your television show—"

"No!" Zoë exclaimed. "I know you think I'm the lowliest person around, but I wouldn't exploit a child for a story."

"I saw J'Ron give you a hug."

"Because we were talking. He's a nice kid. Says you've been a great father figure to him." Zoë's lips curled in a faint smile. "That's high praise, Kahari."

"Flattery will get you nowhere."

"Look, you can't avoid me forever," Zoë said to him.

And Kahari suddenly realized that she was right. He

couldn't avoid her. That had been his problem—trying to avoid the likes of Zoë Andrews and other members of the media out to ruin his reputation. What he needed to do was deal with her straight on.

"All right. You want to talk? Let's go upstairs."

But she wouldn't like what he had to say. And truthfully, if she weren't here in the community center, he would usher her out the door. Instead, he glanced around, wondering who here might be observing his interaction with Zoë, and if anyone would recognize her from TV. The office was the safest place to deal with her.

He placed a hand on her shoulder. "This way."

Kahari led the way upstairs, looking around the facility as he did. Today had been a good day, with no real conflicts to speak of.

Until now, that is.

He led Zoë into his office and immediately closed the door behind her. "Miss Andrews."

"You can call me Zoë."

"Zoë—"

"Uh-oh. I don't like your tone."

"I'm not gonna beat around the bush."

"Please, don't say it." She leaned her butt against the edge of his desk. "You're always saying no to me, but this time it's in your best interest to say yes."

"You think so?"

"Yes. Definitely. You have an interesting story to tell. You've been nominated for this great award—"

"Are you on crack?"

Her eyebrows shot up. "No."

"You sure?"

"Yes, I'm sure. Why would you ask me that?"

"Because now you're talking about how I've been nominated for an award, yet you did everything in your power to make sure I was discredited in the public. Do you think, Miss Andrews, that I have a shot in hell of winning at this point?"

Zoë held up both hands. "Kahari, you've got it all wrong. Estela had a story to tell, and *True Story* let her do that. If anyone's discredited you, it's her, not—"

"I see. So you figure you've got no responsibility in all this, right?"

Zoë sighed softly. "I understand what you're saying. Really, I do. And maybe you were given a bad rap. All the more reason to tell us your version of the facts."

"Nice way to operate. Slander someone first, ask questions later."

"Why didn't you want to talk to me?" Zoë asked him. "In your hotel room?"

After you kissed me to the point where I couldn't see straight? "Miss Andrews—"

"Zoë, please."

"You backed me into a corner, and as far as I'm concerned, the damage is done."

"But it can be undone." Zoë's eyes pleaded with him to see reason. "For all I know, Estela was lying through her teeth." She paused. "Was she?"

Why the hell had he even thought about the kiss at a time like this? This woman was a reporter, plain and simple, with an agenda. Damn the truth and who got hurt in the process.

It was clear he needed to get her out of his office. There was something about her that made him lose all sense of reason.

Kahari walked to the door and opened it. "Good day, Miss Andrews."

She shook her head. "Please, no."

"I feel like I'm going around in circles with you, and that's not a good feeling."

"Then let's start over."

"I'm sorry, but I have to ask you to leave. I have a very busy day."

Kahari stood at the door, his expression hard as he stared at Zoë. Sighing softly, she resigned herself to her fate and started walking toward him.

Thank God, Kahari thought. He made his way to his desk.

Zoë gripped the handle of the door, as though about to open it wider, but instead quickly closed it and threw her back against it.

"Okay," Kahari said firmly. "This game is over. I have no more time for you right now."

"Don't you remember what it was like—before you had all your millions and you just had the dream? How you wanted it so bad you could taste it? You ate it, slept with it, and then, thank God, you achieved it."

"Huh?"

"I know this might come as a shock to you, but I'm not some big-time reporter. Sure, I did this story on True Story, and I've been seen in millions of households. But I just got my big break. Just over a week ago. And the crazy thing is, it came at a point when I thought I'd never work again. I got fired from LASN for asking you that question after the game you played against New England, by the way. I thought my life was over. But strange things happen, and a producer from *True Story* saw a clip of me on ESPN, and suddenly she was offering me an incredible opportunity. How could I pass it up?"

Zoë was talking so fast Kahari could hardly make sense of a word she was saying. "What exactly are you saying?"

"I finally have a job that pays enough for me to get my *own* apartment, which I so badly need right now, since I caught my boyfriend in bed with another woman and I'm practically homeless."

This woman had some serious issues. "What does this have to do with me?"

"I need to keep this job, Kahari. This is my big break, the one I've dreamed about since I was a kid. I always thought I'd be a big sportscaster, but this is what fate handed to me instead. And my producer, she reeeally wants me to get you to do an interview. I tried to tell her it might not work, but she wouldn't take no for an answer." Zoë finally stopped to catch her breath. "Why do you think I was in your room in Vegas? Because I break and enter on a regular basis?"

"How should I know?"

"Kahari, I *need* you to do this interview. I'll be as nice about it as I can, as positive. And I think it'll be great, personally. I don't want to get fired before I have a chance to really shine. Pleeease, Kahari. Please say yes."

Dumbfounded, Kahari simply stared at her.

"If you're not on crack, then you're just crazy."

"Do you want me to beg? Because I will, if that's what it takes."

Zoë started to go down on one knee.

"Get up," Kahari told her.

"I know you're mad at me. I get that. And I admit I formed a certain opinion of you without ever hearing your side of things. That's something I'll work on in the future, because I know a good journalist has got to be objective."

Kahari opened his mouth to say something, but before he could, Zoë continued.

"When I got to this community center and took a look around, something hit me. I don't know what. I only know that it felt really good being here, witnessing the good things you're doing. I see you . . . I see you in a different light now."

Something about Zoë's expression made him swallow. Hard. "So you don't think I'm a slimebag?"

She shook her head. "I guess I don't, no."

"Gee, thanks."

"I know, I know. You think I'm crazy, and maybe I am. But what I really am is desperate. Desperate to keep my job. Ten years ago, I was like one of those teens downstairs, with big dreams I didn't think I could ever make come true. I know you believe in helping people out. This community center is proof of that."

"God, Zoë. I don't know what to make of this."

She clasped her hands together. "I really, really need to do this story on you. And I feel bad for any negativity this has caused you. I'm being serious about that. But think about it." Her eyes lit up. "If you tell your side, I'm sure people will believe you. That's the best I can offer you to make things better, Kahari."

Kahari scratched his head. Part of him realized this woman was right—that he needed to go public to salvage his image. But there was another part of him that was completely wary. And with good reason.

"Why don't we do this?" she suggested. "Let's go out. Have dinner. Talk. No cameras, no tape recorders. You can tell me your side of the story, and we'll go from there."

For a moment Kahari forgot that she was a member of the media out for blood—his blood. There was something about her that got to him on some level. He did believe she was desperate, and he knew this town didn't make it easy for a person to succeed.

But still, she was clearly the enemy.

Even if she hadn't felt like the enemy when she'd kissed him in that hotel room . . .

He cleared his throat as he tried to forget about the kiss. "And the episode of *True Story* airing Estela's bullshit story? We pretend it didn't happen?"

"Like I said, this will be about giving you a chance to be

heard. I know you're up for an award, and I didn't even think about how Estela's story might hurt you. But if you come forward, people will see that you have nothing to hide, and that will go a long way in clearing your name."

"I'll think about it," Kahari told her, "and I'll call you."

Zoë whimpered. "If you're going to give me the brush-off, just say no. Don't lead me on."

Who was leading on whom in that hotel room?

"It's pretty obvious that saying no to you doesn't work." Kahari actually smiled as he said the words. "Damn, I don't know what I'm getting myself into."

Zoë flashed a smile. "So you'll do it? You'll get together with me and we can talk about it over dinner?"

"One dinner," Kahari told her.

"Oh, thank you!" She leapt at him and wrapped her arms around his neck. "You won't regret it, I promise."

Her body, it seemed, was giving him a different kind of promise altogether.

Or was that wishful thinking?

What the hell was wrong with him? This woman was the enemy.

He pulled away from her, not meeting her eyes.

"We can do this tomorrow night," Zoë suggested. "I've been wanting to try that new Italian restaurant, Il Fornello, and this is as good a time as any. Do you know the one? It's on La Cienega?"

"Yes, I know it."

"I'll call tonight and make a reservation for seven o'clock. Is that good?"

"Fine."

Zoë's eyes lit up as she smiled. For the first time, Kahari noticed that her bright eyes were hazel in color.

He turned away from her and made a show of searching

for something on his desk. "Tomorrow, seven o'clock. I'll be there."

"I hope we can get in. Tuesday night shouldn't be too busy. But if we can't get in, I'll call and let you know. Otherwise, if you don't hear from me, it's a go."

"Right, right," he mumbled.

"Well, I'll see you. Thanks again."

"Sure. Do you mind closing the door behind you?"

"Oh. Certainly."

Finally Zoë left, and Kahari's shoulders drooped from both relief and exhaustion. Damn, he hoped he was making the right decision by meeting with her tomorrow.

But like it or not, he was already knee deep in this mess. He may as well use the opportunity Zoë was offering to get himself out of it.

Twenty-seven

Mr. Brown—maybe we could have you standing right here by your staircase. That way, we can get a glimpse of the impressive foyer in the background."

"Sure," Kahari agreed, but only halfheartedly. He was wondering when this photo shoot was going to end. The photographer from the Pass on the Dream Foundation had already taken numerous shots of him on the basketball court in his backyard, at his desk in the den, and he'd even come by the community center earlier this morning to get some photos of him there. As far as Kahari knew, the foundation only wanted one shot of him for the profile. Surely Dennis Claiborne had to have gotten a decent one already.

But Kahari moved to the staircase nonetheless. After all, only five minutes earlier he had changed into a suit sans tie for the next series of pictures Dennis was planning to shoot.

"Keep one foot on the main floor and put the other on the first step," Dennis instructed him.

"Okay." Kahari did as told.

"Now lean your right arm against the banister. Good,

good." Dennis walked up to him and fussed over the lapels on his jacket. Then he smiled. "Yeah, I like this. This'll be the money shot."

Kahari could only hope so.

Dennis snapped off a series of photos. Kahari smiled for some and didn't smile for others—as per Dennis's instructions.

Dammit, he should be more excited about this shoot, but he wasn't. There was no way he could put out of his mind the reality that there was a black cloud hanging over his head and his hero nomination. Estela's story had tainted not only his shot at the hero award, but his and Anthony's community involvement award as well.

Of course, Anthony said it didn't matter, but Kahari felt like crap nonetheless. If they didn't win the award, Kahari would never be sure it wasn't because of Estela, and that was a hard pill to swallow.

"Mr. Brown?"

"Hmm?" Kahari said, his mind returning to the situation at hand.

"Try one for me with your hand on your hip. That's it. Just like that." Dennis snapped off shots. "And give a little smile. Excellent. Now hold it there." After taking another round of photos, Dennis lowered the camera. "That's it. We're done."

"Great." And not a moment too soon.

Dennis shook Kahari's hand. "It was a pleasure meeting you."

"Likewise."

"Good luck. I think you deserve to win, despite all this nonsense in the news."

"I'm glad to hear someone thinks it's nonsense."

"Everyone knows how desperate some women are to land a successful man. Even I deal with the gold diggers, and I'm only a photographer."

"I hear that."

Dennis grinned. "Enough of my rambling. I'll get out of your way."

Kahari followed him the short distance to the door. "Take care," he called as Dennis headed out.

Four more hours. That's how long he had until he met with Zoë Andrews.

Kahari strolled to the mirror and glanced at his reflection. *Not bad,* he thought. Armani had sent this suit to him when they'd learned of the Pass on the Dream nominations, with a note congratulating him. They had sent him suits before, as had other designers, all hoping that if he wore their clothing in a photo shoot or at a high-profile event, he'd give them a plug.

When Kahari had been broke as a joke, no one had given him a penny. Now that he was rich beyond anything he'd ever imagined, he got free stuff all the time.

The suit was definitely sweet, though, and he decided that he would wear it later for his dinner with Zoë.

"Hi." Zoë grinned from ear to ear as Kahari approached the table in Il Fornello. She rose from her chair and offered him her hand. "Right on time."

As Kahari shook her hand, he gave her body the once-over. She wore a light and flimsy dress that flowed around her knees. Orange and mauve swirled in a combination that created a striking yet delicate pattern. The jacket she wore matched the mauve in her dress, as did her purse and pointy designer shoes.

Kahari released her hand. "Have you been here long?"

"Only fifteen minutes. Long enough to order a glass of wine," she added with a laugh. "Oh, sorry. I didn't order any for you. But I don't know what you like . . . "

"That's fine." Kahari pulled out his chair and sat, glancing around the place as he did. He and Zoë had a table on the restaurant's upper level, along the railing that overlooked the first floor.

"It's a great view, isn't it?" Zoë asked him. "I'm excited to be here. I couldn't afford it before, but now . . . " Her voice trailed off as her eyes ran over him. "Wow. You look great."

"It's Armani."

"Of course. I love the lapels, and the shirt without the tie. Very . . . sexy."

"It's kind of crazy. They sent me this suit as a gift."

"You're kidding?"

"When you reach a certain level of wealth and fame, you suddenly get big-ticket items free all the time."

"Must be nice."

"I can't deny it is."

Their talking stopped, and they were left looking at each other. Another beat passed, and Kahari realized they were staring a little too long. He glanced away, reaching for his water glass. "I like your outfit too," he told her.

"Do you?" Zoë asked, her tone sounding totally insecure. "I wasn't sure."

Kahari nodded. "Yeah, I like it."

"Unlike you, I had to pay for it. And I had a fabulous time shopping because for the first time, I could afford to put this purchase on my credit card. And finding the shoes and purse to match was such a stroke of luck!" Her eyes grew wide. "I'm sorry. I'm sure the last thing you want to hear about is my shopping. Oh, great. Here's the waiter."

Kahari turned his head to follow her line of sight over his shoulder. The waiter, a man whose dark hair was slicked back, smiled as he stepped up to the table.

"I see your guest has arrived."

"Yes. Yes, he has."

The waiter handed a menu first to Zoë, then one to Kahari. He gave it a quick glance.

"Let me tell you the specials for the evening . . ."

As the waiter listed dish after dish, Kahari's mind wandered. Wandered as he stole another glance at Zoë, who appeared to be sneaking glances at him over her menu. She really did look amazing tonight. Sexy and flirty. Her hair was loose, and for the first time he noticed that her mahogany tresses were highlighted with auburn. And whatever perfume she was wearing was doing a number on his senses because she smelled incredible.

Incredible enough to kiss again.

"Thank you," Zoë said to the waiter. "Everything sounds wonderful."

Kahari cleared his throat. "Give us a few minutes."

"Of course."

The waiter disappeared as quietly as a cat.

"Isn't it wild?" Zoë said. "This is an Italian restaurant, yet the guy sounds like he's French." She didn't give him a chance to answer before continuing. "I guess it doesn't matter."

"Guess not." Kahari opened his menu. "Do you know what you're having?"

"I'm not sure yet." Then, "Hey—are you okay with this?"

Kahari met her gaze over the top of his menu. "With what?"

"With dinner. With me. I know I didn't give you much of a choice, but I really do appreciate you being here."

"I'm fine," Kahari told her. But he wasn't entirely, and not for the reason he should have been uncomfortable. There was something about Zoë that intrigued him, and he couldn't deny an attraction to her. Which was very odd, since he hadn't been interested in a woman in quite a long time.

And yet he knew without a doubt that if he'd met Zoë under different circumstances, he would definitely want to get to know her better.

"I know we met under weird circumstances, and you

probably think I'm ruthless and calculating, but I'm really not."

"I wouldn't be here if I thought you were those things," Kahari told her, the truth in his statement catching even him off guard.

"Thank you."

Damn, the woman's eyes were so bright and guileless. It was like Kahari could read all her emotions in the depth of her gaze.

"You, on the other hand," she began, "are probably a totally wild playboy, bedding women in every city you visit. That's a joke," she quickly said. "I hope."

"You hope?"

She nodded, then leaned forward. "You're not one of those athletes who has like twenty girlfriends?"

"Twenty!" Kahari exclaimed. "Where'd you come up with that number?"

"It's a nice round number. And a *completely* inappropriate thing to say. I apologize."

"You're actually a little off." When Zoë's eyes narrowed, Kahari continued. "It's twenty-one. Twenty-one girlfriends."

Her mouth fell open, then she laughed. "You *are* kidding—right?"

"Full-time girlfriends, I might add. I am stretched so thin . . . " He puffed out his chest. "But a guy's gotta do what a guy's gotta do."

"I think I'm sorry I asked," Zoë said, smiling as she rolled her eyes.

She really did have nice eyes. Kahari suspected he could look in them all day and not get bored. And nice lips. Full and pouty and definitely kissable.

"Well, I'm starving," he announced, because he had to stop looking at her. He scanned the menu. "I think I'll have the eighteen-ounce steak. Ooh, or the lamb. Yeah, the lamb looks good."

"Lamb?" Zoë asked him, her tone laced with shock.

Kahari lowered his menu to once again look at her. He saw alarm in her eyes. "Yeah, lamb. Something wrong with that?"

Her face twisted in disapproval. "How can you eat lamb? It's just a baby."

"It's delicious, that's what it is."

"Ugh, how can you say that?"

The repulsion streaking across her face made it clear that she was serious.

"Think about it," she went on. "Imagine you're a lamb. A cute little lamb that's just been born. You're enjoying spending time with your mother. You love running and jumping in the meadow. You're enjoying eating grass and dandelions. Then, one day, someone snatches you and *murders* you. And why? So that people in restaurants—who could just as easily eat something else—can eat you."

"We're at the top of the food chain," Kahari said frankly.

Zoë's mouth fell open. "Adult cows, adult chickens, adult pigs—that's one thing. But eating baby animals, not even giving them a chance at life—that's just plain cruel."

"All right," Kahari conceded. "I won't have the lamb." He lifted his menu just as the waiter arrived.

"Sir, madame," the man greeted them pleasantly. "Are you ready to order?"

"Yes," Kahari said. "I'll go with this eighteen-ounce sirloin."

"How would you like that prepared?"

"Rare, please."

"Rare?" Zoë gasped.

Oh, great. "What's wrong with rare?" Kahari asked her.

"Why don't you just go outside and kill the cow yourself? If you're gonna eat it with all the blood oozing out of it—"

"You know what." Kahari snapped the menu shut. "Forget the steak. I'll have . . . " Damn, what could he eat? "Give me a plate of vegetables."

The waiter narrowed his eyes. "Vegetables?"

"A large plate."

"Okay," the waiter said, sounding perplexed. "And to drink?"

"A glass of Chianti, please. Red wine is okay, isn't it?" he asked Zoë.

"Any wine is wonderful."

"You know what? Make that a bottle of Chianti."

"Certainly. And you, madame?"

"I would like the fettuccine Alfredo, heavy on the Alfredo sauce. But I'd like that with rigatoni noodles instead of fettuccine. And to start, an order of your bruschetta. It sounds scrumptious."

"Okay, wait a second," Kahari interjected. "Forget my vegetable plate. I'll have fettuccine Alfredo as well. You serve that with chicken?" He quickly looked at Zoë. "Is chicken okay?"

She held up both hands. "Chicken's fine."

"Don't worry about the chicken," he told the waiter. "Just give me the fettuccine Alfredo, and I'll have garlic bread with cheese as an appetizer. No, two orders of the garlic bread, please."

The waiter took Kahari's menu from him. "Is that everything?"

"That should do it," Kahari answered.

"Do you have mushroom soup?" Zoë asked him.

"Of course."

"Okay. I'll have that."

With the waiter gone, Kahari let out a deep breath. He had a feeling that nothing about Zoë was easy.

"I take it you're a vegetarian," he commented.

"How'd you guess?" Zoë smiled sweetly. "No meat for me."

"No fish even?"

"Nothing that's got to be murdered for me to eat it."

"Wow."

"It's not like there aren't a million other things people can eat—tasty and a lot of times better for you, too—so why partake in the murder of animals? I know I'm not really helping them any, since just as many are slaughtered every day, but it does help my conscience. And you have to do what your conscience tells you, you know?"

"Has anyone ever told you that you talk *a lot*?"

Zoë grinned. "Only when they can get a word in edgewise."

Despite himself, Kahari chuckled. "You can laugh at yourself. I like that."

"Hey, if you can't laugh at yourself, who can you laugh at?"

"You're probably still a little crazy."

"Crazy is the spice of life. Can you imagine how dull things would be if we were all sane? My sister's sane. And dull as dishwater."

"Sounds like there's a story there."

"Oh yeah." Zoë rolled those beautiful hazel eyes of hers. "But I want this to be a good evening, so I promise not to talk about her."

Kahari laughed again. Maybe this evening wouldn't be too bad after all.

"I have to tell you," I say to Kahari once the meal and dessert are done, "I had a good time."

"I had a good time, too."

"But you didn't think you would, did you?"

"Honestly?"

"Honestly."

He chuckles. "Then no."

"Ouch."

"But you proved me wrong," he quickly adds.

There's something really sexy about Kahari when he smiles. He gets these little laugh lines around his eyes that soften his face. And it's an incredible face, much more fantastic in real life than it ever was on TV.

I'm feeling my crush blossoming once again.

"I'm glad I was able to prove you wrong," I tell him. "I think this was a great way to break the ice. And I didn't mention one word about Estela . . . "

"No, you didn't. And believe it or not, you made me forget about her for a couple hours."

"I'm going to take that as a compliment."

"You should. Oddly enough, given everything."

Kahari gives me another of his looks I've caught him laying on me all evening. Where he meets my eyes and our gazes hold for a moment too long. Most of the time, he quickly glances away, like he's uncomfortable.

I know I'm a little neurotic, but every time he gives me The Look, something inside me gets all mushy. And I remember that moment when my lips met his in the hotel room in Vegas . . .

It's amazing that I keep remembering that kiss, because I certainly shouldn't. Yet I do, and I wonder if he thinks about it too.

"When do you head to Oakland again?" I know he told me, but the wine has clouded my memory.

"I head out tomorrow afternoon."

"Then how about we get together in the morning. For a preinterview."

"I thought we did that today."

"Today was about getting both of us comfortable with each other."

Kahari hesitates. "Tomorrow?"

"I'll meet you at the center. If you have time, that is. Maybe watch you with the kids. Then we can talk. I'm thinking this interview shouldn't just be about Estela, the whole he-said, she-said routine. Of course, you'll have the chance to do that, but what I'm thinking of will be a broader interview to show more of who you really are—you know?"

Kahari shrugs. "Tomorrow might be tight."

"Oh, don't say that."

"It's the truth."

"Not if we spend the night together."

"Whoa. What did you just say?"

"Oh God." Did I say that out loud? "I am totally sorry. It's the wine. It's turned me into a moron. That is why," I say as I quickly push my chair back, "I normally don't drink red."

"Wait," Kahari says, because I'm already heading for the stairs. But I don't stop. I know I need to get out of here. Like yesterday.

"Zoë . . ."

"You've got my cell," I say without turning. "If you can meet me in the morning, call me around eight."

"Will you hold up, please?"

I don't slow down even when I reach the top of the stairs. And then my heel or something gets caught on the first step, because I lose my balance—and tumble down the stairs headfirst.

Twenty-eight

My vision blurs as I open my eyes. Several heads wobble around me. After a moment, the heads straighten and I can see clearer. There are faces all around me, filled with concern.

"Thank God."

That's Kahari's voice, I realize. I feel his hands on me, at my neck, holding my head straight. Damn but his hands feel good, even if this isn't how I've fantasized about him touching me.

"What happened?" I ask.

"You fell," he answers. "All the way down the stairs."

"No wonder I hurt," I say, then attempt a laugh. It comes out as a croak.

His lips twist in a crooked smile. "You still have your warped sense of humor. That's a good sign."

"I knew I shouldn't have had that third glass of wine. I told myself, Zoë, you're already giddy, two is enough, don't be crazy—"

Kahari cuts me off. "Do you feel like you can move everything? That was a nasty fall."

I raise my arms, angle my head, wiggle my toes in my pointed shoes. "I think I'm okay."

"Except that you passed out, which means you probably have a mild concussion."

"I passed out?" I ask, surprised. But I know I must have, since I have no memory of the fall.

"Yeah."

"How long was I out?"

"Five minutes."

"Five minutes!"

"Uh-huh. Five minutes of blissful silence . . ." He laughs.

"Oh, I get it. Because I wasn't talking. Aren't you funny? Ow!"

"What is it?" Kahari asks, all concerned. "What hurts?"

"My neck."

"Hmm." I can't read the expression on his face.

"Am I gonna die?" I ask in another attempt at humor.

"No. I've had plenty of concussions from getting hit pretty hard. You'll live."

I try to sit up, and now not only my neck hurts. Pain shoots all down my back. I grip Kahari's arms for help.

"We should get you to the hospital," he says.

"No." With difficulty, I climb to my feet. "I'm feeling better already." And then I let out a groan of despair when my shoe wobbles. "My shoe!" I pull the Jimmy Choo sling-back off my right foot. I gasp in horror when I see that the heel is broken. "Damn! I spent over three hundred dollars on these!"

"You've just taken the worst fall I've ever witnessed and you're worried about your shoe?"

"You don't understand. I had to scrimp and save to buy this pair of shoes!"

"I'll buy you another pair."

A well-dressed man walks swiftly over to us, through the concerned-looking waitstaff. "Excuse me," he says. "Are you all right, Miss Andrews?"

"How do you know my name?"

"I've seen you on *True Story*."

"Oh. I see. Um, yeah. I think I'm okay."

"I'm taking her to a doctor," Kahari announces.

The man reaches into his jacket pocket and produces a card. "I'm Tony Giamatti, the owner. I'm so sorry this happened to you."

"Thanks," I say.

"I've gone ahead and reversed the charge off your credit card," he goes on. "And the next time you come here, your dinner's on the house."

My first free thing! Tonight's dinner was over three hundred dollars!

"I don't know what to say."

Tony grips my hand. "If you're not okay, please let me know. Whatever medical expenses you incur—"

"Completely unnecessary," I tell him. "I'm fine."

"I'll take her to the doctor, Tony. We appreciate your generosity."

"It's the least I can do."

"Come on." Kahari grips me firmly around the waist.

"A doctor?" I ask as I watch the owner walk away. Then I moan softly as I look at my shoe once again. I examine the heel, seeing if there's a way to fix it. Maybe some Krazy Glue?

And then it dawns on me that I can afford a new pair of these no problem with my six-figure salary.

"Zoë, are you spacing out on me? Because if you are, then you need to see a doctor more than ever."

"And I would—if I had medical insurance. But I don't yet, because I'm too new on this job."

"You heard what Tony—"

"Honestly, I'll be fine." As I say the words, I feel woozy and teeter dangerously on my good heel.

"You're obviously not okay."

"All right." I am suddenly aware that all eyes in the restaurant are on me. "I'll call my doctor while I'm driving home. But it's too late to see him tonight—"

"You are not driving anywhere."

I look up at Kahari in confusion. "Then how am I supposed to get home? Or to the hospital if I feel like my brain will explode later?"

"Whether or not you fell down the stairs, I wasn't about to let you drive home. You've had too much to drink." He pauses. "I'll drive you."

"Adding Good Samaritan to your résumé?"

"No arguments."

"I appreciate the gesture, Kahari, but you don't have to babysit me. I can call my friend Rose. No, wait. I can't call her because she's in Jamaica. I can call . . . Well, I can't call Marvin, or . . . "

"There's no need to call anyone. I'm right here." Kahari tugs on my waist. "Look, we've been here forever, and people must think we're the evening's entertainment. I say we go." He starts to move. "Come on now. Nice and easy."

I limp as I walk with him, but that's because I'm only wearing one shoe. I want to protest that he doesn't need to fuss all over me like this, but I kind of like that he's fussing over me. The truth is, I haven't had much male fussing in my life. My exes have all been the ones who expected pampering when they were sick or hurt, but none of them gave me the same kind of treatment.

"My car," I say when the cool evening air hits me in the face. "What am I supposed to do about it?"

"You valet-parked it. It'll be fine."

"I didn't valet-park. I found a spot down the street. It's the first really nice car I've had in my life. I'm feeling a little overprotective."

"You know what—why don't I leave my car here, we'll take your car, and when you're feeling better, you can drive me back here to pick it up."

"Oh." That means . . . "You're coming to my place?"

"You can't be alone tonight."

"But—"

"If you've got something worse than a mild concussion and I let you go home alone to die, I won't feel very good about myself in the morning."

"Well, when you put it that way . . . " I smile.

"Sit here." He deposits me on a bench outside the restaurant.

"How far is your car?"

"Just about a minute walk to the right."

"Okay. Give me your keys, then. And what kind of car is it? Color?"

"A silver Mercedes." I dig inside my Lulu clutch and pass the keys to him.

"I'll be right back," he tells me.

As I watch him head off, his stride strong and confident and sexy as hell, I sigh softly. I saw how women looked at me when I was in the restaurant with him—with envy. That's something I'm not used to. But I could really get used to having a man like that in my life. He's got this sweetheart quality to him, and while I didn't ask him about it, I am curious to know what went wrong with him and Estela.

He certainly doesn't resemble the man she painted him out to be in her interview, but there's a part of me—a very big part—that's not surprised.

Is she just some crazed fan, out for fifteen minutes of

fame? Or is Kahari really the father of her baby and the type of guy who would shirk his responsibility?

A movement across the street from the restaurant catches my eye. As I look in that direction, I see a body slip into a narrow walkway. My eyes squint as a weird feeling sweeps over me.

Was that Colby?

I shake my head. No, it couldn't be. If it was, certainly he'd come over and say hi.

Unless he saw me with Kahari and he's angry because I didn't agree to a date with him.

I stare a moment longer at the walkway but no one reappears. I see no face peering out from the shadows.

Pushing thoughts of Colby and Estela out of my mind, I think about Kahari's smile. He's got that sincere, sexy kind of smile that makes a girl melt. Thinking about him makes me feel good. I don't even know why I feel good—I just know that being around him makes me feel that way.

Maybe it's because you're drunk as a skunk.

Which is probably why I also thought I saw Colby on the other side of the street.

Finally, my car pulls up, and I get a kick out of the fact that the silver E320 is actually mine. As I start to rise, Kahari is already rushing out of the car and toward me.

"Wait for me," he says.

So I do. And then I take his arm and let him lead me to my car, savoring the moment all the way there.

A short while later, Kahari is inside Rose's apartment with me. Standing in the living room, he glances all around. "This place has only one bedroom?"

"Yeah," I respond, looking up at him from the sofa. He's

taken his jacket off, and looks pretty damned sexy with his pressed white shirt and black dress pants. "Why?"

"I guess the couch will do."

"What? You mean you . . . you're planning on sleeping here?"

"I said I'd keep an eye on you tonight."

My heart rams against my rib cage. What can I say—the idea of staying the night in this small apartment with Kahari is too much for me to handle. It's torture, really, considering how my hormones have been raging out of control in his presence all evening.

"I figured you'd stay a couple hours, then I can drive back with you to get your car."

"Remember that lecture about doing what's right for your conscience?"

"Lecture?"

"Well, my conscience says I've got to stay with you the night to make sure you're okay."

"I didn't really lecture you, did I?"

"Imagine you're a lamb," Kahari says, mimicking my higher-toned voice.

I groan with embarrassment.

"Do you do that a lot?" he continues. "Imagine you're a lamb?"

"Okay, shut up."

He laughs, enjoying how he's teasing me.

"Now I know why you think I'm insane. I feel pretty insane right about now. Not to mention bad, considering I somehow guilted you into staying the night with me."

"You didn't guilt me. Besides, I could use a night away from home, anyway."

"Why—the walls of your million-dollar mansion closing in on you?"

Kahari raises his eyebrows at my comment, and I immediately regret my statement. "Sorry. That was out of line."

He eases his body onto the sofa beside me. His masculine presence surrounds me. "I can live without seeing my sister for one night," he admits.

"Ah," I say, understanding. "Your sister drives you nuts like mine does?"

"That's an understatement."

"At least I'm not the only one. Thank God mine doesn't live with me."

"I've been trying to get LaTonya to move out for some time. She came here from Texas about a year ago, saying she was visiting. She hasn't left, and now she's on this kick about being a star. Or a model. Or a best-selling novelist. Like you make a decision like that and it happens at the snap of a finger." He shakes his head.

"You have only one sister?"

"Yeah. She's my baby sister. I love her to pieces, even if she's getting on my last nerve. When I got home from Denver and opened the phone bill, I wanted to throttle her. Damn—I know I make a lot of money, but she's spending it faster than I am these days. And she's always there. I make breakfast, she's there. I work out in my gym, she's there. And my pool—forget about it. She's taken it over."

"My sister only took over my man," I say dryly. When Kahari's eyes widen in curiosity, I nod. "Yep. She slept with him. Then had the nerve to justify it by saying she felt he was her true love. He—well, he justified it by saying she'd tempted him. Lola the temptress. That's what I call her these days."

"Sounds like you don't have good luck with men."

"What are you talking about? I have the best luck . . . choosing the wrong guys." I wag a finger. "It's a talent of mine."

Now Kahari stares at me, and I'm not sure what he's thinking, but I suddenly feel uncomfortable.

"Do you always put yourself down?" he asks.

"I don't put myself down." Do I? "Maybe a little, I guess. Doesn't everybody?"

I don't give Kahari a chance to answer, because I shoot to my feet. "Excuse my bad manners. Can I get you something to drink, snack on?"

"I'm stuffed from dinner. I didn't think it was possible with a vegetarian course."

"Please . . . no more talk of baby lambs." I laugh despite myself.

Kahari extends a hand and I look at it, then back at that gorgeous mocha-brown face of his. Damn if he doesn't give me The Look again. This time he doesn't glance away.

"Sit down," he tells me as he reaches for my hand. "You need to take it easy."

"Right." I slink onto the sofa beside him.

Now what? Lord, now what?

At first I don't want to make eye contact with him, sitting so close to him and all, but the silence is heavy between us, and I sense there's something on his mind.

Nervous, I glance at him and ask, "What?"

"Nothing."

"No, don't say nothing. What were you thinking?"

He shrugs. "I was wondering what we should do to pass the next few hours."

My face flames. "Kahari . . . "

"Oh, hell. That came out wrong." He drags a hand over his face.

"At least now I don't have to feel so bad for that asinine comment that somehow came out of my mouth at the restaurant . . . " I smile softly, and he does too. But I wonder if there isn't a subtext to his words he doesn't want to admit, the way I didn't want to admit that the thought of sleeping with him *had* actually crossed my mind.

"What I wanted to do," Kahari says, shaking his head, "was ask if there's a movie or something we can watch to pass the time."

"Sure. Rose and J.P. have lots of movies. What do you want to see?"

"Anything with Will Smith."

"Oh," I say with interest, "you're a Will Smith fan?"

"Huge."

"How huge?"

"Huge."

"Like if you met him you'd freak out or something?"

"I wouldn't be responsible for how I'd act, no."

"Interesting."

"Why?"

"You're such a huge star yourself . . . it's hard to imagine you losing your head over an actor."

"We're talking about Will Smith," he says as if this is a no-brainer. "Come on."

"Will Smith coming right up." I head toward the entertainment unit where the DVDs are housed. It's kind of nice to know that Kahari is as human as your average guy.

A couple minutes later, I announce, "Offhand, I see *Shark Tale* and *Enemy of the State*."

"Enemy of the State," Kahari says without hesitation.

As I bend to the floor and turn on the DVD player, an idea comes to me. May as well make this a proper movie night.

I turn around and walk toward Kahari. "You put the DVD in. I'll go get some popcorn."

"Why don't you put the DVD in, and I'll make popcorn."

"You don't know where it is."

"I'll find it."

I shrug. "Okay."

Kahari disappears into the kitchen, and I go about inserting the DVD. A short while later, I jump with fright when I stand and bump right into him.

I whirl around. "You're quieter than a cat."

He holds up a Ziploc bag filled with ice. "For your neck," he tells me when I give him a questioning look. "Ice ten minutes, then heat ten minutes. Hopefully you won't feel worse in the morning."

"You're gonna kill me with all this niceness," I joke. But secretly, I am loving his attention.

"I've learned a thing or two being an athlete. And it'll be easy enough to do while we watch the movie." He places a hand on my shoulder. "Come on. Back to the sofa."

Don't touch me like that, please. I know you're just being nice, but when you touch me . . .

"Sit."

I sink into the sofa's softness, and Kahari angles himself so that he's sitting behind me. As I start the movie, Kahari surprises me by holding the bag of ice against my neck. Ten minutes later, he does the same thing with the hot-water bottle.

"Why are you being so nice to me?" I can't help asking.

"I'm out for myself, of course. Trying to make sure you don't sue me."

I spin around to face him. A playful grin is dancing on his face. Despite the fact that he appears to have been joking, I still ask, "Why would I sue you?"

"I ordered that bottle of wine. If it weren't for me, you wouldn't have been tipsy in the first place, and you wouldn't have fallen down the stairs."

"Kahari, you have to know I wouldn't even think of suing you."

"I was kidding."

"Maybe . . . but still, I want you to know."

I turn back to the movie. It's at the part where Will Smith is feeling foolish shopping for lingerie. The salesclerks are clad in an array of skimpy lingerie, and now I try to take note and see if Kahari is suddenly less attentive to me. It's completely silly, and immature, because so what if he's checking out the women. And yet I can't stop myself.

To my delight, he doesn't seem any more interested in this part of the movie than any other.

The issue, of course, is that I'm not as voluptuous as those women on the screen. I don't fill out a lacy bra quite the way it's meant to be filled out. I don't have the kind of figure that has guys losing their heads. I was gawky and awkward as a young girl and couldn't snag a hot guy to save my life.

As the movie plays, I'm not concentrating on the story. I'm thinking about what it would be like to date a guy like Kahari. To live the fantasy of the geeky girl ending up with a dream guy that millions of women would kill for.

It is the last thought on my mind as I drift off to sleep later that night, snug in Rose's bed, knowing that Kahari is out in the living room sleeping on the sofa.

Twenty-nine

I wake up in high spirits. I'm more content than I've been in a long time. There's no stress about money. I'm not worrying about putting a roof over my head or how I'm going to afford a car. And my relationship with Marvin is a distant memory at this point.

And, of course, I'm alive. Which means I probably didn't suffer any internal injuries after falling last night.

I stretch my body beneath the down comforter on Rose's bed, a smile dancing on my lips. *And there's Kahari,* a voice in my head says. *Don't pretend you're not happy because of him . . .*

Remembering the way Kahari alternately held ice and heat against my neck has me getting warm and woozy and even a little turned on.

Yes, turned on. Crazy or not, it's true.

I know it's wishful thinking, because he's a subject and I'm doing a story on him. But at least we've gotten past a hurdle and on some level have become friends.

My eyes fly to the wall clock. It's a few minutes past nine. A part of me is worried about getting to work late—

but only a small part. I don't want to go anywhere, not while Kahari is here with me. And, quite frankly, I can argue that he *is* work. I'm sure Eva would be thrilled to know I spent the night in the same space with him. I've learned that she's the type who doesn't care what you have to do to get the story, as long as you get it. Kahari and I stayed up till nearly one-thirty, watching not only *Enemy of the State* but half of *Shark Tale* as well, before I insisted that I get some sleep.

I wonder if he's awake.

I wonder if he's wondering if I'm awake.

I wonder if he's wondering if I'm wondering if . . .

Just get up already, I tell myself. So I do, and make my way to Rose's closet. I pull a plush terry-cloth robe off a hanger and slip into it.

As I make my way into the living room, I run my fingers through my thick mane, hoping I look presentable. I've never been the vain sort, though, or I would have straightened my hair to comply with America's standard of beauty a long time ago.

Kahari is stretched out on Rose's sofa. One leg is actually resting on the floor. He's on his back, with the comforter bunched around him, but it doesn't cover his chest at all. I can't help staring at his muscular pecs and broad shoulders and well-built arms.

This is so surreal—him being here, sleeping on the sofa in my friend's apartment.

A little sigh escapes me, and I turn to head back to the bedroom.

"Where are you going?"

My body jerks from fright and I throw a hand to my heart. My heart beating rapidly, I spin around to face him. He's got a mischievous smile on his face.

"I thought you were sleeping," I say.

"I know."

I swallow my embarrassment. "Um, how'd you sleep?"

"All right," he replies.

He looks tired. The sofa's fabric left a print on the left side of his face. I'm guessing he's got a bad case of morning breath after all that garlic seasoning last night. And yet he is utterly irresistible right now.

"It's funny, isn't it," he says. "We ended up spending the night together after all."

"Oh God," I blurt out. "You're going to have to forgive me for anything inappropriate I said while under the influence of alcohol."

Kahari sits up. "You made me laugh, at least."

"At me?"

"At myself, maybe. The last few weeks I've been serious, serious, serious. It was nice to relax."

I'm not sure what to make of his compliment, so I change the subject. "You want some coffee?"

"Naw, I'm fine. How are you, though? Any aches and pains this morning?"

"I've had better days," I admit, twisting my neck to test how it feels. "My neck's a bit sore, but not nearly as bad as it could be. Thanks, I'm sure, to your expert hands last night."

My statement hangs between us like a sexual grenade, ready to explode if either of us pulls out the clip.

"Come here." His low voice washes over me like a sensual wave.

"What?" I ask nervously.

"I want to take a look at your neck. See if there's any swelling."

My whole body is instantly alive, and I can hardly take the few steps to the sofa. When I near him, Kahari reaches for my hand and pulls me down beside him.

"Let me see." His gentle hands move my bushy curls out of the way. And then he touches me, and my insides melt.

"How does that feel?" he asks.

Pretty damn amazing! But I say, "Um, okay."

"No pain?"

"Well, it's a bit tender." As is another part of my body right about now . . .

Now his fingers stroke the length of my neck. "I think you're gonna be okay."

Oh, I don't think so. Not after you touching me like that.

He doesn't lower his hand. Instead, he brings his other hand to my neck and gently starts to massage.

Okayokayokay. I'm not sure I can handle this.

"What are you doing?" I ask him, aware that my voice is soft and whispery. Seductive.

"Massaging your neck."

"There's no need for any more guilt, Kahari. You've done more than enough to see that I'm okay."

There's a pause. "You think that's why I'm touching you?"

My breathing becomes shallow. "It's not?"

"What if I said it wasn't?"

Then I'd have to pinch myself, because I'd have to be dreaming . . .

Slowly, I turn to face him. I look into his beautiful brown eyes, and he smiles at me. My bones turn to Jell-O.

"Kahari . . . are you . . . flirting with me?"

"I think we're past flirting."

Now I do pinch myself. Damn, I'm awake. Very much so.

"I don't . . . I don't . . . "

He puts a finger on my lips to quiet me. "Let me just say this. I think you're fascinating."

"Come on," I blurt out in disbelief.

He actually chuckles at this. "I take it you're not good at accepting compliments."

How can he be serious? He can't be serious. "Kahari, don't mess with me."

"I'm not messing with you. And wine or not, I think you were flirting with me last night."

"Ah, I get it. I'm a woman. Women flirt with professional athletes. So you think—"

"This has nothing to do with other women." He pauses. "Am I wrong?"

I whimper softly. "No," I whisper.

"Okay."

"But it's totally inappropriate. I know that. I'm doing a story on you. But I've also had this crush on you for so long. A silly crush. But seeing you, spending time with you . . . I'm sorry if I've crossed the line in any way."

"Zoë?"

I look away. "Yes."

"Don't apologize. I'm feeling something here too. As improbable, as unlikely . . . " He shakes his head, as if he can't believe his own words. "But I want to know what your intentions are."

"Huh?"

"In Vegas, in my hotel room, you kissed me."

"Yes." I groan and cover my eyes.

Kahari takes my hand from my face. "I need to know—did you do that just because of the story?"

"You mean like, try to seduce you to get you to talk?"

"Exactly." He snaps a finger, then points it at me.

"I just finished telling you I've had this crazy crush on you for some time now. You don't think I kissed you because I was attracted to you—"

He puts his finger on my lips again. "Okay, okay. That's all I wanted to know."

I stare into his eyes, a question in my own. "Why?"

"Zoë," he says frankly, "there's something about you. Something about you that touches me, and I have no clue why."

"Maybe . . . " A breath oozes out of me. "Maybe it's just because we're spending time together. And the wine last night. You know." *My God, what are you doing?* I ask myself.

Kahari gets to his feet, giving me an incredible view of him in his black boxer shorts. "You know what—I think you're right."

"You do?"

"Of course. That makes perfect sense." He laughs, sounding relieved, as if he needed some reason to explain his attraction to me.

And, of course, I provided him that.

I could kick myself.

Shooting would be much better, though. End my misery right here.

He walks to the armchair and reaches for his shirt. "Ready to head back to the restaurant so I can get my car?"

Lord, I am such an idiot. I almost had Kahari in reality right where I've had him in my fantasies, and I ruined the friggin' moment. What the hell is wrong with me?

"I, uh, I figured I'd make you breakfast," I tell him.

Kahari shakes his head. "I'll get something at home, or on the road. I have to catch a plane at one."

"Right." My stomach sinks. "Of course." I'm feeling really sad right now, like my lover is about to abandon me.

Kahari slips into his pants. "And I have to pick up my boy Anthony."

"Um, I'll just, uh . . . throw on some clothes."

"I'll be here," he says in a sugary voice.

Which says to me that he can't wait to be rid of me.

Ugh, God.

I head to the bedroom, cursing my bad timing all the way

there. Of all the stupid things I've ever done, ruining the moment with Kahari has got to be the worst.

"Oh, hell no," Kahari says when we arrive at the restaurant less than an hour later. And I instantly see why. The restaurant is closed, and so is the valet stand.

"It's closed." I state the obvious.

Kahari glances at the Mercedes' digital clock. "I don't know what time this place is gonna open, but I can't stick around and wait for my car."

"What are you gonna do?"

"You're gonna have to give me a ride home. If you don't mind, of course."

"Why would I mind?" *Yes! A few more precious moments with Kahari!* "But what about your car?"

"I don't know what your schedule is like, but is it possible for you to come back here and pick up my car?" Kahari digs his wallet out of his pants and takes out a hundred-dollar bill. "Here," he says, stuffing it into my hand. "Use this to pay for a cab."

"That's way too much money."

"Take it anyway."

I know he's totally loaded, but it still seems so unreal that someone can easily give me a hundred dollars for what will be a ten- or fifteen-dollar cab ride.

But I stop thinking about that when I realize that if Kahari wants me to pick up his car, that means he'll have to see me again.

He must read my thoughts, because he says, "We're gonna get together anyway to shoot this interview, right?"

"Sure." I try not to smile from ear to ear. "Right."

"So it's no problem?"

"No, not at all." I pause. "You live in Beverly Park, right?"

"You've been there?"

"No, but like everyone else in the L.A. area, I've heard about it." I don't add that I'm dying to see the houses, which I know must be magnificent. Maybe I'll even glimpse Eddie Murphy . . .

"It's a great spot."

As I pull away from the restaurant, my temples throb. I need coffee. "I know you want to get home right away, but do you mind if I stop at Starbucks?"

"Sure, go ahead."

Five minutes later, I'm pulling into the parking lot of a Starbucks. "You want anything?" I ask.

Kahari shakes his head.

I sprint inside the building. The smell of all those coffee beans has me sighing in relief.

Because I can afford it, I order a caramel macchiato. I also buy a piece of lemon cake and orange juice for Kahari.

"Here," I say a short while later, passing him the orange juice.

"You didn't have to."

"You need something."

"Thank you." His lips curl in a soft smile. Then he says, "Hey, why don't I drive? I know where I'm going, and you've got that piece of cake to eat."

"That's a great idea."

We get out of the car and switch sides.

When we're settled in our seats, Kahari starts to drive. I sip my caramel macchiato and moan in pleasure. "This is so good. Have you ever tried a caramel macchiato?"

"A caramel what?"

"Caramel macchiato. It's got espresso, whipped cream, and lots of caramel. It's sort of a dessert coffee."

"I'm not big on coffee."

"No," I gasp.

"I've never liked the taste. Plus, caffeine's not that great for you."

"Nonsense! This is the best."

Kahari smiles, and so do I. We're silent and I munch my cake and sip my coffee. I gaze at the street as Kahari turns onto Beverly Drive. One perfectly pruned palm tree after another lines the street. It's a subtle touch that lets you know you're now in a ritzier area.

"Tell me more about Zoë," Kahari says.

I wash down the last of my cake with a sip of my specialty coffee. "What do you want to know?"

"Everything, I guess. Where'd you grow up, how many siblings you have . . . You mentioned having a sister."

"I only have one sister, Lola, and we're as different as night and day. We even have different fathers, but that's another story."

"Not an uncommon one."

"No, I guess not." Should I tell Kahari about my father? That he was once a star in the league?

"So one sister, and you're not particularly close."

"No. I love her, of course, but we don't get along. I think she was always trying to prove her self-worth in all the wrong ways. Like how many men she could steal from her friends. Maybe because her father was in and out of her life. But mine was never in my life and I didn't behave like that. And why am I even telling you this?"

"Does she live in L.A.?"

"No, she lives in Cleveland, which is where I grew up. A boring town if ever there was one."

"I've been to Cleveland. I liked the downtown area. The Rock and Roll Hall of Fame, the restaurants on the waterfront . . ."

I shrug. "I guess it's all right. But I had big dreams. Ones I couldn't achieve in Cleveland."

"So you came to L.A., where everyone with big dreams comes."

"Yeah." I pause. "What about you?"

"Wait a second."

I finally pay attention to where we are. We're at a large wrought-iron security gate, complete with a security guard in one of those little houses.

Kahari rolls down the window. "Hey, Lou."

"Kahari," Lou sings. "You've got a different ride today. I can hardly keep up with all your cars."

"This one's not mine. It's my friend's. Zoë, this is Lou."

I wave. "Hi, Lou."

"Hello, Zoë." And then in a quieter voice he says, obviously to Kahari, "She's cute."

Kahari chuckles. "See you later, Lou."

He drives into Beverly Park, which is full of lush foliage and a stunning display of palm trees. I am literally breathless as I stare out at the landscape.

When the first house comes into view, I can't help saying, "Oh my God."

"That's something, isn't it?"

"That's not a house. That's a palace."

"The homes here are definitely spectacular. Some might say excessive, and I can't blame them, but for me, my house is about realizing a dream. I grew up in a house that was falling apart in Fort Worth. So many of the kids in my hood never thought they'd get out of it. They didn't aspire to greater things. But I always knew, I always believed, that if you wanted something badly enough, you could have it. And now I do."

"Wow," I say softly. "Talk about the American dream."

"That's exactly what this is for me. The American dream."

I continue to gawk at palatial estate after palatial estate

until Kahari slows down. He turns into the U-shaped driveway of a house that has a sprawling, pristine lawn, complete with large palm trees and a large flower garden. The driveway seems to go on forever. I imagine it can hold thirty, maybe forty cars.

"Is this your house?" I ask. I can't hide the awe from my voice.

"It is."

I check out the house. It's two stories, expansive, and pale brown in color. More like a peachy brown, really. The main level has several archways on the right-hand side, where the door and veranda are. Hanging in the middle of each archway is a pot of colorful flowers. The porch wraps around to the side of the house. I can't see where it ends. I imagine all those archways allow a nice breeze to flow onto the veranda if you're sitting out there in the evening having a glass of wine. Not to mention if he were to open any of the dozens of large windows.

It reminds me of the kind of place one would find on a hillside in the Mediterranean. Or in the Caribbean.

"Kahari . . . this place is . . . I can't find the words to describe it."

Kahari's eyes light up like a little kid's at Christmas. In his eyes, I see that this house is exactly what he said it was—about the realization of a dream, and not ego.

"Wait till you go inside."

"You want me to come inside? Don't you have to . . . to get ready?"

"Yeah," he answers as he opens his door, "but I've got time to give you a quick tour."

Kahari walks around to my side of the car and opens the door for me. Then he takes my hand and helps me out.

A surge of heat shoots through my body. Lord, I could get used to him touching me.

"You've got to hear this," Kahari says as I follow him to the front door. He presses the doorbell, and the theme music from *Monday Night Football* plays. "Is that cool, or what?"

His excitement is contagious. "That's cool," I agree.

We step into the house. As Kahari disables the alarm, my mouth falls open. The foyer is massive. It looks more like the type of foyer you'd find in a posh hotel lobby. Above us is an enormous crystal chandelier in a silver-colored metal. Twin staircases lead to a large landing that overlooks the lower level. The banister is dark, probably cherrywood, with black iron spindles. And now this is something I haven't seen before—each step is black marble. So is the floor.

It looks amazing.

Kahari points straight ahead, past the area beneath the landing. "That's a sitting room."

"One of many, I'm guessing." It's elegantly decorated with a red lounger sofa. A gold-colored vase sits on a coffee table and is filled with flowers.

"Uh-huh."

I can't imagine Kahari being able to give me a quick tour of this place. It's too large.

"Let me show you the back," he says.

I walk behind Kahari through the sitting room, noticing two sixteen-by-twenty-inch framed black-and-white photos. One is a picture of three young black boys, laughing. The other is an elderly black woman sitting in a rocking chair on a warped wooden porch.

"I love these photos," I tell him.

"The boys are my young cousins," Kahari explains. "And that's a picture of my grandmother. Rita Brown." A smile touches his lips. "That's the house where I grew up. Not much more than a shack, really. But I have fond memories of the place and my grandmother. I've invited her here to live with me, but she refuses. She loves that house. She was born there, and says she's gonna die there."

These human touches make it obvious that Kahari is normal. More than normal, really. He's caring, and sensitive, and has a strong sense of family.

My crush on him grows stronger.

"And this," he announces, "is the kitchen."

"Wow." The kitchen is as huge as his foyer, and has black marble floors, black granite counters, and white cupboards. It also has a large stainless steel fridge. But my favorite part is the center island. I wonder if Kahari actually uses it to chop vegetables and chicken.

How cute would he be, in boxers and an apron . . .

I turn to the left. Okay, I know I just said my favorite part of the kitchen is the center island. But I have to take that back, now that I see the café! Yes, a café! It even has leather sofas, cozy tables, and a fireplace. My God, it's like a Starbucks in your own home!

"I thought you don't drink coffee," I say when I see the coffeemaker and cappuccino machine.

"Sometimes. But I like tea. And my friends drink coffee. I find the café is great for entertaining."

"You have quite the house."

"Come see the backyard."

Kahari opens the shutters and I peer outside. "Oh my God, this is paradise!"

"This is a great spot to entertain, and also to relax."

"I'll bet." The backyard boasts a large pea-shaped pool surrounded by lounge chairs. One corner looks like an island oasis, with leafy plants and water cascading over rocks. The entire backyard is surrounded by abundant leafy plants with colorful flowers mixed in. I honestly feel like I'm on a Caribbean island. The tiki bar and tables with straw umbrellas add to the Caribbean flavor.

"And look at this view of the valley," I comment. "But this backyard . . . it's like being on an island. The only thing that's missing is music."

"Which I have, of course. If we had time, I'd let you hear the stereo system. I've got different theme music. Reggae, for an island feel. Mediterranean. Soft jazz . . . "

For romancing. I swallow, wondering how many women Kahari has entertained here.

"I love it. I mean, what's not to love?"

"Maybe you'll come back when we both have some time."

My heart starts to pound. Does he really want me to do that? Spend more time with him?

I know we had a pretty nice evening together, but it's hard to believe this. I mean, I'm Zoë Andrews. Nothing extraordinary happens to me.

"I'm sorry, Zoë. But I've got to get ready."

"Right," I say, and spin around. I head back into the house.

Moments later, I'm about to reach for the front door's knob when Kahari rushes to open it for me. Clearly someone raised him right.

"I guess I'll see you when you get back to town," I tell him.

"Yep."

"All right." I smile softly, then start for my car. I'm almost at the car when I glance over my shoulder to see if Kahari is still standing at the door.

He is.

Yes!

Thirty

I am deliriously happy the next three days.

Eva is happy too, because I've told her that Kahari has said yes to doing the story. I'm going to try and arrange it for next Tuesday, when I know he'll have the whole day free.

This is a huge career coup. But as much as I should be excited about it—especially since Eva is so pleased with me—I almost couldn't care less about the story. What I care about most is the fact that doing this story means I get to see Kahari again.

I know, pathetic. And certainly unprofessional. But the guy makes me come alive in a way I've never experienced before. How can I *not* be excited at the prospect of spending more time with him?

And maybe, just maybe, I'll have a chance to redeem myself and regain the opportunity I so horribly blew.

It is almost impossible to concentrate on work, that's how excited I am to see him again. I'm even more excited because Kahari called my cell yesterday and left a message. "Here I am, supposed to be concentrating on my game, but

I'm thinking about you. So I thought I'd call. I'm looking forward to seeing you again."

I know the message verbatim because I've listened to it at least a dozen times.

The week is hardly going by fast enough. Last night I decided that I'll go back to the Rita Brown Community Center to get a better feel for the place. I know Kahari is in Oakland today, and that's fine because I *should* be concentrating on finding the best angle for the story, anyway.

There's only one thing I need to do before heading to the center, and that's go see an apartment I called about yesterday. I can only stay at Rose's place for so long. This apartment is close to Lankershim—and more importantly, close to Starbucks.

I shower and change into black slacks and a burgundy top, and pull my hair back into a ponytail. I complete the outfit with black flip-flops. The weather's gotten a bit cooler over the past couple days, but the sun during the day makes flip-flops doable.

When I reach the apartment's front door, I slip my sunglasses on and head for my Mercedes. *My Mercedes.* I'm not sure I'll ever get used to the sound of that.

I'm almost at my car in the visitors' parking row when a sound makes me halt. Raising my head, I look all around. I see nothing, but the bushes to my far right are rustling. No surprise there, since there's a light breeze today.

I keep walking, hitting the unlock button on my remote control key. And then my cell phone rings.

I dig it out of my purse. "Hello?

"Zoë?"

"Yes?" I don't recognize the female voice.

"This is Estela. Estela Rivera."

"Oh, Estela." It's amazing that I'd all but forgotten about her. "Hi. How are you?"

"Not too good."

I lean my hip against my car. "Why? What's the matter?"

"You promised me this would work. That I would get Kahari back."

I have to pause for a couple seconds to try to make sense of what she's saying. "You mean—"

"You know what I mean! And I've been getting all these nasty calls, and letters. People who hate me for smearing Kahari's name. I could deal with all of that if he would just come back to me."

Well, I certainly never promised Estela that sharing her story would win Kahari back, and even if that's what she hoped, she had to know the risk. Besides, I'm not sure I believe her story entirely anymore. I've spent time with Kahari, and he seems nothing like a first-class jerk.

"Look, Estela. If he hasn't called you already, then maybe . . . maybe it's time to move on."

"How dare you! My son needs a father."

"And you're sure Kahari's the father? Because he says he's not."

"Oh—now you believe him, do you? So what was Vegas about? Spoiling me with that suite, the first-class ticket home. You said you cared about me, Zoë. And I believed you."

Estela is raising her voice, and she sounds half hysterical. "Calm down, please. I do care. That's why I did your story. But . . . Kahari's denying he fathered your child. It's he-said, she-said right now, Estela. Unless . . . "

"Unless what?" Estela asks, her voice piquing with interest.

"Unless you get a paternity test," I finish. "Force his hand. Prove that the baby is his, and with the public watching, he'll never be able to deny you." And I can imagine Eva's delight if *True Story* snags the right to do this on national TV.

"No," Estela replies without pause, sounding indignant.

"But Estela, don't you see? If we can force him to take a paternity test—"

"I said no."

"Why not?"

"I will *not* put my baby through that kind of pain just because his father doesn't want to acknowledge him. Sooner or later, he will have to do the right thing on his own."

A weird sensation flutters in my belly. And now I know that I didn't ask that question purely for Estela's sake, or the show's. I asked because I needed to know how she would respond.

It's kinda like that story in the Bible, with two women claiming a child is theirs. When the judge orders the baby to be split in half, the one woman quickly agrees, while the other woman says no, to give the baby to the other woman. It's pretty clear who the real mother is in this scenario.

It's pretty clear to me why Estela doesn't want to force a paternity test.

I suddenly feel sick.

"Zoë, are you there? Zoë, you answer me!"

I blow out a hurried breath. "Estela, let me talk to my producer. I'll see what we can do." But we can hardly force Kahari to admit he's the baby's father just to please Estela.

I wonder if the woman's crazy, or just desperate.

No sooner do I end the call and slip into the driver's seat than I hear a pounding on the car window. I scream as my head whips to the left. Pain shoots through my neck, as it's still sore from the fall I took at dinner with Kahari.

There is Colby, standing beside my car and staring down at me.

He holds up both hands. "Calm down. It's just me."

I climb out of the car and walk a few feet away from the door. "You scared me."

"Sorry."

"Where were you? I didn't see you here." And what the hell is he *doing* here? In the parking lot of Rose's building, as though he's stalking me or something.

"I live right across the street. I cut through this parking lot all the time. You didn't see me because you were talking on the phone."

"Oh." I'm not sure I believe him, however. There's a twig stuck in his hair, and I can't help thinking he was hiding in the bushes. I remember that sound I heard before my phone rang.

He folds his arms over his chest. "You haven't returned any of my calls."

"I've been busy."

"Yeah, I know. I saw you on *True Story*. Great gig."

I detect a note of anger beneath his words, and maybe that's what this is about—that I didn't tell him about my new job. "It all happened so fast, Colby. One minute I was getting fired from LASN, and the next my agent got me this great opportunity."

"And now you're too busy for your old friends."

"Of course not," I reply, a tad defensively. Gee, it's not like Colby and I talked every day. It was more like once in a while, whenever I saw him around. I certainly don't owe him any explanation.

"But I *am* busy." I hope he gets the point. "I've got to be somewhere in twenty minutes." I refrain from telling him I'm looking for a new place. If he's stalking me here, I don't want him to know I'm moving.

I step toward the car door, but Colby scoots in front of me, forcing me to stop. "I guess you and Marvin broke up," he says.

"Why would you think that?"

"Because I called there, and he said you moved out."

"Oh." That made sense. "Yeah, I did. I caught him cheating on me. Long story, and I have no time to tell it now." I step to the right—but he matches my move, as though we're dancing.

"You're just gonna take off? You don't want to get a coffee or something?"

I glance at my watch. "I told you. I have an appointment."

This time, I take a step to the left. Again, Colby blocks my path.

I raise an eyebrow, and he shakes his head at me. "You've changed."

Great. This is the last thing I need. "I got a job, Colby. A demanding one."

"And suddenly you're too good to go out with me."

"What are you talking about?"

"That's why I was calling you. To see if we could get together for coffee. Or dinner. You know." He shrugs. "Kinda like a date."

"A date . . . "

"It's over with Marvin. You can't give me a chance? *I* would never cheat on you."

"Uh, I . . . I'm concentrating on my career right now. I don't really have time to date." This time, when I sidestep him to get to my car door, Colby doesn't get in my way. He does, however, hang over my shoulder.

"Are you gonna pretend you don't have feelings for me?" he asks.

The accusation is so . . . bizarre I'm floored. Too floored to pick up my jaw off the asphalt.

And suddenly Colby is standing at my open car door, one arm on the roof of my car, the other on the door. He's standing so close to me I feel very uncomfortable.

My patience is wearing thin. "Colby, what are you doing?"

Now he smiles, but it's forced, and there's almost an evil quality to it. "Just trying to talk to you."

"Well . . . I have some research to do, and I have to report in to my producer—"

"The life of a star, huh?"

"I'm hardly a star." *And why are you being so freakin' strange today?* "Look, I'd really love to stay and chat—"

"Would you?"

I glance at my watch, this time being obvious. "Colby, I'll call you, okay?" He doesn't move. *"Okay?"*

Slowly, he moves away from my car. "Nice car," he comments.

I slip into the seat. "Thanks."

"I hope you do," Colby says. "Call me."

At his comment, I throw a glance over my shoulder. Again, he's doing that evil smile thing.

"Sure," I tell him.

But I can't help feeling like I've just been threatened.

Thirty-one

"Hey, J'Ron." Kahari wrapped an arm around the smiling boy. "How ya doin', my man?"

"I'm cool, Kahari. Real cool."

"Good to hear, Shorty."

It was Monday afternoon, and Kahari had gotten back to Los Angeles a little over an hour before. He had headed straight to the center, while Anthony had opted to head home and check on his pregnant wife first.

J'Ron gave his arm a playful punch. "Guess your arm's finally feeling better, huh?"

"My arm?"

"My cousin said that last week your arm was sprained, and that was why you didn't play so well. But you played a great game yesterday. Two touchdowns!"

J'Ron raised a hand and Kahari gave him a high five. Then Kahari made a show of rotating his right shoulder. "Yeah, my arm," he said. "It's much better."

He felt slightly bad lying to J'Ron. But this was better than admitting the truth—that he'd underperformed during last week's game because he'd been distracted.

"Hey," J'Ron said. "That woman came by again."

"What woman?" *Lord, not Estela . . .*

"Zoë."

Kahari whipped his head around, his sense of dread replaced by a sense of anticipation. "She's here?"

"No, not right now. She came by a couple days ago."

"Looking for me?" Kahari asked, happily surprised. Maybe she was thinking about him as much as he'd been thinking about her. Still, she knew he was in Oakland for the weekend, so why would she come here?

"Naw, she didn't come looking for you. She said she came to hang out with the kids. But I think she's got a thing for me." J'Ron grinned widely.

"You got a thing for the older ladies, huh?"

"She *fine*."

"Yeah, I guess she is." Kahari rubbed his knuckles against J'Ron's head. "So, she came to hang out?"

"Uh-huh. She talked to a lot of us. Shot some hoops. She's pretty good."

"What'd she talk about?"

"What we like about coming here. What we wanna be when we grow up. That sorta thing."

"I see."

"Oh, and she helped some of the younger kids do finger paintings. Stuff like that."

"Hmm," Kahari said thoughtfully. "Thanks for telling me."

"Are you gonna start dating her?"

"J'Ron . . . "

"Hey, if you're not interested . . . "

"You're too much," Kahari told him. "I'll see you a little later, Shorty. I've gotta go upstairs."

As Kahari headed off, his thoughts turned to Zoë. So she had come by on Saturday? Interesting indeed.

He would call her as soon as he got into his office. He had to arrange to get his car back.

Which was an excuse to see her, of course. He could have taken a cab from the restaurant back home that day instead of having her drive him to his house. But he knew then that he wanted to see her again.

He didn't think the desire was one-sided.

"Zoë," he said, grinning. He made his way to the office, determined to call her.

A couple hours later, Kahari looked toward the front doors of the center to see Zoë walking in. He smiled immediately, and placed his hands on his hips as he watched her glance around the place. After a moment, she saw him, and her eyes lit up.

They walked toward each other, meeting near the edge of the basketball court. "Hey, Zoë."

"How are you?"

Kahari crossed his arms over his chest. "I'm all right."

"I brought your car. It's a nice ride."

"You came alone?"

"Yeah, but I'll catch a cab back."

Kahari nodded. "I hear you're pretty good on the basketball court."

"Oh." A laugh escaped Zoë on a shaky breath. "Who told you I was here? J'Ron? It was probably J'Ron."

"I think he's smitten with you."

Zoë's eyes suddenly widened in alarm. "Please don't get the wrong idea. I came to hang out, play with the kids. Get to know more about the center. That's all."

"I didn't think there was another reason."

"Good." She took a deep breath. "Look, I'm sure you have lots to do, so I'll just call for a cab—"

"Whoa, whoa, wait a second." Kahari took hold of her arm and looked at her with concern. "What's up?"

"What do you mean?"

"If you don't want to hang around and chat, then something's wrong." He said the words lightheartedly, but Zoë didn't even crack a smile. That wasn't like her. "What is it?"

She glanced downward. "Nothing, really."

Kahari placed his thumb on her chin and angled her face so she had to meet his eyes. "Tell me."

"You'll think it's stupid."

"Now I really want to know."

She exhaled softly. "It's my birthday today. I'm the big three-oh, and no one's called me. Not one person."

"It's your birthday? Happy birthday."

"It's no big deal."

"You're upset. So it's obviously a big deal."

"I'm disappointed."

"Thirty," Kahari said. "You're on the top of the hill now, about to go down the other side."

She made a face at him. "Ha ha. Very funny."

"It's not as bad as they say."

"And what are you—like thirty-two, thirty-three?"

"Thirty-one. And I'm well aware that I'm going downhill now—in terms of football."

"That's not true. You had one bad game."

"I mean in terms of the life of a ballplayer. We only have so many years playing the game."

Zoë's lips curled in a soft smile. "But you're fabulous. You'll be around forever." She suddenly frowned. "It's amazing how everyone you know can forget your birthday. I know I'll hear from my mother later, but . . . "

"And your father?"

"Uh, I don't think so."

Kahari narrowed his eyes as he stared at her. "You say that like the two of you don't get along."

"We don't talk," Zoë replied in a tone that said she didn't want to discuss the matter.

All right. They didn't have to talk about it. "Are you telling me you have no plans for tonight?"

"No, I do have plans."

"Ah . . . "

"I'm putting down first and last on a lease for my new apartment."

"That's your plan?"

"Hey, it's not so bad. Like a milestone, really. I'm thirty. I have a great new career. I'm getting my own place. It's like turning the page on a brand-new life."

"No, no, no." Kahari shook his head. "That won't do."

"It's just another day. I'm not even sure why I'm letting this get me down. My friend Rose is out of the country, and it's not like I even want my ex to call me—"

"Let me take you out."

Zoë's eyes were guarded as she looked at him. "What?"

"You have to do something for your thirtieth birthday."

"You don't have anything better to do?"

"Like call up one of my twenty honeys and see who's free tonight?"

Zoë laughed. "I thought it was twenty-one?"

"Nothing gets by you, does it?"

Silence passed between them, then Zoë said, "You're doing that Good Samaritan thing again."

"Let's make some definite plans," Kahari said, ignoring her comment. "Name the place you'd like to go, and I'll pick you up."

Zoë thought for a minute. "You think Il Fornello is ready for us again? No, let's go somewhere different."

"What about Ambience?"

"Oh yes. Another place I've heard great things about. But busy, too. Busier than Il Fornello. It might be hard to get in last minute."

"Consider it done."

"You say that like—"

"—I can pull a few strings?" He nodded. "Usually I can."

Zoë's mouth fell open in surprise. "Wow."

"Eight o'clock okay? You're still at your friend's apartment?"

"Yes, I am."

"Great," he said. "See you then."

I'm a nervous wreck for the next few hours. After signing the lease for my new place and getting the keys, I went right back to Rose's apartment, where all my stuff is. Over the last two hours, I've tried on at least eight different outfits, none of which seem good enough for a birthday outing with Kahari Brown.

I can't believe he's taking me out for my birthday! In fact, I can't believe much of what's happened over the past couple weeks. I know I'm letting my guard down where Kahari's concerned, but he's more than a subject to me. More than a guy I'm doing a story on.

How much more, though, I'm not sure. I know I have a crush on him, but how does he feel? I think there's a hint of attraction. Why else would he want to take me out tonight?

It's almost amazing, considering how we first met and that he was initially so angry with me I never thought we'd get past that. Who would have thought that we'd be enjoying dinners together like friends?

And maybe more . . .

"Dammit!" I glare at my reflection. "Why doesn't *anything* look good on me?"

For the next ten minutes, I debate between a red pantsuit

that screams, *I WANT TO GET LAID,* and a pair of black slacks that make my ass look fabulous, complemented perfectly with a white ribbed top.

I finally decide on the pants and top, because I don't want to look desperate. Besides, the pants and top can be dressed up or down, depending on the shoes and purse you accessorize with.

The apartment's buzzer buzzes.

Oh my God, oh my God.

I inhale deeply. I'm ready for this.

I have to be.

My birthday date with Kahari Brown.

I grab my clutch and head for the door.

"Wow," I can't help saying as the host leads us to our table. "This place is fabulous."

The lighting is dim, the colors vibrant. The place has an upscale funky feel. "I see why they named this place Ambience," I point out.

"You'll be happy to know I made sure to ask for a table on the first floor," Kahari jokes.

I throw my head back and laugh.

The host leads us to a booth near a window. There's a picture of Miles Davis on the wall above our table. In fact, all around the restaurant there are a host of black-and-white photos of all the great jazz artists.

No sooner are we seated and I lift my menu than Kahari says, "Here."

I lower my menu to look at him, and he's pushing a small box wrapped in gold foil across the table to me.

"Kahari." Butterflies flutter in my stomach. "What is this?"

"Open it and find out."

I need no further encouragement. I open the box with the

excitement of a kid at Christmas. Inside the wrapping paper is a blue Tiffany box.

"Oh my God."

"Go on," he says.

Slowly, I lift the lid. And gasp when I see the silver chain-link bracelet. It has the cutest trinkets on it. A smiling sun, a banana-shaped moon, the astrological sign for Scorpio.

"Kahari—"

"It's white gold."

Another gasp. "It's too—"

"I hope you like it. As soon as I saw it, I thought of you."

And damn if it isn't exactly my style. I carefully lift it out of the box. "That was so sweet of you. And you didn't have to."

"I wanted to."

My eyes meet his, and a jolt of electricity passes between us. A breath oozes out of me.

"Here. Let me put it on."

"Okay," I say nervously.

I pass the bracelet to Kahari and extend my left wrist. He clips it on. Even in the dim lighting, it sparkles like it cost a million bucks.

"It's beautiful," I tell him, meaning every word. "I love it."

Another look passes between us, and I have to glance away, it's so intense.

Thankfully, the waiter arrives, and Kahari orders a bottle of Merlot. I'm grateful for the diversion, because it keeps me from thinking about the emotions swirling inside me right now.

It keeps me from wondering if my crush on Kahari has just kicked up a notch.

Thirty-two

Nearly two hours later, Kahari pours the last of the Merlot into my glass and asks me, "If you had one wish for your birthday, one thing you'd want to do, or receive—what would that be?"

I fiddle with the stem of my wineglass. "Other than tonight? Because this evening has been pretty great."

"Dinner's just dinner. There's got to be something else."

No, having you take me out for my birthday is pretty much a fantasy come true . . .

Kahari takes a sip of his wine. "Come on," he says. "Maybe something you've never done before?"

"Okay, let me think." I look at the garnet-colored liquid in my wineglass. "Okay, I got it." My eyes raise to Kahari's. "Now don't laugh."

"Go on."

I lean one cheek against the palm of my hand. "Oh, you'll probably laugh. But what the hell. I've always wanted to go on a Ferris wheel."

"What?"

"A laugh would be better than pity."

"You've never been on a Ferris wheel?"

"Never. I've always been too scared!" I speak a little too emphatically, courtesy of the wine.

"Then we have to find a Ferris wheel for you."

"There's a fair going on right now, in Santa Monica—"

"Let's go."

My eyes widen. "What?"

"Let's go."

"Tonight?"

"Why not?"

"Because . . . " *Because what?*

"It's your birthday," he tells me. "Your thirtieth birthday. I say it's time to experience something new."

Something new . . . How about a six-foot-one wide receiver who goes by the name of Kahari Brown?

Before I can say anything else, Kahari is getting the waiter's attention. He settles the bill in cash, then stands and reaches for my hand.

"You really want to do this?" I ask him. "I'm wearing the worst possible shoes for this. Look at all these straps."

"I love the straps."

My heart skips a beat. "You do?"

"Oh yeah."

I giggle. "Okay then. Let's go."

We take a cab to Santa Monica, because Kahari didn't want to risk driving and I certainly was in no shape. In the backseat, we hold hands. Or maybe I hold his and he doesn't want to embarrass me by letting go. Whatever the case, I'm savoring every moment of my time with him. Of all my birthdays, this is the best one by far.

"Ah, there it is," Kahari says as the fairgrounds come into view.

"Oh God. I can't believe I'm going to do this."

Kahari passes the taxi driver some money. "Buddy, do you mind waiting here for us? I'll make it worth your while."

"Kahari Brown, right?" the driver asks.

"Yeah," he replies. "That's me."

"I think you're awesome. Great game on Sunday."

"Thanks." Kahari slides across the backseat of the car. "So you'll wait? We'll probably be half an hour, maybe less."

"For sure."

Kahari exits the car, then reaches for my hand. "I think you're pretty awesome too," I whisper. "Doing all this for me."

"No one should spend their thirtieth birthday alone."

Minutes later, we're inside the fairgrounds. Holding my hand, Kahari starts to run toward the Ferris wheel.

"Kahari, I'm not so sure about this—"

"You're gonna love it!" He sounds as excited as a kid in a candy store. He doesn't stop running until we reach the Ferris wheel.

He hands our tickets to the young girl standing there, saying, "She's a virgin."

"Kahari!"

"Never been on a Ferris wheel, I mean. So make it really special, okay?"

"Kahari, what does that mean?"

"Nothing."

"Kahari . . . " He tugs on my arm, leading me onto the platform and into this cagelike contraption.

I grip his arm as the Ferris wheel jerks to life. Soon we are moving, heading backward. I squint my eyes as I look down at all the people and the lights. It's quite a marvelous sight.

The Ferris wheel reaches the top, and as we make our descent, I close my eyes and scream.

"It's great, isn't it?" Kahari asks me above my bloodcurdling shriek and other people's.

"I don't know . . . "

The Ferris wheel hits the bottom and swoops back up again. I open one eye.

When we hit the top, the Ferris wheel stops. Now I open both eyes and glance around in a panic. There's no doubt about it—we've stopped. We aren't going anywhere.

"Kahari . . . " I dig my fingers into his arm. "Kahari, what's happening? Why did we stop?"

"I don't know," he replies, but he laughs.

Our cage teeters and totters and we spin end over end. I scream as though I'm about to be pushed off the plank.

"Kahari! Oh my God. We're upside down! What's happening?"

Kahari wraps an arm around me and holds me tight. "It's all right," he whispers. "This is part of the fun."

"I'm not so sure I should have done this!" I shriek as we spin end over end once more. I lean against Kahari's strong chest and hold on to his arms for dear life.

Finally, we turn right side up, and I sigh with relief. But my relief is short-lived when I open my eyes and glance outside and see just how high off the ground we are.

"This is insane. I'm *never* doing this again."

"But you're having a good time, right?"

"The best," I respond without hesitation.

I ease my face off of his chest and look at him. His eyes are filled with something, an expression I can't quite read. Happiness? Attraction? I'm not sure.

And then it happens. Something between us changes. I get lost in his eyes, and he's lost in mine, and we are moving our faces closer and closer together as if there's nothing right now that can pull us apart.

As his lips brush against mine, I gasp softly at the pleasure of it. The pleasure of those thick, soft lips moving against mine in a slow, seductive manner.

The kiss deepens, and this time when I grip Kahari, it's not because I'm afraid. It's because my body craves the feel of his against mine.

Lord, this man is delicious. He nips my lips with his teeth, he suckles my mouth with exquisite gentleness, until I am wet and wondering if anyone has ever made love in a Ferris wheel cage.

And then the Ferris wheel jerks, startling us both, and I squeal as it starts to drop.

I still hold Kahari's hand.

This is the best birthday I have ever had.

By the time we get back to Los Angeles, Kahari is no longer under the influence, and I'm pretty much sober as well. So we have the taxi drop us off at Ambience so Kahari can get his car, which happens to be a red Porsche.

"Thank you so much, Kahari. I had a great time."

He throws a sideways glance at me. "No problem."

I lean my head back. "I didn't mention this before, because this dinner wasn't about business, but the head at *True Story* wants me to get that interview with you right away. So I was thinking . . . wondering . . . could we do it tomorrow morning, at the community center? Before you head for Oakland?"

"Tomorrow morning?"

"It'll be quick, I promise. And this way, we can get it over and done with. And you can tell the world how incredible you are."

"Ah, so now you think I'm incredible?"

"I do," I tell him, meaning every word. Then I sigh. "If you want to know the truth, everything that happened with Estela seems like a lifetime ago." I glance at his side profile as his eyes are on the road. "And there's something else. Something else I should tell you."

He throws a quick look my way. "Go on."

"I . . . I spoke with Estela over the weekend. She called me, pretty upset that she hadn't heard from you. She figured her telling her story to the world would force you to do right by her."

"And?"

"And I guess she's angry at me. Because the plan didn't work."

"Do you and Estela know each other?"

"No! I only met her when I saw her at the hotel in Vegas. I recognized her as being the woman who claimed you'd fathered her baby. And when you wouldn't talk to me . . . "

"You figured you'd talk to her instead."

A moment passes, and Kahari doesn't look at me. Damn, I've gone and spoiled the mood.

"I want to tell you not to be angry with me, but you have every right."

"What else did Estela say?"

"Oh, right. Well, I told her that you'd denied her claim, and she got even more upset. So I told her she should force you to do a paternity test if she was certain you were the father—"

"And she said no."

"Yeah," I say. Kahari meets my eyes as I ask, "How'd you know?"

"Because I'm *not* the father of her baby," he answers, and it's obvious he's got no more patience where this subject is concerned.

"I know that," I say softly.

"Oh, damn," he mutters. "I'm fucking heading to my place instead of your friend's. I wasn't even thinking."

"Did you hear me?" I ask.

He doesn't answer right away, but then he says, "Yeah, I heard you. Too bad it took her saying no to a paternity test for you to believe me."

"Kahari, no. That's not true. I believed you when . . . well, when you told me you weren't the father. And then seeing the kids at the community center . . . It didn't make any sense. Why would you do so much for the community yet deny your own child?"

He doesn't say anything, but makes a U-turn on Beverly Boulevard.

"I can see why you don't believe me, though. And I can't blame you. But trust me, if I truly believed you were anything like my father, I would have stayed away from you like the plague."

He looks at me. "Your father?"

"I shouldn't have said that."

"Tell me about him."

I sigh heavily. "He was never there for me. He was . . . he was a football player. Played for Dallas for many years as their quarterback. Led them to four consecutive Super Bowls."

Kahari's eyes widen. "Andrews," he says thoughtfully. "Sean Andrews' daughter?"

"Uh-huh."

"The white guy."

"Ta-da. I'm biracial."

"I figured that." He pauses. "But last I heard, Sean Andrews was married with a family. His children are blond-haired and blue-eyed."

"He had an affair with my mother but didn't want to marry her. He denied me for nineteen years, pretty much. Who knows—maybe he found God now or something because he apparently wants to be in my life. I tried, but it didn't work out. I don't think I'll ever forgive him. Could he not deal with having a biracial child? Was it something else?"

"You've never asked him?"

"God, no."

"Maybe you should."

"Honestly, I want to forget about him entirely. I don't even know why I'm telling you all this. I don't like to talk about it."

He surprises me by reaching for my hand. "I'm glad you are."

"But you're mad at me. You probably hate me."

"I don't hate you."

My heart starts to beat faster. "You don't?"

"No," he says softly. And then, "Maybe we should get a nightcap."

"Um . . . "

"Unless you don't want to. Don't worry. Forget it."

"No, no. I'd love to. I was just thinking . . . maybe I can show you my new apartment."

"Your new apartment?"

"Remember I told you I was signing a lease today?"

"That's right. Where is it?"

"In NoHo. Not too far from where you picked me up earlier. It's actually the top level of a house, and it's furnished."

Kahari's eyes dart from the road to mine at that tidbit, and I'm suddenly getting turned on at the thought of sleeping with him. Because I'm pretty sure that's where this is going to lead.

"It's a nice spot," I say.

He faces the road again. "Sure."

I give him directions to get to my new place, and fifteen minutes later he is pulling up alongside the curb. He looks toward the house, then glances at me. I swallow and open my car door.

"I don't have any wine," I admit as we start to the door.

He puts a hand around my shoulder. "I'm sure we'll be fine."

Ooh, yes. He's thinking the same thing I am right now. He's got to be. I can hardly wait to get upstairs.

I fumble with the key in the lock. "This has been a dream birthday," I tell him. "I appreciate it."

"Just open the door already."

I look over my shoulder at him and smile. And then I open the door. "It's this way. Up the stairs on the right."

I am aware of every one of his movements, every one of his breaths, as we walk up the stairs.

"This is it," I announce when we reach my door. "My new home."

I quickly open the door (much more smoothly this time!), but before I can flick on the lights, Kahari sweeps me into his arms. I gasp softly in surprise. And then he is kissing me. Kissing me and walking me backward against a wall. Kissing me and linking our fingers. Kissing me and kicking the door shut with his foot.

"Mmm," I moan. Every part of me is electrified.

"Ahh, Zoë."

We kiss deeply and slowly and feel each other, relishing every moment. God, I love how he touches me. Feathery strokes along my neck and face, gentle touches beneath my top.

He's not rushing. He's seducing me.

He eases me off the wall to loop his arms around my waist. I slip mine around his neck. With the moonlight as our guide, we kiss our way to a sofa where he sits while I still stand. He lifts my top and kisses my belly, a long, lingering kiss that makes me shiver. His teeth nip at my protruding belly button, and I imagine his mouth going to work farther south.

His hands trail the length of my upper body, up over my rib cage, then to my breasts. He tweaks my nipples through my bra, and I moan in pleasure.

"Are you sure?" he whispers.

"Are *you* sure?" I ask him. It's pretty obvious why I want to sleep with him. But I don't know why he wants to sleep with me.

"Oh yeah," he answers, low and guttural. "I'm sure." He kisses my belly again. "But I should probably run to the store. I don't have any condoms."

"I do." His eyes meet mine in the moonlit room. "And not because I'm a slut," I point out. "But I did bring a box of things over with me, and I've had the condoms in that box since I packed my stuff and left my ex. All of which is too much information. The point is—"

He pulls me down onto the sofa with him and shuts me up with a kiss.

Thirty-three

Kahari could be making the biggest mistake of his life, but right now he didn't care.

And he didn't think it was a mistake. There was something sweet and vulnerable about Zoë Andrews, and he was attracted to her beyond all reason.

He watched her on her knees, digging through the one box in the corner of the living room. Damn, he liked the way her ass filled out those pants she was wearing. The moment he had seen her tonight, he'd wanted to sink his teeth into her.

"Found them," she said, turning to look over her shoulder.

"Them. Very good."

She laughed as she made her way back to him. "I like the way you think."

He pulled her forcefully onto his lap and kissed her. He wasn't patient with her this time. He wanted her in the worst possible way.

But she pulled away from him, and Kahari groaned his displeasure. She looked at him from eyes that were fogged with desire. Desire for him.

Taking his hand, she brought it to her mouth, then she kissed each finger. Slowly. She kept her eyes steadfast on his as she took his thumb in her mouth and sucked gently.

"Holy, baby." Who would think that something so simple could make him feel so turned on?

"Come here." He got to his feet, pulling her up with him. He swept her thick curls to the side and kissed her neck. Then he inhaled her scent.

"That feels so good," Zoë told him.

"I'm gonna make you feel a whole lot better."

He spun her around in his arms and rained hot kisses along her neck while he slipped his hands under her shirt. He lightly touched her skin, enjoying every moment. He wanted to take his time with her, spend the whole damn night making sweet love to her.

And he would. Until she begged him to stop when she'd had too much.

He moved his hands upward, and this time pushed her bra out of the way to feel her breasts. They were small and soft, but the nipples were large and hard.

She shuddered as he tweaked them. "Oh, Kahari . . . "

His erection straining against his pants, he pulled her shirt over her head and tossed it onto the floor. Then he spun her around and lowered his head to one of her breasts, taking the nipple into his mouth and suckling.

"Oh, oh, oh," Zoë panted.

"You're driving me crazy, Zoë."

She arched her back, offering him more of her. So he suckled her other nipple, and her heated moans made him feel like he would explode.

"I love your breasts, Zoë. I love your nipples."

"Mmm . . . "

"Damn, where's the bedroom?"

"Over . . . there . . . " She pointed.

Kahari took her hand and led her across the living room. He opened the first door he saw, then drew up short when he realized it was the bathroom. He moved down the hall to the second door and opened that one.

There was a queen-size bed in the middle of the room.

He gave her a tender kiss before leading her there. He couldn't remember the last time he had wanted to kiss a woman as much as he wanted to kiss Zoë, but he knew he could kiss her all night and not get bored.

At the edge of the bed, she undid her pants. Kahari unbuttoned his shirt and threw it off, then unbuckled his belt. Zoë was wearing red lacy panties that matched her bra, and damn if she didn't look like a million bucks.

As Kahari undid his pants, Zoë placed her hands on them. She pulled them down the length of his legs, then kissed her way back up his thighs. She ran a finger along the length of his erection.

"I want you inside me." She kissed him through his boxers.

Kahari pulled her to her feet, then eased her backward onto the bed. Their lips met and their tongues tangled as they ran their hands over each other's bodies. Zoë put her hands into his boxers and dragged them off of his butt. Kahari slipped his hand between them and teased her mound with his fingers. She matched his movements, reaching for and stroking his penis.

A ragged breath escaped his lips, and he grabbed her hand. "Let me do the teasing, Zoë. I don't know how long I'll last if you continue to do that."

He took her arms in his hands and pinned her to the bed, climbing on top of her. He kissed her neck again, and she giggled.

"Mmm . . . is that a sweet spot?"

"One of," she answered.

"Then I'll have to find the others."

"Take your time . . . "

He couldn't take his time, though. He needed to be inside of her *now.* "The condoms?" he rasped.

"I dropped them on the bed."

He found the string of condoms and ripped one off the perforated fold. Zoë's eyes locked with his, he pushed his boxers down to his knees and rolled the condom on. He reached for her and massaged the folds of her sex to see how ready she was for him. He felt a strong pull in his groin when he felt just how wet she was.

"Kahari," she whispered, her voice hoarse with sexual longing. "You're driving me crazy."

But he didn't enter her yet. He lowered his body beside her, continuing to feel her while taking a nipple in his mouth. A rapturous moan escaped her before she reached for his face and lifted her mouth to his.

"Kahari, don't make me wait . . . "

She moaned in disappointment as he turned her over onto her stomach. Slowly, he ran one finger down her back, and over her barely covered butt. Lowering his head, he kissed one cheek above the lace panty.

"You are so beautiful. So incredible."

"Baby . . . "

He turned her over, then settled his body on hers. Zoë pulled his head down to meet her lips. As they kissed, he entered her, filling her slowly. She moaned into his mouth.

"Oh yeah." God, she felt wonderful. He eased himself farther, going as deep as he could go.

Zoë buried her face in his neck. "Ohbabyohbabyoh-baby!"

Kahari picked up speed. Zoë arched her hips to match each of his thrusts. He looked at her, deep into her eyes, wanting her to know this was personal. He wanted her to know this was about a connection between them, not just casual sex.

He kissed her again, tweaking one of her nipples as he did. And then Zoë was crying out, a loud, euphoric moan.

"I'm coming . . . "

Her walls tightened around his shaft, and he could no longer hold on. He drove himself into her soft, deep place and succumbed to his own orgasm.

Their ragged breaths filled the room.

"I'm sorry," he said after a moment, his lips near her ear. "I didn't last as long as I wanted."

She framed his face. "Are you crazy? That was . . . pretty damn amazing!"

He chuckled softly, her compliment making him feel warm inside. "You're not just saying that, are you? So you don't crush my ego?"

"Come on, Kahari. I'm the one who should be worried about disappointing you."

"Not a chance," he said. He captured her lips in a hungry, breathless kiss. "And don't you think I'm through with you yet."

"Promises, promises . . . "

"This is one promise I assure you I'm gonna keep."

We make love three more times. The second time we go much slower. We savor each other like old lovers reuniting. The third time, Kahari wakes me up for a quickie. And the fourth time we make love in the shower in the very early morning. Of course, there are no towels, so we snuggle under the comforter until we dry off.

I feel amazing. Freakin' amazing. Honestly, I haven't ever felt better in my life.

I had no clue that sex could make a person feel this way. Trust me, I've had enough experience and I *should* know.

Not that I'm any sort of tramp, but I'm thirty, and long ago gave up on the hope of saving my virginity for Mr. Right, when it's pretty obvious that most of the men out there are Mr. Right Nows.

I stretch my body against Kahari's, noting that my vagina still tingles from the night of illicit bliss. Kahari Brown is a man who definitely knows how to perform on the field—and in the bedroom.

He lifts our joined hands and kisses the top of mine. "What time do you want me to do that interview?"

"I can call the producer anytime and have her get a camera crew together. We could probably set things up for nine or ten."

Kahari glances at his watch. "It's not quite seven yet." He yawns. "I'm tired, but if we do it at nine, nine-thirty, that'll give me time to go home and get changed."

"Plus drop me off at Rose's."

"Right."

Silence. I'm thinking about the fact that Kahari and I actually had a serious lovemaking session last night. I wonder if he's thinking the same thing.

"And then," I say, "you head off to Oakland."

"Yeah."

I moan softly. "I miss you already."

"I know what you miss." He strokes the mound between my legs, and just like that, I'm hot and bothered again.

"Kahari . . . "

"I know." He sighs in frustration. "I guess we'd better get up. And next week"—he kisses my hand again—"we'll pick up where we left off. I promise."

"You *are* good at keeping your promises."

Kahari eases up onto an elbow. "Hey, what are you doing this weekend?"

"Besides getting settled in my new apartment?"

"Why don't you come up to Oakland? Watch my game."

"What?" I couldn't be more surprised at his offer.

"I'll leave a ticket for you at the Will Call window. And I can make flight arrangements for you tonight."

"Kahari, you don't have to do that."

"It's not like I can't afford it."

"This is true."

He fully sits up, and the comforter slips down to his waist. One look at his chest and I remember every carnal moment spent in his arms . . .

"What do you say?" he asks.

The thought of spending five days without him is already unbearable. How can I say no?

"I say why not?"

He grins from ear to ear. Sitting here like this, naked in bed with Kahari, it almost feels like we shared more than just sex.

It kinda feels like I'm his girlfriend.

Thirty-four

Kahari pulled his Ferrari up to the gate in front of Anthony's house. Before he could even press the intercom system, the gate started to open.

He hit the gas, pushing the car to the limit and whizzing up the long driveway. In less than five seconds, he was outside Anthony's front door.

Damn, he loved this car.

Anthony emerged from his house, dressed casually in an L.A. Lakers jersey, an Oakland Raiders baseball cap, black sweatpants, and blue-tinted sunglasses.

Lecia's head appeared in the doorway. She smiled and waved at Kahari. He waved back.

"Hey, Smooth." Anthony folded his body into the Ferrari's passenger seat. "What's up?"

"Nuthin' much, T."

"I see you brought out the Queen."

"The Queen" is what Kahari affectionately called this car, as it was regal and sexy. "She was itchin' for a ride, and I figured we could have some fun on our way to Van Nuys."

"Too bad we can't take her all the way to Oakland, not just the airport."

"I know." Kahari revved the engine.

"Wait!"

Both Kahari and Anthony looked to the right at the sound of Lecia's voice. She was doing this waddle-run type movement as she hurried down the walkway. At the car, she handed Anthony a brown paper bag.

"I almost forgot," she said, grinning at her man.

"Thank you, babe." Anthony leaned toward her for a kiss.

The kiss went on for a few seconds, and Kahari looked away. But he felt a pull in his gut. He couldn't help remembering Zoë, and the incredible night they had shared.

Kahari had seen his friend's life change for the better after marrying Lecia. And while Kahari didn't often confide this to anyone, he wanted to find his soul mate too.

Some of his teammates called him soft, mostly the guys who had a different woman for every day of the week. They loved their star status because of the "perks"—women who would do practically anything for them.

But Kahari had never gotten into that game, and the few times he'd taken advantage of easy sex when it was offered to him, he hadn't felt good about himself in the morning. What he wanted most was a domestic partner, a woman to come home to. A sense of normalcy in his often hectic world.

Had he found that woman in Zoë?

It was a crazy thought, wasn't it? After all, he hadn't known her that long. Yet there was something about her. Something unique, and special. Intuitively, he felt they were good for each other.

"Have you two come up for air yet?" Kahari teased, turning his head back toward them. Only then did Lecia and Anthony pull apart, Lecia grinning in embarrassment.

Kahari shook his head. "You two."

"Hey, what can I say? I love my man."

"Where's *my* brown bag?" Kahari asked her.

She gave him an apologetic grin. "Tony can share his with you."

"I ain't sharin' nuthin'."

Lecia shrugged. "I tried."

"Hey, I'm used to it." Kahari put the car into gear. "See you later, Doc."

"No one calls her Doc but me," Anthony protested.

"See what I mean?" Kahari said to Lecia.

She giggled. "You two be careful. Call me when you get in, sweetheart."

Kahari hit the gas, which sent both men flying backward against their seats. Anthony's sandwich smashed into his mouth.

"Hey," Anthony protested.

"Sorry, bro."

"You sure about that?"

"What does that mean?"

Anthony paused. "You sure there's not something you want to tell me?"

"Like what?"

"Like about your love life."

Kahari whipped his gaze to Anthony's before driving off the property. "My love life?"

"I've been waiting for you to tell me. I thought we were tight."

"Whoa, wait a second." Kahari held up a hand. "What the hell are you talking about?"

"Lecia showed me the paper this morning. I saw the picture, bro. The one with you and that reporter all cozy at some fair in Santa Monica."

Kahari stared at his friend in disbelief. "There was a picture of me in the paper?"

"With Zoë Andrews. That reporter you were bad-mouthing only a couple weeks ago."

Ah, hell. "I told you about her, T. That she wanted me to tell my story on her show."

"And your exact words, if I remember correctly, were 'Hell no.' "

"I said that?"

"Uh-huh." Anthony munched his sandwich.

"That was probably a little harsh . . . "

"You seein' her now?"

Kahari hesitated, not sure what to say.

"Wow."

"She's pretty cool," Kahari said. "Not at all like I thought her to be. In fact, I shot an interview with her earlier today."

"Wow," Anthony repeated.

"What'd the article say?" Kahari asked.

"It speculated that you'd found love. Then it went on to talk about the hero nomination. Nothing negative."

"Surprise, surprise."

"Personally, I think that whole Estela story is dead in the water. And it sounds like you think so too."

Kahari felt Anthony's eyes boring a hole into his right cheek. "All right," he finally said. "Zoë and I . . . we've gotten pretty tight."

"Damn."

"In fact, she's coming to the game this weekend."

"It's that serious?"

"You know how it is when you meet someone, and your

brain tells you to stay away but your heart . . . your heart says you click? It doesn't make any sense, but—"

"Your heart? Man, this *is* serious."

"Am I crazy?" Kahari asked, throwing a quick glance at Anthony.

"Naw," he replied, smiling. "I know exactly how you feel, cuz that's how it was for me when I met Lecia. I knew we shouldn't have been together. Swore up and down things wouldn't work out. But look at us now."

"I know," Kahari said. He faked a shudder. "Scary."

"Shut up, dude." Anthony playfully punched him on the shoulder. Then he and Kahari laughed.

Thursday afternoon, I'm in my office at the *True Story* studio when my phone rings. I grab the receiver on the first ring. "Hello?"

"Damn you, Zoë."

Oh God. Not Estela. "Hello, Estela."

"I can't believe you. I fucking can't believe you!"

"This is about last night's show, right?" I know it has to be, and part of me expected to hear from Estela.

"What the hell do you think it's about?"

"You shared your side of the story with us. My producer wanted me to get Kahari's side too—"

"You people are all a bunch of bullshitters!"

"Calm down, Estela."

"Calm down? You paint Kahari out to be this wonderful guy and make me seem like some crazy bitch."

"That's not what we were trying to do."

"And now you're sleeping with him?"

My stomach sinks. She must have seen that picture of us in the paper.

"My whole life is falling apart," Estela continues. "I

should just kill myself. Is that what you want? I'm sure that's what Kahari wants."

"No!" I scream into the phone. "Estela—"

"I'll kill the baby, and I'll kill myself, then we'll both be out of your way!"

"Estela, please don't say that. No one wants that."

"I've got a gun here, for protection." Estela bursts into tears. "I'm gonna go get it."

"Estela, pleeeease. Please just calm down. I'm on my way over, okay? Right now."

She sniffles but says, "Okay."

OhmyGodohmyGod, I think as I grab my purse and run for the door. I'm barely finished closing it when I realize I need to let Eva know what's going on. I don't have time to see her, so I dig my cell out of my purse.

"Eva Raines," she says.

"Estela's gone over the deep end, and I think she's gonna kill herself! I'm heading over there right now to talk her out of it. I don't know—should I call the police, or a priest, or what? I've never dealt with this kind of situation before."

"You think she's really gonna do it?"

"I don't know," I answer as I rush through the studio's front doors.

"This is *huge,*" Eva says. "I'm gonna hang up and call Rusty."

"Rusty? Eva, maybe you don't understand how serious this is. Estela said she's got a gun and she's gonna blow her brains out!"

"And she's not going to want to do that with a camera crew there. Trust me, Zoë. I know what I'm doing."

And if she *does* blow her brains out? What spin will Eva put on that story before she airs it on TV? Because I know it wouldn't be beneath her to capitalize on Estela's suicide.

As I round the corner in the parking lot, I halt as I see my

Mercedes. A month ago, I was driving a clunker of a car with no real prospects of ever making a decent living. Now I'm driving an E320. A dream come true, certainly, but I'm suddenly very aware that my success is at the expense of other people's pain.

"I feel awful," I confess to Eva. "I don't want this woman's suicide on my conscience."

"Relax. You're going to see this woman, and tell her how sorry you are that she hasn't really been heard. And you're going to offer her the chance to tell her story again, assuring her that this time the public will believe her."

"What?"

"It'll calm her down, Zoë. What she wants is to be heard."

"But we just aired Kahari's story. And it was very compelling. Estela's story has holes you could drive a Mack truck through. I don't want to make her more promises we can't keep."

"So many questions," Eva says. "You've just got to trust me."

That's the problem, I think as I end the call and get into my car. I don't.

I start my car, but suddenly realize I don't know where Estela lives. I pick up my cell phone and call Eva once more.

"Eva Raines."

"I don't know where Estela lives. I only know she's somewhere in Compton."

"Rusty's getting the van ready. Come back inside. You can ride with him."

One way or another, Rusty is clearly going to be there. I curse under my breath as I head back into the studio.

When I get to Estela's front door, she opens it before I can knock. I gasp softly when I see her, because she's normally so beautiful, but with her eyes bloodshot and puffy and all that gorgeous black hair in knots, she looks nothing like her normal self.

"Estela." I pull her into a hug.

"Why doesn't he love me?" she cries.

Over her shoulder, my eyes scan her house. It's small and cramped, and I can't help feeling bad for her. She's obviously got it rough, and maybe she sees Kahari as a way out of poverty for her.

"I don't know, Estela."

"I gave him everything. And that night we made love . . . it was the best night of my life."

That *night* they'd made love? In Estela's interview, she'd said they'd been involved six months. Surely if they had been, they would have made love more times than one.

However, I don't point this out.

"What am I supposed to do now?" she asks me, looking absolutely crushed. "I can barely afford formula for the baby."

"Is he here?" I ask softly. "The baby."

Estela wipes at her tears. "Yes. He's sleeping."

"Can I see him?"

She nods and leads the way. I glance over my shoulder and hold up a finger to tell Rusty to wait. I don't care what Eva said. I'm not about to exploit this woman's pain.

Estela leads me to a very small bedroom. It's painted a vibrant blue, and decorated with various cartoon character decals. I peer inside the crib and see the most adorable little baby, fast asleep. He's on his back, his arms spread out beside him.

"Ohh," I coo, "Estela, he's beautiful."

"I would never hurt him," she says over my shoulder. "I know I was upset when I called you, but I'd never hurt him."

My heart aches as I turn to face her. "Estela, I'm going to see to it that you get some money, okay? You deserve as much, for telling your story."

"What I want is Kahari."

"You need to think about your baby," I tell her frankly. "He's the most important thing." And now, because I know it will make her feel better, I lie. "If Kahari doesn't want to be a part of your lives, then it's his loss. Remember that. I got by just fine without a father."

I lie because there's no doubt in my mind that the baby is not Kahari's. While it's not impossible, he looks more Hispanic than black. And completely adorable nonetheless.

"Are you seeing him?" Estela asks me pointedly.

My heart slams against my rib cage.

"Someone called me. Said they saw a picture of you and him in the paper."

"I . . . " I swallow as I think of what to say. The last thing I want to do is make her feel worse. "I went out with him to try and encourage him to do the right thing by you."

"You did?"

"Yes." *I'm gonna burn in hell . . .*

"And what did he say?"

I reach for her shoulder and give it a squeeze. "I don't think it's gonna work out, Estela. I'm sorry."

Sniffling, she looks into the crib. "I tried. But I can't make him love me."

"Exactly. Sometimes, Estela, no matter how much you want something, you have to give it up. If it's not working, what can you do? And you deserve so much better. You deserve a man who loves you with all his heart. A man who will love you and your beautiful baby." I smile as I glance into the crib again. "Look at those little hands. He's so precious."

Now, she smiles. "He is, isn't he?"

"Oh yes. And you're gonna be okay. I promise you that."

"I hope so."

I reach into my purse and take out all the money I have. It's only sixty dollars, but it's better than nothing. I push the money into her palm. "Here."

"You don't have to, really. I'll get by."

"Take it. For the baby. And I'm going to make sure there's more where that came from." I offer her a soft smile. "Trust me."

I don't feel good as I leave Estela's place, but I feel better than I did when I got her call earlier. The crisis is averted. At least for now.

"What's happening?" Rusty asks me when I return to the van.

"We're leaving."

"What?"

"She doesn't want to be interviewed again. And can you blame her?"

Rusty shrugs nonchalantly. "Whatever."

"Let's head back to the office."

I hope Eva's not upset. But then again, I don't really care.

Thirty-five

I don't tell Kahari about Estela. Not when I was in Oakland and saw him after the game. And not now that he's back in town and I'm in his incredible house with him.

It's not that I think he'll be angry. I guess I want to protect him, really. And I figure it's best to leave well enough alone. I don't want him calling Estela out of pity, and possibly stirring up her romantic feelings for him. I'm really hopeful that after I saw her, she's going to make an effort to move on.

And if she doesn't . . .

Kahari drapes an arm across my waist. We're snuggled close in the middle of his extra large bed. I say extra large because I'm not sure what its official size is, considering that it's round. It fits in a curved alcove near the window, and even has a rounded headboard made of mahogany.

"Are you awake?" Kahari asks.

"Uh-huh."

"What are you thinking about?"

I stroke my fingers along his arm. The room is dark, and

it's not quite morning. I would be sleeping if thoughts of Estela weren't keeping me up.

"I'm thinking about how much I like being here," I tell him. "With you."

"I like you being here."

Damn. Should I ask him about Estela—about how involved they actually were? Because it's obvious they were.

What are you trying to do, Zoë? Ruin a good thing that's developing? Don't be so fucking stupid!

"You're being unusually quiet," Kahari says. "Are you sure there's nothing else on your mind?"

"I'm just thinking about . . . your place. Talk about incredible pads! I still can't get over this bed. And it rotates!"

"I saw it in a movie and had to have it."

"I could stay here forever and not get bored." It suddenly dawns on me that he might think I'm talking about our relationship, that I'm ready to take it to the next level, so I quickly add, "You know. Anyone could. I mean, how could you not? This place is magnificent."

"It's a little something I picked up."

"Ha. A little something. Right."

Kahari pulls me onto him. My breasts crush against the hard wall of his chest. He runs his hands over my hair, then frames my face in the dark room.

"Are you sure there's nothing wrong?"

"How serious was your relationship with Estela?"

Oh God. Tell me I didn't just ask him that!

"Estela?" he asks, shocked. "You're asking me about Estela?"

"I know you're not the baby's father, but you *were* involved, right? She's so into you."

Kahari sighs softly. "If I answer your questions, can we drop the subject of Estela once and for all?"

"Yes."

"Estela and I went out a few times, slept together once, and that's it."

"Why didn't things work out?"

"Because I realized she wasn't the right woman for me. There was something a little off about her. Like she wasn't quite operating with a full deck. She had our whole lives mapped out in a freaky kind of way."

"I kinda feel sorry for her," I admit.

"Yeah, me too."

"You do?"

"Uh-huh. And her kid. I figure she was hoping for a relationship with me because she wants to escape her life. She doesn't have much."

"I . . . I know."

"And that's why I've set up a scholarship fund for her kid."

My eyes widen in disbelief. "You have?"

"Yes. Not because the kid's mine, but because I do care about her, even if we only dated for a short time. There have been other people, people I considered friends, who tried to get money out of me. They told stories to the media, or threatened to. That kind of thing happens when you reach the level of success I have."

"And yet you still set up a scholarship fund for Estela's child."

"I don't think she was like the others. She wasn't vindictive. In a weird way, I think she really cares about me."

"You're really . . . something," I tell him.

"I want the best for Estela. I did like her. It's not like I didn't want things to work out. But it didn't take long for her to become extra clingy. Real needy."

I've heard enough. I don't want Estela in bed with us anymore. So I say in a brazen voice, "I'm needy too."

"You are?" Kahari asks.

"Uh-huh. I need something from you right now." I take his penis in my hand and coax him into erection.

"Ahh. I see."

I nip his chin. "I might need a lot of this before I'm satisfied."

"Well, we *have* only made love once tonight. I'm falling short of the standard I set last week."

"Which is very, very bad of you."

"Let me fix that," he whispers hotly against my ear.

"You'd better," I tell him.

His tongue enters my mouth at the same time his penis enters my vagina. And I'm lost.

I wake up smiling. But my smile immediately disappears when I roll over and realize that Kahari isn't beside me.

Alarm sweeps over me. I have to say, despite my attempt to show the world that I'm confident and in control, I'm hopelessly insecure. So my first thought is that Kahari has gotten out of the bed because he's upset that I questioned him about Estela and he can no longer stand to be near me.

I am so certain that this is the case that when I see him enter the room with a tray of fresh strawberries and pineapple, I actually breathe a sigh of relief.

He must sense my wariness, because he says, "Why are you looking at me like you're shocked to see me."

"I . . . I . . . "

"You thought I took off?"

I decide to be honest. "I guess I thought maybe you woke up and you were a bit mad at me."

"So mad that you thought I'd leave my place to you?" he asks, smiling playfully.

"No, no of course not. But you could have always gone to another room."

It is clear that Kahari is not listening to my nonsensical

ramblings, which is probably a good thing. I'm pretty sure I could talk him out of feeling good about what's happening between us because I'm so bloody insecure.

But all negative thoughts soon flee my mind as Kahari plants the tray on the bed. "I hope you like this. I asked Starbucks for the recipe, but they wouldn't give it to me."

My eyes light up as they land on the covered silver travel mug. "What is this?"

"My attempt at a caramel macchiato."

"Oh my God!" I squeal in delight. "You made one for me?"

"I tried. I don't know how it will taste."

"You didn't have to go to all this trouble. Regular coffee would have been great."

"It was no trouble. I hope it's all right."

I lift the lid off the travel mug and take a sip. "Mmm. I love it!" How thoughtful is this man?

"As you can see, there's a variety of fresh fruit. A nice, healthy breakfast. Vegetarian."

"Ah! Right." My heart fills with warmth as I look at him. "You're a total sweetheart." *How could anyone ever let you go?*

"It was the least I could do. After last night . . . "

My cheeks flush at the memory of the scandalously wonderful night we shared. "You didn't actually prepare this, did you? I mean, I'm sure you had your maid put this together . . . "

"I prepared it. I do have a housekeeper come in three days a week, but I'm not so useless I can't make my own meals."

"I'm sorry. I didn't mean to—"

He silences me with a kiss. Mmm, I could get used to this.

Kahari sits next to me on the bed. And there's something seriously wrong with me, because I suddenly wonder if he ever did this for Estela, or other women. Why the hell am I thinking about this right now, when Kahari is being so wonderfully sweet to me?

"About last night, me asking about Estela—"

"I thought we were through talking about Estela."

"We are." I sigh. "I just want to thank you. You've been more than up-front with me about everything."

"You're welcome."

We eat in silence for a few minutes, then I say, "I'm sure you have a busy day ahead of you, so whenever you're ready to tell me to get lost, I'll understand."

He looks at me quizzically. "Now why would you say that?"

"I'm sure you won't want to play house all day."

"No, why would you think I'd tell you to get lost? As though you're a dime a dozen to me?"

Damn, he's right. He figured out the subtext of my comment so well. But why am I feeling insecure all of a sudden? Like what's happening with Kahari is too good to be true?

But I tell him, "That's not what I meant."

Kahari pops a piece of pineapple into his mouth, chews and swallows, then speaks. "I know ballplayers have a shitty reputation, but I'm not like that. I don't bring a different woman home every night of the week."

"Just every other night." I smile to soften my words.

Kahari surprises me with a soft kiss on the cheek. "Believe me, that's not how I operate."

If he keeps surprising me with moments of total romantic behavior, I'm likely to believe anything he says.

He is smooth. Maybe too smooth? I want to think the best about him, but I'm also a bit of a skeptic. I've had so many failed relationships.

"We're taking things one day at a time," he tells me, as if

sensing my thoughts. "And the way I see it, we're heading in the right direction."

My stomach flutters. "Are we?"

Kahari's lips lift in a smile. He really does have the sweetest smile. The kind that can make you feel warm and fuzzy and hotter than fire at the same time.

"Yeah," he says. "I think we are." He takes the tray off the bed and places it on a table near the door. When he comes back to me, he reaches for my hands, saying, "Come here."

I take his hands and move to sit beside him.

"I know you've been hurt. We all have."

"Someone broke your heart?" I ask disbelievingly.

"Yeah. Definitely."

"Who?"

"I was engaged once. Five years ago. It was someone I'd met in Oakland. She worked for the team's office. Things were cool for about eight months. But after I proposed, she was increasingly insecure about my career. Hated that I traveled on the road so much. Hated that women threw themselves at me wherever I went. And then she started accusing me all the time of cheating on her. I never did cheat on her, not once."

"So you ended things?"

"I couldn't live my life like that." He eases me backward on the bed, then lies beside me. "I want you to know that when I'm involved with someone, it's only her."

"So you've dumped your other twenty girlfriends?" I ask playfully.

"Just last night. Before you came over."

I laugh, then frame his face. "I do like you, Kahari. And if we don't get up right now, I'm going to be tempted to throw myself at you—again."

"I like when you throw yourself at me."

"Talk about something. Something unsexy."

"Like what?"

"Like . . . like football."

"Oh, but football is very sexy."

I shrug. "I guess. All those hot men in tight outfits . . . "

"That's not what I mean."

"Oh?"

He runs a finger along my inner thigh. "The game of football is easily compared to a woman. In fact, women and footballs are pretty much the same."

I look at him skeptically. "Oh? How so?"

"Well . . . " Kahari's fingers tickle my inner thigh as he moves them higher, to my center. As he rubs his thumb over my nub, he whispers, "You both have a sweet spot."

He's looking right into my eyes as he says this. His gaze seems to say that he's going to own me completely, and as I stare back at him, I know my eyes tell him that he already does.

"The key to success on the field and with women," he continues, still stroking me, "is to find the sweet spot. And when you do . . . "

His fingers move over me gently, skillfully. I swear, I am already at the edge of orgasm, and it never happens this quickly for me.

"And when you do, what?" I ask.

He eases one finger inside me, and I moan softly. "When you do, you're in sync the way you're supposed to be." He slips another finger into my wetness, and I can't help thinking that right now I'd let him do whatever he wanted to do.

"When you're in sync, with the ball or with a woman, it's pure magic."

"That's your secret. To success."

"Mmm-hmm. But don't tell anyone."

This is the most erotic, intense fingering I've ever experienced.

Kahari lowers his head to my ear and whispers, "Tell me when I've found it." He nibbles my earlobe. "Your sweet spot."

And then I'm coming, and coming, and he's staring into my eyes and stretching his fingers deeper inside me, making the pleasure even more intense.

I've never been so exposed in all my life. And yet I don't look away. I don't want to look away. And what I see in his eyes makes this so much more meaningful. I see that he's riding this wave with me.

As the wave of pleasure subsides, I can't help calling out his name. "Kahari, baby . . . "

I feel as close to anyone as I've ever felt.

And I wonder, does he feel the same?

Because what's happening between us does feel like magic. It has a life all its own and it can't be explained.

Smiling up at Kahari, I reach for him, taking his arousal into my hands. He's so hard, so large. So utterly magnificent.

I urge him onto his back and climb on top of him. "Let me ride you."

Within seconds he is inside me, and the pleasure is more delicious than anything I have ever experienced before him.

He holds my hands as I ride him, and I swear, this feels so right.

And as he pulls my head down for a kiss, I can't help thinking that this is more than sex.

A whole lot more.

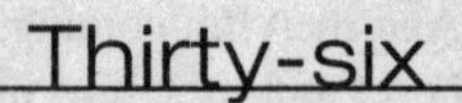

Thirty-six

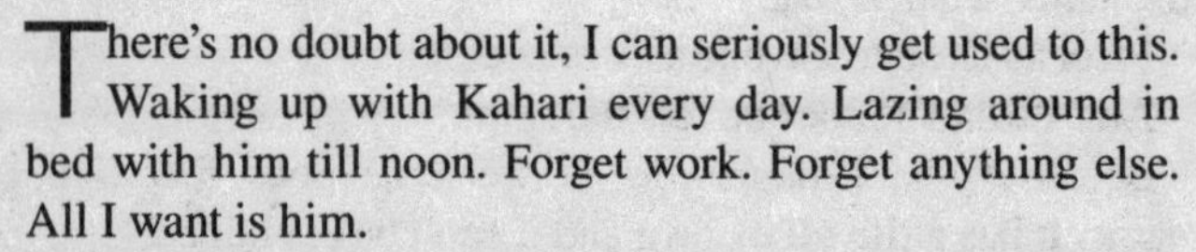

There's no doubt about it, I can seriously get used to this. Waking up with Kahari every day. Lazing around in bed with him till noon. Forget work. Forget anything else. All I want is him.

I know I swore I'd never give my heart to another man, but I'm pretty damn close to giving it to Kahari.

The man makes me feel so incredible, and not just sexually, though we seriously connect that way. He makes me laugh. He doesn't hate my quirkiness. And somewhere along the way, he's gotten under my skin.

And the hell of it is, he's a professional athlete, but he's so *not* like my father. I sense instinctively that if I were to announce to him that I was pregnant, Kahari would stand by my side.

"Are we ever going to get out of this bed?" Kahari asks. "Not that I want to, but I'm sure you've got to go to work."

"Well," I begin slowly, "technically you could say I am at work. You're my assignment," I add, chuckling softly. "Actually, I got up earlier and called my boss. She knows I'll be late today." Eva knows I'm with Kahari and gave me her blessing to stay and do "research" as long as necessary. Of course, I'm not here for the research. I'm here because I love being with Kahari.

He trails a finger along my jaw. "I like lying here. With you. Like this."

"I like it, too," I say breathlessly.

Kahari links one of his hands with mine. "Tell me something you haven't told anyone else."

"Like what?"

"Whatever. Something you think I'll laugh at. Something you think I'll think you're crazy for."

"If you don't think I'm crazy already—"

"I'm serious," he tells me.

"I don't know. Oh, okay. I got it. And I feel really bad about it now, but when you're ten, you don't see past your own wants and needs."

"What'd you do?"

"I flushed my sister's goldfish down the toilet. We'd been fighting, and I did it to get back at her because she destroyed my favorite doll's face with a blue marker. Even now, I still feel guilty. She cried so hard."

"Whoa."

"Now you think I'm some sort of psycho creep, don't you?"

He kisses the inside of my wrist. "Of course not."

"Maybe that's why she stole my man." I pause. "What about you? What's something you did that you haven't told anybody?"

Kahari's lips twist as he thinks. "Once, in college, I had someone write a paper for me. And what I'm telling you, I don't want to read about in the paper or see on TV."

"Kahari. Of course not. I don't want you to think I'd ever do that."

"I know. I was only teasing."

"So—this paper?"

"It was a history paper, and I didn't have time to write it because of football. I started it, but couldn't finish it. I got an A plus on the paper," he adds.

"That's not so awful. At least you didn't murder something."

"Maybe not, but it was the only A plus I ever got on a paper. I still feel bad about that."

"Most people wouldn't give that a second thought. But you're not most people, are you? Someone raised you right."

"My grandmother. And to this day, if she caught me doing something out of line, she'd whoop my ass."

Kahari and I share a chuckle over that.

"There's one other thing I want to tell you," he says.

"Oh, I can just imagine. You stole the teacher's apple, or something wretched like that."

"No . . . Though I did steal a kid's eraser once. But I was going to say"—he takes a deep breath—"I've never lain in bed with a woman after sex and talked to her the way we are now. I haven't really wanted to."

That floors me. "Get out."

"I'm serious. I'm not saying I just picked up and left. But I didn't feel one hundred percent comfortable lying like this, and talking."

"Even with your fiancée?"

"She didn't like to cuddle much."

"Now that's just freaky." I snuggle my body closer to his. "I love to cuddle."

"And I like when you look in a woman's eyes, and she gives you a steady look back. She's not afraid to let you see into her soul. You probably think I'm a nut now."

"No, I think you're romantic. Most guys don't talk the way you do. I wish they would."

Kahari suddenly says, "Tell me about your father."

"My father?" I stare at him in confusion. "Where's that coming from?"

"I don't know. I'm curious."

"There's nothing to tell."

"You mentioned you'd tried to have a relationship with him."

"And it was a disaster." My chest feels like it's being crushed by a heavy weight. "I don't want to talk about this."

"I know you don't want to, but maybe you should."

I eye Kahari warily. "Why?"

"Zoë, I've been there. I grew up without a father for most of my life. I know how that hurts. Why do you think the community center matters so much to me? So many of those kids need a father figure the way I did."

"I'm beyond that. I'm a grown woman, doing my own thing."

Kahari doesn't say anything for a moment, just stares deeply into my eyes. "I'm going to say something," he begins cautiously. "Give you some advice."

I sigh and look away from him.

"No, look at me."

I hesitate a moment before meeting his gaze.

"I know you're angry with him. He left you and your mother and only contacted you when you were an adult."

"Too little, too late."

"Hear me out."

"I know what you're going to say. What my mother always says. That I should forgive him. But that's easier said than done. And some things in life can't be fixed with a Band-Aid."

"That doesn't mean you can't try."

"Kahari," I groan. I don't want my time with him ruined over talk of my father.

"I definitely can't tell you what to do, and I'm not saying you have to forgive him." He pauses. "Like I told you, my father wasn't around for most of my life, either. I resented him for that, for barely being there for me. Then, when I got drafted in the NFL, we started talking again. I didn't exactly open up to him, figuring he was in touch because I'd made the pros. Three months later, he died in a car accident. And suddenly all my anger, resentment, my second-guessing his motives—none of that mattered. What mattered was the reality that it was too late for my father and me to ever have a relationship."

I don't say anything. Surprisingly, Kahari's words cause a tinge of melancholy to chip away at my shield of anger toward my father.

"You don't think I wanted a relationship with him?" I ask. "But he walked away from me—"

"I understand that. I hear you. And all I'm saying is . . . life is short. I care about you, Zoë. I know what it feels like to lose a father for good. I wouldn't want you to ever go through that."

He really does care. I can see it in his eyes.

"And this isn't really about him. It's about you. What if you establish some kind of relationship with him and he's able to answer questions you have? Questions you might not even know you have, or think don't matter to you anymore?"

"Well." This is almost uncanny, how he can read me so well. "I can't say you don't understand."

"I don't know what you're going to do," he continues. "That's your decision to make. I guess I just want you to know I'm here for you, if you want to talk to someone about it."

My God, he's amazing. Amazingly tender, amazingly caring, amazingly insightful. Amazing, period.

I think this is the moment. The moment I know for sure that I've fallen in love with him.

I give him a soft kiss on the lips. "You really are special. Pretty damn near perfect, as far as I'm concerned. How did your fiancée ever let you go?"

"I'm not perfect."

"Are you kidding me? Okay, so you leave the toilet seat up. Big deal."

"Seriously, Zoë. I've done things in my life I'm not proud of. I haven't always been the best boyfriend."

I give him a questioning look. I'm about to ask if he wants to tell me more when I hear my cell phone ring.

I groan. "That's probably work."

I climb off the bed and grab my purse, then dig out my phone. "Hello?"

"Thank God I reached you."

Eva's voice sobers me a bit, brings me down from my high. "I'm sorry, Eva. I . . . I'm running later than expected . . . "

"I have a story for you, Zoë. A *huge* one."

I cover the phone's mouthpiece and turn to Kahari. "I'm gonna go into the hallway."

He nods.

I start for the bedroom door, comfortable with my nakedness in front of him. "You have a story for me?"

"It turns out Kahari Brown isn't so innocent after all," she says in a singsong voice.

I open the door and step into the hallway. "What are you talking about?"

"Another woman has come forward. Someone else he got pregnant and abandoned."

I frown. "That's a little convenient, isn't it? Estela's story went national, now someone else wants to cash in?"

"Which is why I had a research team check her out. She was Kahari's high school sweetheart."

Now my stomach lurches. "She was?"

"They dated for four years."

I think of everything Kahari and I have discussed. Is this the woman he was engaged to? No, it couldn't be. He said he met that woman in Oakland. So why didn't he mention a longtime high school sweetheart?

"She . . . she could be lying," I tell Eva.

"She's not. I have a picture of her and Kahari together. He's touching her pregnant belly in the photo."

No, this can't be. Kahari and I have talked about a lot of things. He'd tell me if he got someone pregnant. And furthermore, he's not the type to abandon his child.

"Eva, I find that a little hard to believe. Maybe the photo was doctored?"

"It's legit, Zoë. Why are you questioning me about this?"

Because I've fallen for Kahari.

And when has anything ever worked out for you?

Now my hand starts to tremble. Was I wrong about him? Have I shared my body—and my heart—with a man who's no better than my father?

You know your judgment in men sucks. Let's face it.

"Zoë, are you listening to me?"

"Sorry. I . . . I . . . "

"I'm booking you on a flight this evening."

"You are?"

"Yes! I don't want anyone else getting this story before we do. You have to head to Dallas as soon as possible."

Dallas. Ohmygod. The very mention of the city makes me sick, as it always has. It's where my father lives.

"You want me to interview her," I say, almost in disbelief.

"Yes. And there's something more you should know. Not

that I want to distract you, but Estela overdosed on sleeping pills."

"What?"

"She's gonna be fine. But she's in the hospital."

"And the baby?"

"I'm sure Children's Aid has him."

"Oh my God."

"I know it's awful, Zoë, but you have to pull yourself together. You have a job to do."

"I'm not sure I can do it now," I whisper.

"You have to."

"You don't understand. If what you're saying is true . . . How could I have been so wrong about him?"

There's a pause, then Eva says, "Oh, Zoë." Her voice rings with understanding.

"I'm fine," I tell her. "I will be."

"Are you there right now?" she asks me. I wonder how the hell she knows, but then, Eva's as successful as she is because nothing seems to escape her.

"Yes."

"This was a job, Zoë. You got emotionally involved and you shouldn't have."

Thanks. What a way to make me feel better!

"But you're not the first one," Eva tells me in a surprisingly gentle tone. "You'll get over this. We all learn the hard way."

Her words, this unexpectedly soft side of Eva, only make things worse. The tears fall now, and I angrily brush them away. I'm not sure why I'm crying. Maybe because I don't know what to believe. I want to believe Kahari, but what if all that pillow talk and eye-gazing is part of his game? One he plays as well as he does the sport of football?

"What's her name?" I ask.

"Denise Williams."

"What time's my flight?"

"In just over four hours."

I nod. "Okay." I can do this.

"You sure you're okay?"

"Yes. I can do this." I have no choice. And this time, I'm not going to let anything like emotions get in the way. I have to distance myself from what I experienced with Kahari romantically in order to be objective.

And my God, what if Estela was telling the truth all along, and because I refused to believe her, she overdosed on drugs? Can I live with that?

"I'm sorry," Eva says. "I know this isn't easy."

"Please, no more pity. What's happened has happened and I'm ready to move on."

"Good girl. I knew I hired you for a reason."

Eva's vote of confidence fills me with pride—until I hear the dial tone. I have to go back into Kahari's room, and Lord help me, I don't want to face him now. But I have no choice. My clothes are in his room, and I need them to get out of the house.

Still, I hesitate before going in. Nausea washes over me in waves and I grip my stomach. Kahari's words of only a short while earlier sound in my head.

I've done things in my life I'm not proud of. I haven't always been the best boyfriend.

Is that what he didn't get to tell me?

Should I even believe what Eva's said?

But she sounded so certain . . .

Why—why did this have to happen now, after I've given Kahari my heart?

Get over it, I tell myself. *If what Eva told you is true, then you have to lick your wounds and move on.* After all, that's exactly what I told Estela she needed to do. If the advice is good enough for her, it's got to be good enough for me.

"Zoë?"

My eyes fly to Kahari as he opens the bedroom door. He grins when he sees me, his eyes sweeping over my naked body.

"That's a long phone call, baby."

Damn, the way he calls me baby sounds so friggin' right I can't take it. I wish he'd blown me off the morning after my birthday so I could think of him as a first-class jerk. That would make it so much easier to deal with the news Eva has told me.

"I know," I say.

"You have to go?"

I nod. "Yeah, I do."

He reaches for my hands. "So this means you can't spend the afternoon with me in bed?"

"I'm tempted."

"What's wrong?" he asks me. "Why do you sound so down?"

Right now, I would love nothing more than to go back to bed with Kahari, lie with him, and tell him what Eva has just told me. I want him to wrap an arm around me, hold me tight, and tell me that Eva is wrong, that there is no other woman he's screwed over in the past.

Then we'll laugh about the absurd allegation and make love.

And that's exactly the problem. Anything he said to me I'd want to believe. Around him, I lose all objectivity. So I can't stay. I have to talk to Denise. Get a feel for the woman and her story before I share any of this with Kahari.

"Hmm?" he prompts. "You seem upset."

"It's just . . . I have to go to Dallas." I study his face to see if he reacts. But there's nothing, not even a flicker of unease.

And then he says, "Ah. Now I see why you're upset. Because your father lives in Dallas."

"Yeah."

He wraps his arms around me and pulls me close. "I've already said what I wanted to say on the subject. But don't let it get you down. You do what you have to do."

"Thanks." I swallow. "For caring." I step away from him. "And now I have to get ready. I've got to be at the airport in a couple hours."

Kahari catches me off guard with a soft kiss on the lips. "When will you be back?"

"Probably tomorrow night. When you're already back in Oakland."

"It's Miami this weekend. You could meet me there . . . "

"Oh, I don't know."

No more VIP lounges. No more watching my man from his reserved seats. One phone call, and I've lost so much.

Just ask him. Ask him about Denise.

I want to. Lord, I do. But I can't do that yet, not until I talk to this woman and hear what she has to say. I can't let my feelings for him cloud the truth.

I head back into his bedroom, toward my clothes, because if I don't leave now, maybe I never will.

"I'm sorry, Kahari," I say. "I really am."

I've never spoken truer words.

Thirty-seven

The first thing I notice about Denise is that she is drop-dead gorgeous. Just like Estela. Are these the normal types of women Kahari prefers, and if so, why did he ever get involved with me?

Unlike Estela, however, Denise is clearly doing all right financially. I can tell that from a quick look behind her into her modest-looking apartment. Her furnishings are run-of-the-mill and the paintings are the type that stores sell everywhere for ten bucks or so. So she's obviously not well off or anything, but she's not in rough financial shape.

"Hello, Denise." I extend my hand, and she shakes it. "I'm Zoë Andrews, from *True Story.*"

I smile, trying to appear pleasant and confident, even though my stomach feels like it's full of snake venom. On the plane, I told myself that I would give Kahari the benefit of the doubt, but seeing Denise has sent me teetering on the emotional brink once again.

"Hello," she says, meeting my eyes for a moment, then looking away.

"It's okay," I tell her. "The interview will be harmless."

"I've never been interviewed on camera before," she says. "I guess I'm nervous about it."

"Don't worry. Within a few seconds you won't even know the camera is there. Just talk to me like it's only the two of us in the room."

"Okay," she agrees, her voice shaky.

She invites me and my camera crew in, where I introduce her to everyone. Then I ask her if she's got a favorite spot in the apartment where she'd like us to set up.

"I got new furniture in my living room just a couple months ago. It's nice."

I glance around. The living room is small, but for our purpose, it certainly doesn't need to be big. It has a warm and cozy feel, which is a good thing.

"This is great. Let's set up here."

Normally I'd spend some time doing a preinterview with her, but I don't really want to stay here all that long. And can you blame me? My heart is aching, and I'm doing everything I can to try to keep it together.

Besides, Eva faxed me a bunch of notes at my home which I was able to look over on the plane. So I pretty much know this story inside out.

Even though I wish I didn't.

The guys have fitted Denise with her microphone, and they've set up two cameras to tape the interview from two different angles.

"All right," I say. "Let's get started."

The guys have rearranged the furniture so that the leather armchair and sofa are angled next to each other. I sit on the armchair, and Denise sits on the sofa at the edge closest to the armchair.

With the sound tested and adjusted, I get right down to business. "Denise, you were involved with Kahari Brown?"

"Yes."

"Will you please tell me the extent of your relationship?"

She nods. "We practically grew up together. We lived in the same town, just a couple blocks away from each other. We went to the same grammar school, the same high school."

"You were high school sweethearts? Or did your romance begin before that?"

"Well, that's kind of interesting. Even though we grew up in the same area, we didn't really know each other until high school. It was our senior year when we started dating, and we continued to date even when he went to Notre Dame."

"So you had a long-distance relationship?"

"Yes."

"It sounds pretty serious, then." I swallow hard.

"It was very serious." She pauses, glances down. When she looks up again, her eyes are shimmering with tears. "I loved him with all my heart. I thought he loved me, too. But then . . . "

"Then what?"

"I thought we were gonna get married, but as soon as I got pregnant, he dumped me."

"After you'd been dating him for years?" I can't help sounding incredulous. But I'm not angry on her behalf, I'm angry on mine. How could I have so easily trusted him? A few nice chats and dinners, a few romantic gestures, and I was putty in his hands.

"Yes. I couldn't believe it. Then I figured he was just scared, you know? Not ready to raise a baby because he was about to be drafted into the NFL."

"And was he?"

Denise shakes her head. "No. It took me a while to accept the truth, but he just didn't care about me. I guess I was fun while it lasted, but he didn't want anything permanent."

"I'm not sure I understand."

"I told him if the commitment to a child was too great, then I would raise the baby alone. That he could send me whatever support he could, when he could, until he got a decent contract. I even told him that I didn't expect him to marry me just because of the baby. I tried to do everything I could to make sure he didn't feel pressured."

"And that didn't satisfy him?"

"No."

"Denise," I begin slowly, "what happened to the baby?" I ask because I have to, but I already know from Eva's fax that she lost it.

Denise lowers her head as she begins to softly sob. "There is no baby."

I cover her hand with mine in a gesture of support. "You lost it?"

She's crying harder now. "Kahari . . . He—he—"

"What? What did he do?" This I ask with serious concern, because I only know that she lost the baby, but not how.

"When I told him I wouldn't have an abortion, he shoved me down a flight of stairs."

My gasp is completely genuine.

"I started bleeding, and I lost . . . I lost the baby before I made it to the hospital!"

Denise is crying hysterically, and I signal to Rusty to stop rolling the tape. Denise is going to need a moment. Quite frankly, so am I.

But then I wonder—is she telling the truth? Kahari told me that people who were once his friends had come forward with stories, hoping to make a buck off of his success.

But I specifically asked Eva if Denise was being paid for her story, and she's not being paid.

She extends her hand. "You see this—the way my wrist is a little deformed?"

I look at her wrist, and see that her wrist bone does indeed seem a bit deformed.

"My wrist broke when he pushed me down the stairs, and it didn't heal properly."

I offer Denise a Kleenex, saying, "I'm so sorry."

"I know it was years ago, but that's not something you get over, ya know? I loved that baby with all my heart . . . "

"Of course." I can't imagine what Denise went through. But I can't help thinking about what my mother once confided to me—that my father had told her to do the same thing—have an abortion. She stood her ground, choosing to raise me alone.

I almost didn't come into existence.

It's the reason I'm antiabortion, and I can never be with a man who would want his child murdered.

Or who would so cruelly push his pregnant girlfriend down a flight of stairs.

I have heard enough, but I have to continue. For the show's sake, I can't do half an interview. But what I want to do is run from this place, check into my hotel room, and down a bottle of tequila.

The rest of my time with Denise is a blur. I can barely remember specifics, only that she painted the picture of a man who is entirely charming on the outside but has an awful, secret dark side. Denise also said something about his own father abandoning him, and that that may be at the root of his problems.

My father abandoned me, but I didn't turn into a creep.

You don't know if she's telling the truth, a voice says as I lie in my dark hotel room.

I want to believe that, because the Kahari I've gotten to know—the one I've fallen for—in no way resembles the one Denise described, or the one Estela described.

But I've messed up before. I can't exactly trust my judgment.

What do I do, God? What do I believe?

Later, in my hotel room, I find myself dialing my father's number.

It's because you need a distraction after today. And this is as good as any.

But I know that's not entirely true. I remember the talk I had with Kahari, how he encouraged me to call my father. Try as I might to forget him for the time being, I can't get him out of my thoughts. Even with what Denise has told me, I think about the positive ways Kahari has touched my life.

"Hello?" a woman says on the other line.

"Um. Hi. Is Sean there?"

"Who is this?"

Sean's firstborn child, I think sourly, but I say, "This is Zoë."

"Oh, Zoë. I'm Tara, Sean's wife."

"Is he around?"

"He's working on something in the garage, but I know he'll want to take this call."

A minute later, I hear his voice. My father's. "Zoë?"

"Yes, it's me."

"What a surprise. A pleasant one."

There's a moment of awkward silence. Then I say, "I want to say something before I lose my nerve. When we were first in touch years ago, the mistake you made was trying to be my father. Telling me your opinions, giving me unsolicited advice. I don't need a father anymore." I pause. Close my eyes.

"This is why you called? To tell me that?"

He sounds disappointed, and pain stabs at my heart. "No," I answer softly. "I called to say . . . I know you were trying to make an effort to repair our relationship. I guess I wasn't ready. But now . . . I'm willing to open communication between us. See where it leads."

"Zoë. I'm so happy to hear you say that."

"I'm in Dallas right now," I find myself saying. "If you want to get together."

"Name the place."

I give him the name and address of my hotel.

"But you have to understand," I go on, "I'm an adult. I don't need guidance anymore. You didn't give that to me growing up. But I suppose it doesn't hurt to have . . . a friend. A friendship with the man responsible for my life. We can work on that."

"You bet we can. I'll see you soon, okay?"

"Okay."

"And Zoë?"

"Yes?"

"Thank you. Thank you for calling."

"Sure." I actually feel the sting of tears, something that surprises me.

Time will tell how it all works out, but I'm willing to keep an open mind. I suppose that's half the battle.

If only I could keep an open mind where Kahari is concerned.

I want to, but my hope is dimming.

Thirty-eight

I don't call Kahari for the rest of the week, and I don't return his calls, either. I need time to think, to put some distance between us.

I also convince Eva that we should wait to air the tape of Denise's interview until the following week, when Kahari is back in town. What I really want to do is talk to Kahari first.

I'm going to do that. Tonight. Because I finally called him this morning and we're meeting at Il Fornello for dinner.

As Kahari sees me heading toward his table on the ground floor, he smiles and gets to his feet. My stomach twists painfully, because he always gives me this sweet look, like he deeply cares about me.

Is it a lie? Was everything with him a lie?

Be calm, I tell myself. *Be rational. Do* not *lose your head . . .*

"Hey, babe." He takes me in his arms and kisses me.

"Hi."

"I've ordered wine," he tells me. "It's on its way."

I nod. Then I try to swallow the lump that's formed in my throat as I sit down.

He reaches for my hand. "I missed you, babe. What have you been up to?"

I look him directly in the eye. "I'm going to ask you something, and I want you to give me an honest answer."

His smile wavers a bit. "Of course."

"Did you ever date a woman named Denise Williams?"

Kahari's eyes fill with shock, but he answers, "Yes. I'm not gonna lie."

Oh my God.

"Did you get her pregnant?"

Kahari sighs wearily. "She claimed it was my baby—"

"Like Estela claims her son is yours?"

"That's what you were doing in Dallas. Talking to Denise."

"Good guess."

"So you've judged me, is that it? You've already made up your mind?"

"Did you push her down the stairs?"

Kahari exhales loudly. "What happened that night . . . maybe I handled it the wrong way."

Something inside me snaps. Forget calm. Forget rational.

"You son of a bitch." I grab my water glass and splash the contents in his face.

Kahari reels backward as the cold water hits him. His eyes narrow as he reaches for his napkin. "What is wrong with you?"

My chair scrapes loudly against the hardwood floor as I push it backward and shoot to my feet. "I can't believe I fell in love with you."

He glances around uneasily. "Zoë—"

"I almost didn't come into existence. I almost didn't have a chance at life, and do you know why? Because my father wanted me aborted. I could never be with a man who could try and kill his own child!"

I am aware that every single eye in the place is on me, and while I felt powerful throwing water in Kahari's face, I suddenly feel awful. Dammit, people will recognize me from TV. I have to get out of here.

I grab my clutch off the table and spin around.

"Zoë, wait."

I start to run. How did this happen? How did I fall in love with a stereotypical philandering ballplayer?

"You don't care about my side of the story?" Kahari asks as he pursues me. "You don't care what I have to say?"

Oh, I can imagine the excuses. *I was young, Zoë. Too young to handle the responsibility of a child.*

Thank God the restaurant door is in sight. I reach for it, but before I can open it, Kahari's hand slams against it, keeping it shut.

And now I know I'm crazy, because there's the slightest part of me that's happy he's prevented my getaway. Maybe he cares about me more than he's cared about anybody else.

And then I feel sick. How desperate am I?

"Let me leave," I warn him.

"Fine. We'll both leave together."

Before I can protest, he hustles me onto the street. "You want to know about Denise—"

"I don't want excuses."

"We got into a fight, okay? We were arguing—"

"Oh my God."

"Dammit, Zoë. Let me finish!"

There's a flicker of movement behind Kahari, and the next thing I know, he's lurching forward with a startled look on his face.

He groans and falls onto the ground.

For a moment I am too stunned to comprehend what's going on. But when he doesn't get up, I scramble to his side. "Kahari! Kahari!"

I look up to see Colby standing a few feet away. He's brandishing a knife that is covered in blood. His eyes hold mine for a moment, and then he starts to run.

"Oh my God!" I gather Kahari in my arms. "Someone get help! Call an ambulance! *Pleeeease* . . . "

"Denise and I were arguing—"

My heart thunders in my chest as I stare down at Kahari. "Please, don't talk."

"Because I found out the baby wasn't mine. She'd slept with a buddy of mine, and he's the one who got her pregnant. I told her I didn't love her anymore, that I wanted nothing to do with her. And then she threw herself down a flight of stairs."

"Oh my God." A crowd has gathered around us. "Kahari, we can talk about it later."

"She's been telling that story for years—that I pushed her—to anyone who will listen." Kahari inhales a deep breath. "But when she realized it was over for us . . . that's when she threw herself down the stairs to kill the baby because she said she didn't want to live without me."

Holy shit. I feel like . . . I feel like the biggest idiot in the world.

"It was drama. Denise is drama with a capital D."

"You wouldn't lie about that, would you?" I ask.

"When I'm lying in the street probably dying? Zoë, when are you gonna start believing me?"

As I look at the blood pooling around him, I hear the wail of sirens. "Please don't die, Kahari. I'll make this up to you. I swear."

"It matters to me," Kahari says. "Before I die, tell me you believe me . . . "

"You're not going to die."

He grips my hand. "Tell me . . . "

"I believe you."

Kahari's eyes flutter shut.

"No," I utter desperately. "No, Kahari. Please don't die. I have so much to tell you. To thank you for. Because of you, I called my father. And I think maybe we'll make things work this time. Kahari? Kahari!"

Paramedics push their way through the crowd. Arms wrap around me, pulling me away from Kahari.

"He's gonna be okay, right? He's gonna be okay!"

No one answers me, and my heart nearly splits in two.

Then Kahari opens his eyes as he's being placed on the gurney, and relief like I've never known washes over me in waves.

He lifts his hand, as though reaching for me, as the gurney starts to pull away. His lips move, but I don't hear his words.

It doesn't matter, because I read his lips.

He said, "Don't leave me."

Thirty-nine

I wait in the hospital for hours while the doctors operate on Kahari. Because of Colby, he suffered a collapsed lung.

I feel like shit. If I hadn't run out of the restaurant, if I hadn't been arguing with Kahari on the street, Colby would never have been able to come up to us from behind and stab Kahari.

Lord help me, Kahari's going to hate me for this.

I'm at the hospital when Kahari comes out of surgery after 9 P.M. But the doctor tells me that he'll be out for a while, and I should go home.

So I do.

I can't help wondering if I should even come back.

I do, of course. Even if it's the last time I see him, I have to apologize.

When I arrive on Kahari's floor, I see a throng of people. Reporters, I realize instantly.

Damn, I should have known.

I walk up to the nurses' desk. "Hi, I'm here to see Kahari Brown."

"If you're a reporter, wait there like everyone else."

"No, I'm . . . I'm his girlfriend."

The woman's face brightens with a smile. "Zoë, right. You're one of three people Kahari has said he wants to see."

"So I can go right in?"

"Yes. But keep the vultures out."

I make my way through the vultures, feeling bad that I'd become one of them. That's not what I wanted. Never in a million years.

I open Kahari's door, and they all start to speak. I quickly slip inside and shove the door closed behind me.

"Holy crap!" I exclaim.

"Finally," Kahari says.

I whip my head in his direction. Damn if he isn't smiling at me.

"How are you?" I ask as I make my way to the bed.

"I've had better days, that's for sure."

"I am *so* sorry, Kahari."

"It's not your fault."

"That's where you're wrong. It is. It's totally my fault. The guy who stabbed you—he's a friend of mine."

"Huh?"

"He *was* a friend, I should say." At Kahari's confused gaze, I quickly add, "It's not like I set you up or anything. Colby—he's sort of obsessed with me. He was following me around, and was pissed that I wouldn't date him. But never, ever in my wildest dreams did I think he'd take things this far."

"So he was jealous when he saw me with you?"

I nod. "Yeah. I guess."

Kahari groans. "Damn."

"You're okay, though. Right?"

"I'll lose out on my chance at being voted this year's MVP. But yeah, I'm okay."

I slump into the chair beside his bed. "I feel awful. Really I do."

"I'll probably be out for the rest of the season."

"I'm sorry. I couldn't be more sorry. I've made such a mess of everything."

"It seems so."

And now I know, Kahari putting me on the list of people he'll see—this must be about closure. He wanted to see me not because he cares, but because he wants to tell me it's over.

I can't say I blame him. But my heart. Oh, my heart.

I summon all my courage. "I quit *True Story.* This morning."

"You did?"

"Yeah. My producer wanted me to bring a camera when I came to see you. I couldn't."

"Well, thanks. Though there's no shortage of reporters hoping I'll talk to them. I think if I never see another reporter as long as I live, it'll be too soon."

"I also told her Denise Williams is a liar, but she might run the story anyway . . ."

"I can't believe you went to see her."

I look away. My courage is starting to ebb away, and I might just start crying. Which would be completely crazy, because all of this is my own fault.

"Well, I know it won't change things, but I *am* sorry. That's all I can offer you." I get up from beside his bed and quickly turn my head to the door so he can't see my tear-filled eyes.

I start to walk, and he doesn't say anything. I should be grateful for that, but I'm not.

God help me, it's over, and I'm not sure my heart will ever recover.

"You're wrong about that," Kahari says when I've reached the door. "There's something else you can do to make things better."

I whirl around. "Anything." And I mean it. "*I'll* tell my story to *True Story,* to the *Daily Blab*, about how insecure I am and how I blew the best thing I ever had. How I should have trusted my heart, and trusted you . . . "

And I will, if he wants me to. Call me insane, but this is what love does to you, I realize suddenly. It makes you willing to do crazy things to hold on to it. It makes you willing to let your vulnerable side be exposed, because the reward of being in love is so great.

"You'd do that for me?" Kahari asks.

"Yes."

"What about doing something else?"

"You name it, I'll do it."

"All right. Then marry me."

"Marry you! Kahari, I know I hurt you, and I said I'd do anything, but isn't that too harsh—" I stop abruptly, suddenly realizing what he said. I'm not sure what I thought he said, except that I expected something really awful. But I'm pretty sure he didn't just suggest something wretched. I think he just asked me to marry him.

He waves a hand in apology and then looks away. "Now I'm the one who's sorry. I guess I thought . . . "

I leap toward the bed. I put my finger on his chin and force him to look at me. "I'm nuts. I think we both know that. But I figured you were going to say something else—you know, suggest I do something really embarrassing to prove my regret. But you didn't, did you? I think you said—"

But he couldn't have, could he? Surely my mind is playing

tricks on me. I'm now hearing voices, on top of everything else.

Oh for God's sake—just ask him to repeat it!

I take a breath, swallow. "Kahari, will you please repeat what you said?"

"Well . . . I suggested you could make things better by marrying me. I know, crazy idea."

"No, it's not crazy!" I know I'm smiling like an idiot, but I can't help myself. "Well, maybe it is crazy, but since when am I not up for crazy? But how will that make things better for you?"

"If I'm married, maybe the press will leave me alone from now on. You know, find a promising rookie to slander instead."

My happiness deflates like a balloon that's just been pricked by a pin. "Oh. I—I—I see."

I move backward, standing up fully.

"Zoë . . . "

"No, no please. I can't." Maybe months ago I would have married him, hoping that one day he'd grow to love me, but somewhere along the line I've grown some balls and I am going to stand up for myself. Not accept less than I deserve. "I could never be in an arranged marriage, or worse—one for publicity."

Kahari drops his head back on the pillow and roars with laughter.

"This is funny, is it?" I say, growing angry.

"An arranged marriage? Come on, baby. Do you think I'm asking you to marry me for any other reason than the fact that I love you?"

He loves me . . . Warmth spreads through every fiber of my being.

"You love me?"

"Do you think I would even allow you in my room right now if I didn't?"

He's got a good point.

"But I brought all this chaos to your life. Hell, I got you *stabbed*."

He flashes me a mock scowl. "No you didn't."

"Well, practically. I mean, this is what happens to people when they know me."

"Ah, so there have been other stabbing victims?"

"No, not that. But bad things." Whoa, what am I trying to do? Talk myself out of an engagement?

Kahari reaches for my hand. "You remember the first time you kissed me?"

I groan as I cover my face. "God, how can I forget?"

"Don't do that. Don't hide your face."

Reluctantly, I lower my hand. "It wasn't my classiest moment. I know that."

"I liked that kiss."

"You did?"

"Hell yeah."

I can't believe Kahari and I are talking as if . . . as if we're not over. As if we have a future. "And all the bad stuff—you're just forgetting that?"

"You know what they say about keeping your friends close, but your enemies closer?"

"Kahari . . . I wish you wouldn't joke at a time like this. Unless . . . unless you're not joking."

A playful smile dances on his lips. "I'm joking. Of course I'm joking."

"Oh."

"Look, you've brought some chaos to my life, yes, but a lot of excitement too. A lot of passion."

"Excitement?"

"Mmm-hmm. I can't exactly say my life is dull right now."

"Come on—you hated every minute of everything that's happened. The interviews, my insecurity. And now you want to marry me?"

"Mmm-hmm."

My breath oozes out of me. "You're serious."

"As a heart attack." Kahari pauses, and a lopsided grin spreads across his face. "But I do have an ulterior motive."

"Ah, here we go. I knew there had to be something."

"Of course. If I marry you, then I can keep you locked up in my house where I can keep an eye on you—and keep you out of trouble."

A beat passes, and then he starts to laugh. So do I. He's joking. Of course.

Even if he shouldn't be.

"I think and breathe you, Zoë. No matter what I do, you're in my heart. And I know this is really fast to fall for someone, but sometimes you just know. You know?"

I nod. "Yeah, I know."

"We can have a really long engagement, but my gut tells me things are gonna work out. And I always trust my gut."

He extends his hand, and I take it. "You know," I begin, "maybe that's not such a bad idea what you said, about having me where you can keep an eye on me. Keeping me locked up for a while will no doubt keep me out of trouble." And I can think of a lot worse punishments than being locked away with the man I love.

"That's what I was thinking."

"Were you also thinking that you'll keep me locked up in your bedroom most of the time?"

"Only if you're really, really bad."

"In that case"—I lean forward to nibble on his earlobe—"I will do my best to be very, very bad."

Kahari chuckles as he wraps one arm tightly around my waist. "Does that mean you'll marry me?"

I ease my body onto the bed beside him. "I think, Kahari Brown, that you're possibly as crazy as I am."

"Dammit, woman. Is that a yes?"

Love fills my heart as I smile down at him. I run my finger along his face, feeling the stubble. And then I say, "I can't think of a better way to spend my life than with you."

Kahari slips his hand around the back of my neck and pulls my face down to his.

And then he kisses me, the kind of kiss that says I'm *not* crazy. That I've finally found the kind of love I've been searching for all my life.